Carol Wahlenmayer spent her career as an English and writing teacher in Western New York schools. She is the mother of two adults who make her feel optimistic about the future of a troubled world. Four grandchildren call her Grandmoo. She is the author of several articles published in children's magazines and professional journals. She lives in Florida and spends her summers in her native Western New York.

To Jerry—first in all that matters.

Carol Wahlenmayer

Second Chances

Austin Macauley Publishers™
London • Cambridge • New York • Sharjah

This is a work of fiction. Names, characters, businesses, places, events, locales, and incidents are either the products of the author's imagination or used in a fictitious manner. Any resemblance to actual persons, living or dead, or actual events is purely coincidental.

Ordering Information
Quantity sales: Special discounts are available on quantity purchases by corporations, associations, and others. For details, contact the publisher at the address below.

Publisher's Cataloging-in-Publication data
Wahlenmayer, Carol
Second Chances

ISBN 9781649798909 (Paperback)
ISBN 9781649798916 (ePub e-book)

Library of Congress Control Number: 2022923270

www.austinmacauley.com/us

First Published 2023
Austin Macauley Publishers LLC
40 Wall Street, 33rd Floor, Suite 3302
New York, NY 10005
USA

mail-usa@austinmacauley.com
+1 (646) 5125767

I want to thank the friends who encouraged me when the year I had allotted was over and the book wasn't finished. Thanks to my first and special reader. I recall with delight the writers' society at Canisius College and the Writers' Club at Orchard Park High School, which re-named itself The Writers' Sodality when I was out of the room. Both groups kept me writing at a time when I had hundreds of papers to correct. Last, thanks to my indomitable mother, who inspired the fictional Anna. I have been blessed.

Chapter 1
Monday Night

The sound creeps from the top of the stairs. It begins softly, like a whisper, then crescendos as it gains confidence in its power over the girl huddled on the couch in the living room. Anna won't raise her eyes to the staircase. Perhaps if she stays really still and compacts herself into the smallest form possible, it will stop.

Shewwillnotevenblinkhereyes.

Silence in the dark room. Then it begins again, like a net thrown oh-so-softly then pulling you ever closer with a dragging sound. Then, the final, resounding thump.

A dim light shines at the top of the stairs where Anna, just yesterday morning, had expected to be sleeping soundly tonight. The light wavers, suggesting movement. An illusion. Anna knows that nothing alive is moving in that room—her room. How could she sleep in that room ever again—the same room where…

The sound again. The whispered beginning, like a mother's endearment, but treacherous as a siren's call, followed by the dragging, the thump. The pump relentlessly goes up and down, drawing blood from her mother's body and replacing it with embalming fluid—sucking away everything that had been her mother and leaving…what?

The sound of the pump squeezes Anna's mind and she is afraid. At the same time she's ashamed to be afraid because, after all, that is Mama up there, or it had been Mama just yesterday. She is thirteen—not a baby, after all. Anna longs to see her mother, but she can't bear the thought of what the machines are doing to her, so she huddles under her blanket wishing the night away. Giving up on sleep, she forces her mind back to Sunday afternoon when the world still held the illusion of rightness.

Chapter 2
Sunday Afternoon

The feeling in the big Packard, rumbling along central Pennsylvania's back roads, could be sliced evenly between the front seat, where thirteen-year-old Anna snuggled happily between her parents and the back seat where three more older children glowered. Helene, seated behind her father, the Reverend Ezekiel Hiram, pouted as she looked first at her perfectly manicured nails, and later in the mirror at her pretty face, so naked without the makeup that her father generally failed to notice but made her scrub off today. There were at least three good looking young men who could have given Helene, a worldly seventeen, a better Sunday afternoon than a ride with the family in their "new" car. Ham, gangly at fifteen, sat in the center, his knees pushed almost up to his ridiculous bow tie by the rise in the floor. "Move over, Helen," he said, pushing her to the left. "I have to get my feet off this thing. My legs are cramping up."

"Get your hands off me, you oaf. And how many times must I tell you I prefer Helene to Helen?" Her words dripped with disdain that proclaimed younger brothers a curse to an older sister. Helene planned to be out of this family circle and soon! Out at eighteen, just like her sister, Norma.

On the right side of the back seat, eighteen-year-old Quentin was having his own space problems, which he handled with a sharp elbow into his younger brother's side. He actually admired the big buggy his father had come up with, picturing a young lady or so in the passenger side of it beside him some day. "How old did you say the car was, Sir?" he asked his father.

"Oh, I think about eight years old, but she's kept like new. The price Harold Jurgens gave me—it's close to a tribute," he glowed. Tribute was the word the reverend liked to use for the gifts given him by his wealthier parishioners. Most of the family's acquisitions came from the benevolent obligations of the congregation. The single six had been made for the first time in 1920 and this car had been made two years into production, so the reverend was quite close when he estimated eight years. "Do you feel that breeze, Aletha?" he asked his wife, sitting on Anna's other side. Mama smiled, the gentle smile that was almost always on her face as she pushed strands of honey-colored hair from her face, and peered from under her bonnet with wide blue eyes that saw no evil. Aletha was one of those women who glowed, even when she wasn't pregnant. It was, however, hard to find two years in a row when she wasn't "in the family way."

Ten Hiram children had survived and Aletha had miscarried four others since Anna's birth. Aletha's face always had a pinkness to it, and it flushed easily to a deeper rose as it was doing now. The reverend looked through round, wire glasses across Anna at his wife and for a minute Anna thought he might pull over and send them all scurrying away to be alone with her. Today, however, it was a new love that claimed his attention. Harold Jurgens III, having inherited the Packard 1922 single six from his father, was looking for a quick sale, already owning the luxurious twin six himself. Luckier than most, Harold realized there were few buyers in the present economic climate, so he thought of the church as an alternative and priced it accordingly. The car's roomy four door styling accommodated the remaining Hirams so the reverend bought it on the spot.

"Oh, Reverend," Aletha had cautioned when he came home and told her about it. "Do you think we can afford such an extravagance?"

"The Lord placed me in its path, Aletha," he said, whisking her around the kitchen in a sort of mixture of a polka and a waltz. As usual, the decision was already made.

Anna was enjoying the ride. For once, she didn't have Helene asking her to lie for her as she snuck out to see Harold, or Sam, or Edwin. As the tenth child, this was the closest Anna got to having per parents all to herself as her siblings were intent upon torturing each other in the back seat. The boys could pick on each other something awful, but as quick as that, they'd be ganging up on anyone else—especially a younger sister.

The family had been dropping off potatoes, corn, and clothing donated by some of the church members as well as some of Aletha's famous pies to some of the less fortunate families in the church. This was usually done from a pull cart, pulled by whichever family member was unlucky enough to be around when it needed doing. It gave considerable incentive to be busy with schoolwork or anything that looked productive. Whoever was doing the delivery was expected to sing as part of the job. Sometimes it constituted a duet if the load was particularly heavy, but today's recipients, parishioners too old or frail to attend church, were treated to a chorus of six singing "The Old Rugged Cross" or "Amazing Grace". To Anna, it seemed more like fun and less like a penance when they all were doing it, but she knew in her heart that the pull cart would be back in action as soon as the novelty of the car wore off. Anna heard her mother humming "the old rugged cross" softly, under her breath. Her customary smile was on her face and Anna couldn't help but smile too. Aletha's hand was on her breast as if pledging allegiance to the song she sang "and I'll cling to the old rugged cross." Her whispered voice was barely audible, and Anna felt her turn toward the window as she exhaled a note it seemed she couldn't let go of right away. Mama's weight pressed against her, but it didn't feel like snuggling—more like pushing. As Anna was forced over toward her father, he greeted her encroachment with a stern look. Anna got a look at her mother's face, now tipping back into her view. The bright blush of the afternoon was gone, replaced by a flat gray. She was falling, harder and harder on Anna, making no move to catch herself. Aletha's navy straw bonnet with the gray feather fell and landed on Anna's feet as she writhed to free herself of her mother's weight.

"Papa, something is wrong with Mama," Anna gasped. "We have to help her."

"Aletha, what is the matter?" Getting no response from his wife, the reverend lurched to the side of the road and hurried to the passenger side door. He reached for Aletha, pulling her off Anna. Her blue eyes were open, but she didn't see. Her lips seemed to be still reaching for a word of today's songs. Apart from the ashen grayness of her skin, she was still his Aletha. He pulled her warm body into his arms urgently. For the first time, he didn't feel the welcome response of her body.

The reverend handed the car over to Quentin, who was strictly forbidden to drive under all circumstances and blew air into his limp wife's mouth. The only sounds in the car were his deep breaths as he futilely tried to share them with his Aletha.

Chapter 3

"Carry her up to Anna's room, boys. Helen, you call doctor Rothsberger." Helene obeyed without arguing the pronunciation of her name.

Anna had never heard her father's voice so wooden. He was giving orders, as usual, but it sounded like he was doing it from a land far away. His characteristic movement was a swagger and the usual vibrance of his eyes made people feel singled out in joy or pinned by guilt. Now he shuffled pathetically beside his sons, holding Aletha's hand and getting in their way as they carried her.

"It's going to be alright. Dr. Rothsberger is coming. Be of good faith, Aletha," he pleaded as the four of them crowded the stairs. Ham and Quentin knew better than to argue, although they looked at each other without hope. Anna remembered how she had hesitated when Mama had sent her to fetch apples in the cellar just the other day. She should have not only gotten those apples but helped Mama peel them for the pies she was making. What had she done instead? She couldn't even remember. Her mind grasped the fact that she would now never learn how to make those wonderful pies and it seemed so very tragic.

Dr. Rothsberger's visit was brief, confirming what everyone except the reverend already knew. Aletha was gone, and had probably been gone when Anna had first felt her weight in the car. Anna felt the burden of loneliness as if Mama was dying right now…right this very minute.

Reginald Artine of Artine's Final Rest had a somewhat lengthier visit that day. The undertaker came immediately upon hearing of Aletha's death. "I am unspeakably sorry about your loss, Reverend." Like everyone else, Mr. Artine called him Reverend. There was something about the way Papa looked at people through his round, wire glasses that dis-invited first names. The Reverend Ezekiel Hiram seemed ever on a mission from God. "I have come to help you with the arrangements," Mr. Artine assured. "There will be many people coming to pay their respects to such a prominent woman as your wife.

You will require the Repose Room, I expect. For a small extra charge we can bring in upholstered chairs for your guests' comfort. You will want the deluxe Dream Away Casket, I am sure and, of course, an innerspring mattress for the comfort of the departed." His gold pen with RAA on it bulleted points in an open notebook as he spoke. He looked up with an ingratiating smile, his speech robed in an air of benevolence.

"We can pick her up tonight and have her properly prepared for viewing tomorrow. In our care, she will look like a young girl."

Papa looked at the undertaker with disbelief. "What do you mean, pick her up? This is Aletha's home. This is where we were married, where her children were born. She will not be removed from her home," he declared. "People can come here and pay their respects!"

"Of course, we could arrange an in-home viewing, but first we must prepare her body. She will have the look of a young girl," he repeated. Now, only his mouth participated in his forced smile.

At once, THE REVEREND was back. He pulled his normally erect posture to military proportions and his voice took on its usual commanding timbre. "NO! HERE! Aletha is going nowhere." Anna knew there was no arguing with that voice, but Mr. Artine didn't know it quite yet. Turning to his youngest daughter he continued, "Anna, you will have to sleep somewhere else for a bit. We need your room for Mama." As the youngest of ten children, privacy was something largely unknown. Anna had shared a room with Helene as long as she could recall. Eighteen months ago, however, Norma had eloped, vacating the room she had to herself since Edith had left to marry Bob Bedwin. Helene had immediately confiscated the room, a sort of eminent domain, with a flourish of belongings and a rolling of eyes. With Helene gone, it became apparent how little Anna owned. It was nearly a convent cell.

As Mr. Artine continued his fruitless attempt to change her father's mind, Anna climbed the stairs and haltingly approached her room. The dwindling sunlight made golden threads of Mama's hair as she lay on the bed. The bluish gray of Mama's face had been replaced by a hue for which Anna had no name. She had an urge to climb on the bed and put her head on Mama's chest as if she was a little girl, but she was thirteen, so she just lifted the strangely cold hand and kissed it above the amethyst ring, given to Mama by her mother. Then Anna gathered her few clothes from the chest of drawers and reached under the bed to get her favorite books of mythology. Clutching them to her she proceeded down the hall to the cedar closet. A chill glanced her neck as she thought of going back to her room late at night.

Downstairs, the conversation intensified. "Reverend, I strongly suggest against that," Artine maintained with an attempt at more authority. "While the preparation is quite customary to professionals, it can be extremely upsetting to the bereaved—not to mention that our permanent equipment at the funeral home is more effective. I really could not guarantee the best results using the portable unit. Off-site embalmings are usually done only in extreme cases, and then the burial is expedited to no more than two days."

"You WILL prepare her here. We WILL have a full three days of viewing. She WILL look like a girl as you have promised," proclaimed The Reverend. He looked at a place on the wall beyond Mr. Artine. His voice had the same finality with which he pronounced judgment upon the sinful. Negotiations were ended.

Anna deposited her clothes in the cedar closet then wandered into her parents' room. There the violets still bloomed on the wall paper. The windows still beamed with the late afternoon sunlight, framed by the Priscilla curtains Mama favored. Not sure why, Anna crossed the room to Mama's dresser. A brush with strands of her hair still rested on an oval mirror. Anna slid the top drawer open and fingered a filmy blue nightgown, saved by Mama for special occasions that never came. Anna clutched it to her, inhaling the fragrance of sachet, which always seemed to cling to Mama. Closing the drawer, she carried the filmy nightgown to the cedar chest and added it to her things.

Helene's room was the next one down. Anna saw her sister sitting on her pillow-laden double bed painting her fingernails. There were skirts and blouses from the Bon Ton Shoppe where Helene worked strewn around the room. Anna stopped at the door and paused expectantly. It would be nice to be with someone tonight. As unwelcome as she always felt with Helene, Anna didn't want to be alone. Barely looking up, Helene began her diatribe. "Sure, the old bastard wants her laid out in the house. That way he can bury her on the cheap and the church ladies will provide everything for the breakfast. Would you close that door when you leave, Anna? The sound of him makes me sick."

Since then, Anna had slept on the couch.

Chapter 4

Anna tiredly finished the last of the supper dishes. As usual, Ham and Quent disappeared right after dinner. Helene had moved out to marry Edwin Lord, one of her admirers, within a few weeks of Mama's death. Until then Anna slept on the couch every night and no one seemed to even notice. Anna looked at her reddened hands and sighed at the thought of the work that remained before bedtime. She had always been taught that it was what was inside that counted, so she could hardly be accused of vanity, but the constant burden of work in the big house was wearing her down. Her fourteenth birthday had come and gone without the birthday cake Mama always made. Nor was there a single gift. Although gifts were never lavish, until now, a birthday had always been a day made special with favorite foods and the feeling that you were a blessed gift to the family yourself.

Anna diligently read the recipes that Mama had prepared with such magic, but they were full of "a pinch" of this or "enough" of that, so they never turned out the same when she made them. Papa did the necessary shopping, but he never asked what was needed so Anna tried to do the best she could with what he bought and what came to the family through the generosity of parishioners.

Seven months after Mama's death, Anna had awoken to a bed fresh with blood stains. Horrified, she looked for an injury, but the blood seemed to be coming from inside her. Her pants were soaked with blood. Anna was unsure of whether she should be more worried about where the blood was coming from or what Papa would think about the ruined sheets. She didn't feel sick; there was just a heaviness around her lower stomach, so she stripped the bed, wrapping the clean part around the outside, and headed to the cellar laundry tubs. Anna had learned in the months of laundry that stains got worse in hot water, so she soaked the sheet in cold water. Her pants were in worse shape so she used the bar of lye soap, rubbing the redness into pinkness. With each rinse the stain was more faint until it was like the memory of a nightmare upon waking. Anna knew that Papa would see it as the Finger of God pointed at her—for what, she didn't know.

In any event, she knew they would have to be dry in two days or she wouldn't have any clean underwear. Now she could feel a warm drizzle making its way down her leg, curling its way down her upper thigh then plopping onto the cellar floor. Looking around the cellar, Anna spotted the basket of mending Mama worked on in the evenings. There were socks from Quentin and Ham which Mama would darn over a wooden egg, making them useful again. Anna took two socks and pushed them up between her legs. She tore a clean strip from the soaking sheet to tie the socks in place. Back in the sewing basket was a large pin to secure her makeshift bandage. A few days after she'd learned how to deal with this unexpected problem, the bleeding would stop. She never mentioned it.

Anna's clothes were getting too small as well. Small and compact, Anna had always been able to wear her sisters' hand-me-downs and once or twice a year Mama would sew a new dress for her. Helene was the last sister to leave, and she took everything when she left. Anna had grown about two inches since her thirteenth birthday, the last time she'd received any clothes. Only two dresses fit her at all, so she carefully alternated between the blue sailor dress and the yellow floral print. Each was too short and tight under the arms. Papa didn't seem to notice, and it only really bothered Anna when she bent to scrub floors or reached to retrieve Mama's home canned vegetables. Papa's expectations had left less and less time for schoolwork, so it had been some months since Anna had been to school. "After all," Papa stated, "you know how to read and write now. There are other more important things for girls to learn around the house."

Anna certainly did know how to read. She had been one of the best readers in her class, in fact. She had a special fondness for the Greek myths they had studied, and she could recite any of the stories in her Myths and Legends book, which nestled conveniently under her bed in Helene's old room. It still felt like Helene's room to Anna, even though it had been months since Helene left.

For a while Miss Proctor, Anna's teacher, had stopped by to inquire about when Anna would return to school. Anna was never allowed to talk to Miss Proctor, but she did overhear her conversation with Papa. "Anna is one of our best students, Reverend Hiram. We surely do miss her and look forward to her return. May I see Anna and leave some work for her to do at home until she is with us again? Papa just told her that I was very busy and he evidenced no interest in the books she was leaving." For a while Anna spent some exhausted evenings pouring over the discoveries of Cabaza de Vaca and William Bradford while baking bread for the next day, but eventually Miss Proctor stopped coming and Anna gave up looking forward to returning, realizing that she was falling behind her class and would be assigned with a totally new, younger class if she did somehow return. After a while she even stopped thinking about her day in terms of where she would be if she were in school. Her life dissolved into a blur of work.

Chapter 5

The dinner table was smaller than it once had been but it still took all of Anna's patience to coax dinner out of Mama's ornery, old stove. Ham was working at the Market Basket now and Quent was promoted to assistant foreman at the sportswear factory. Anna had bested the old washer and the cut-glass dishes in the dining room sparkled as they had when Mama was alive.

The best nights were when it was just Anna and her two brothers. Papa had taken to escorting some of the church ladies to the suppers in the area. It was good for contributions, he had maintained. Certainly, the gifts of coffee cakes and pies had increased as a year passed and the Reverend was perceived as an eligible man once again. Anna was disgusted to see former friends of Mama's clustered around her father in a way she considered shameless.

"Is Pa out again tonight?" Quent asked.

"Yeah, I think it's the widow VanHorn. Some sort of Christian song fest," said Ham, "Is there any of that custard pie Miss Wagoner brought left? No harm intended, Anna, but your pies are…well, I mean, uh…is there any left?"

"It does seem in this town pie is the way to a man's heart." Quentin smirked at his brother. "That may just leave you with no prospects, Anna."

Anna didn't say anything. It didn't seem to matter to her brothers that Papa was forgetting all about Mama. Anna had served tea to Ruth VanHorn four or five times in the last month. One time she even brought her snooty daughter, Bette, whom Anna remotely remembered from her past life at school. The way they sat in her Mama's parlor, sipping tea while she waited on them would make you think they owned the house and she was a maid. Most of all, Anna hated the way Papa joked and winked, patting Mrs. VanHorn's arm, and guided her to her chair where his arm would linger on her waist longer than Anna thought was necessary. Bette strutted around the room in her watered silk dress, taking in all the beautiful dishes Mama's mother had hand painted, while helping herself to biscuits from the best cut-glass plate. Anna had to clench her teeth to keep from screaming as Papa complimented the VanHorns on their clothing, their manners, their church attendance, while his eyes kept darting to the cleavage Mrs. VanHorn so generously shared with him by leaning further forward than she needed to while retrieving a sugar cube.

"Poor Ezekiel," she cooed with a voice low enough to be a contralto in the church choir. "No woman to take care of your needs. How are you surviving?" Just then she seemed aware of Anna's presence. "I am sure little Annie does her best, but you know…there are girls and there are women." She slowly looked up at Papa through downcast lashes. Papa seemed totally charmed by it, although Anna saw manipulation of the most obvious sort.

"Anna," Anna corrected.

"The Lord provides," said the Reverend, coating his words with layers of meaning.

"Perhaps the Lord will provide abundantly and variously if we place our faith in Him," continued the low, silky voice.

"My name is Anna," repeated Anna, only to be ignored again.

"It is a lucky man who enters into the Lord's lap of abundance," Anna's father replied, looking deeply into Mrs. VanHorn's knowing eyes.

"God lovingly opens to he who wishes to enter in," she replied, as if it were only the two of them in the room.

"Anna," Anna repeated more loudly. Startled, they unlocked their gaze.

"What is it, girl?" asked her father, clearly annoyed.

"My name is Anna, not Annie."

"Of course it is, no doubt about it." His voice responded, but his eyes remained locked on Ruth VanHorn. His hand was on her arm, grazing her amble breast as she inhaled deeply.

"Anna is the name given to me by my mother, in honor of her mother!" Anna shouted as she raced from the room. They hardly noticed.

It surprised no one when the Reverend and Ruth VanHorn became engaged. After that Ruth was always in the house, fingering the things that had belonged to Mama. Anna even heard her telling Bette that these would all be hers someday.

Wherever Anna was, she seemed to be in the way, interrupting their privacy. Anna didn't know which she found more disgusting—the way her father, so masterful with everyone else, followed Ruth VanHorn around like a puppy or the thought of Ruth VanHorn in her mother's bed.

Chapter 6

Anna unsnapped the right fastener on the old, tan suitcase. The left one didn't fasten at all, so she untied the string she'd wrapped around that side. The worn, leather tag still read Aletha Hiram, 105 Paxon Ave, Strykersville, PA although Anna's mother had been dead for two years now. The suitcase looked awfully worn out considering that Anna had seen her leave the house only two times during the thirteen years they were together. Each was to assist an older sister giving birth. The two years had robbed Anna of the exact shade of her mother's blue eyes and sometimes she couldn't recall exactly what Mama had said during a remembered event. Nevertheless, rubbing her hand along the imitation leather case gave Anna some sense of peace. Burdened for two years with the responsibilities of an adult, Anna wished she could return to the security of being a child in her mother's home.

Those days were gone. Sighing, Anna took her mended wool stockings from the suitcase. She had two pairs of ragged underwear that barely fit. As with all her needs, Papa saw nothing to worry about. Like the one she wore, the dress in the suitcase crushed Anna's chest, and the waist crept up to an uncomfortable place just under her ribs. Thank heavens her growth spurt seemed to have stopped.

Anna placed her meager belongings in the drawer Helene had assigned her. She fingered the lace of the nightgown she'd taken the night Mama died. She wished Mama had had a special occasion to wear it, but she felt sure she didn't. The filmy blue silkiness seemed to put Mama in this strange room with her. Gently, she added it to the drawer which easily held all she owned. Mostly, the drawer was full of torn sheets for when the bleeding, now an accepted regularity, came each month. The only things left in the suitcase were her mythology books. She slipped them under the bed.

Anna couldn't believe Helene had agreed to having her visit now that Papa was married again. Her oldest sister, Rachel had begged off with a house full of children, including four-year-old triplets. "It is a shame about Anna," said her sister Edith, "but I have Bob to worry about." Anna's third sister, Norma, had successfully put the desired distance between herself and her father. She moved to Buffalo, New York. There was, of course, no expectation of any of the boys, so it was to Helene that Anna was assigned.

"She'll be a help to you with that big house and all," Anna heard Papa say. It really wasn't a request or an invitation, but to everyone's surprise, Helene didn't put up any fuss at all.

To Anna he'd said, "It's best you stay with Helene for a while. Ruth needs to feel at home and that's hard for her. A visit will do everyone good." He followed with one of his rare smiles. It didn't come naturally to him. It seemed like something his mouth did in rebellion to his face.

Ruth seemed at home enough to Anna. Whenever she came upon Anna, it seemed she was surprised to find her still there. Anna had the feeling that wherever she was in the house was the wrong place. Papa must have thought so too, for here she was at Helene's.

Her new room was big with a double bed covered by a fluffy white quilt with red poppies. Two large windows opened onto the roof of the front porch. There was a writing desk and a heavy rocker. Anna had only one dress to hang. It was a good thing since being next to Helene's "boudoir" as she called her bedroom, the closet was filled with the overflow from Helene's closet. Anna had never heard of a boudoir before, but she guessed it was a lady's bedroom. Helene's husband, Edwin, had his own room farther down the hall where he stayed when his business allowed him to be in town.

Edwin was home today. Anna heard muffled voices from the boudoir. The house was too well built to hear all of what they said, but she heard Edwin say "keep you company" in the same sort of voice Papa used with Ruth. Helene's sharper tone included "earn her keep" which made Anna think they were discussing her. Seconds later there was a rap on the door, which immediately sprung open as Helene breezed in. Anna closed the closet where she had hung her dress, somehow feeling as if she had been snooping.

"So, Anna, you are here. Did you find places to put your things?" Helene's hair was swept up with tortoise shell combs which exactly matched the mass of well-planned curls they held. As she reached out, Anna looked with astonishment at her long, oval, rose colored nails, which exactly matched the flowers on her dress. Could this lovely woman truly be her sister? Anna felt awkward, realizing that they were strangers although they had once shared a room. In spite of her beauty, there was a slight downcast to Helene's eyes, a crease on her brow, and a tone in her voice making it seem as if something not quite identifiable was wrong. It made Anna feel that she should apologize for something, but she didn't know what so she just nodded.

Edwin stuck his head in the door. "Welcome, Anna. We're glad to have you." Anna noticed that Helene said nothing of the kind. Instead, she seemed to be looking around the room for any changes Anna's arrival might have caused. Suddenly her eyes focused on Anna and lit in recognition.

"Oh my God, Anna, that dress you're wearing was mine—and Norma's before me. I sewed that rick-rack on the collar so I could pretend it wasn't a hand-me-down. That cheap son of a bitch. Didn't he get you anything of your own?" Truthfully, Anna hadn't had anything new since Mama had sewn her one other dress on her thirteenth birthday. It now hung in the closet and was equally small. Fortunately, Mama had put a large hem in it.

Anna felt uncomfortable with Helene's talk, so she tried to avoid it. "I had better say goodbye to Papa," she said.

"The old buzzard is long gone—back to his frosty Ruth who has him by the pants," Helene chuckled. "Dear old Dad's idea of parenting ends with conception. I bet Mama would be alive today if he'd given her a year off from being pregnant. But no, the horny old bastard had his own version of the finger of God, and she was too meek to take control of her own body."

"Helene, watch it. Anna's just a kid," Edwin cautioned.

Helene drew a pack of cigarettes from her pocket and handed Edwin a slender silver lighter engraved with an H in a fancy script. Edwin lit her cigarette. "Time she grows up, then." She took a deep breath and blew the smoke toward the bed. "She needs to find out sooner or later what part of their bodies men think with, doesn't she?" She took the lighter from her husband and spun on her heel. "Come on downstairs, Anna. We'll find you something to eat."

"Anna, I'm glad you are with us. I hope you'll be happy here." He smiled and Anna noticed that his bland face transformed when he did. "And Anna, don't let Helene take advantage of you." It wasn't long, however, before Anna came to know he couldn't follow his own advice.

That night Anna ate with an appetite she'd forgotten she had. It was the first time in over a year that she'd eaten something she hadn't cooked herself. As it happened, it would be the last for some time too.

Chapter 7

For over twenty years Bea Schott had lived across Park Street from the Bingham house. She guessed she should be thinking of it as the Lord house, since it was now owned by Edwin Lord and his wife, Helene. The house had been owned by Lloyd and Delia Bingham until Lloyd died and Delia went to Pittsburgh to live with their daughter. That had been over three years ago and Edwin Lord had come looking at the house shortly after. It had seemed strange, an unmarried man buying such a big house, but Edwin was a nice fellow, he was. Contrary to her nature, Bea had trouble liking the young woman he married. Helene was pretty, all right, too pretty for her own good, judging from the visitors Bea had seen coming and going when Edwin was out of town. Helene always seemed to be in the shortest shorts or the tightest sweaters. Bea doubted Edwin could pull in the reins on his wife, even if he was home more often.

Now there was the girl. Bea had seen the poor thing arrive. An older man in a dark suit with a cleric's collar brought her and was out of there like lightning. The girl looked pathetic, she did. Her curly brown hair looked like it had never been cut. It was pulled back into a thick mass that made her freckled face look like all angles. Her clothes looked two sizes too small and certainly hadn't been bought to favor her. In the weeks she had been on Park Street, Bea had seen her wear only two dresses. It wasn't in Bea's nature to snoop, but something about the girl caught her interest. She'd learned that the girl was Helene's sister, but she seemed more like a live-in maid, always working on that house. One day she'd be scrubbing the large windows with ammonia and polishing them with newsprint. Another day she'd be scrubbing the front porch on her hands and knees. She pulled the weeds from the Lord's gardens until it looked like they had a full-time gardener. Helene was never working by her side, but sometimes she sat on the porch, a frosty tea by her side, pointing out a missed spot with a polished, red nail.

Even more than the working, Bea noticed the sadness about the girl. It was as if a large rain cloud floated over her head. If the corners of her mouth ever formed a smile, Bea had yet to see it. Bea had taken to smiling at her, since they were sometimes outside working on the flower beds at the same time. Once Bea had taken an extra pair of garden gloves over for her. The girl's hands were red and her nails split and dirty, but she pulled on the gloves, thanking Mrs. Schott. Bea noticed she'd worn the gloves each time after that.

One really hot day the girl was outside planting bulbs for Helene. She wiped moisture from her face with the back of her arm and sighed as she looked up. It was hard to know if the moisture was perspiration or tears. She straightened her shoulders and tugged at her dress. It was hard to know how old she was—mid teens Bea decided. *She should be in school, she should,* Bea thought.

Anna looked up from her planting to see the sprightly woman who lived across the street approaching. "Young lady, I know just what you need, I do!" proclaimed Bea Schott. With that, she produced a broad-brimmed straw hat, tan with a plaid ribbon around it. "This will take care of that hot sun," said Bea as she placed it on Anna's head. In the shadow of the brim, a smile finally played around Anna's mouth and the angles of her face were softened into a kind of prettiness. Seeing how little it took to please her, Bea was touched. "What's your name, child?" she asked.

"I was named Anna in honor of my grandmother," Anna replied.

"Anna," Bea repeated. "A lovely name. And mine is Bea—Bea Schott. What do you do, Anna, when you are not helping Helene?"

"Mostly, I read," she said and the little smile returned as she thought of Juno and Zeus, Ashley and Melanie, Echo and Narcissus.

"Do you think you might have some time to come over to my house and help me out a bit? I could really use your help, and you might just like to have some extra money to spend on yourself."

The concept of money was incredible to Anna. She had never had ANY money of her own. It had been expected that all Hirams old enough to work would hand their pay to Papa. Out of this, Papa would dole out a meager amount for "mad money" as it was called. Anna would have expected the same except she had never reached an age where she worked anywhere other than in the house. There was no pay for that.

In the month since she'd been with Helene and Edwin, it appeared Helene felt Anna owed them something for her room and board. Anna tried to eat as little as possible, trying to minimize the feeling of indebtedness until Papa returned to take her home.

Anna entertained the possibility of having actual money to spend on herself. She could buy some penny candy at the shop at the end of Park Street. She could wear underwear without mended holes. She might even be able to get a dress no one had worn before her! But that was crazy. Helene would never let her spend time working for someone else…and Papa was surely coming to get her soon.

"Thank you, Mrs. Schott, but I don't think my sister would want me to do that." Her brown eyes, alive with golden flecks for a bit, returned to flat and downcast.

"Maybe she wouldn't mind at all," Bea said. It seemed to her that Helene was a woman who might just have good use for private time, especially during her husband's frequent absences. With the right approach, she might be all too willing to have Anna out of the house for a while. "But how about you, Anna. If your sister agreed, would you like to come over now and then? I could use your help and I would love your company. I always wanted a daughter, I did, but after my Johnny was born there never were more babies. I could wait forever for Johnny to bring a young lady around."

Anna was obviously warmed by Mrs. Schott's enthusiasm, but life's events had indicated that things this good did not happen to her. "I'd love to, Mrs. Schott, but I doubt my sister will let me. Thank you, though." With this she started to hand the hat back.

"Oh, no, Anna girl. That is for you, it is. Wear it when you're working in the hot sun. It makes you look pretty, it does."

Anna couldn't believe her good fortune. She touched the hat, tenderly, trying to shield it from the dirt on her work gloves. "Thank you, Mrs. Schott, It's wonderful." Apart from her two books and Mama's nightgown, which she removed from the drawer and carefully placed on the chair each night, it was her most precious possession.

"It was made for you, it was, Now, don't let me disturb you further. I will be over to talk to Helene, I will. Goodbye for now, Anna girl." With this, Bea Schott returned to her house to refine her idea.

Chapter 8

Several days had passed and Mrs. Schott hadn't come over to talk to Helene, so Anna stopped hoping she would. While she was clipping around the trees or polishing Helene's perfume bottle collection, she allowed herself the luxury of considering just what she would do if she had any money of her own. Actually, Anna had very little knowledge of what things cost, since she'd only shopped at Dinghen's Market and Mr. Dinghen put everything on the Lords' bill. A bag of apples or a tray of pork chops was only so many notes on a sheet of paper to Anna. She was sure those would not be the kinds of purchases she'd make anyway. That week, as Mr. Dinghen filled Helene's order, Anna looked around with more interest than usual. There was Pond's cold cream to make your skin soft. Anna's skin still had the blush of youth on it, but she imagined it could use some softening. There were no books for sale at Dinghens, but Anna would dearly love to own another book. Perhaps she could buy a bookplate too—one that was inscribed "Property of Miss Anna Hiram."

As Bea Schott left the Lords' front porch, she couldn't stop herself from grinning. "You handled that pretty well, old girl, you did," she thought to herself as she recalled the conversation she'd just had with Helene. Bea had waited until Edwin was gone for a few days before approaching the young woman. Although she seemed to have an endless supply of chores for Anna, Bea had seen a look of restlessness on Helene's face and the company she'd entertained during her husband's absences had dwindled since Anna's arrival. When she saw Anna heading down the street with a list in her hand, Bea started across the street to the Bingham – No, the Lord – house where Helene sat on the glider with one smooth leg swinging across the other. She held a movie magazine, but her eyes darted around and her long, pink fingernails drummed a rhythm on its pages. "Helene, I thought you could use a cold lemonade on this hot day, I did." Bea held out a frosty glass she had brought with her.

Helene looked at it longingly, but she looked away almost immediately. "It sure looks good, but today is Monday, and I only have water and bouillon on

Monday. I was up a pound today, and a girl has to watch her figure, although sometimes I wonder why," she pouted. Her hand patted her trim midsection where she seemed to feel the offending pound was hiding.

"Well, it's very clear how you keep that pretty shape, it is. Do you mind if I sit with you a bit?"

"Suit yourself," Helene replied. "There's a chair right over there."

"It looks like your Edwin is off making money again. He's a hardworking man, he is," Bea began.

"Yeah, that would be Edwin—always somewhere else. Today, he's in Scranton, I believe. I can hardly keep track—but he calls me. He misses me something terrible."

"I can see he would," agreed Bea. "So, you're on your own a lot, or at least you were before your company arrived."

"You mean Anna? She's not much company I can tell you. She's a little mouse with her nose buried in a book all the time. My father dumped her on me so he can have his privacy with his new lady. Randy old prick! My mother wasn't dead six months before he started up with her. Having Anna around wasn't convenient so he brought her here for a "visit". He could care less about what is convenient for me. I've got enough to do, handling this big house without having her around all the time."

"She's a growing girl, I bet she eats you out of house and home," stated Bea.

"You've got that right. Now there are more dishes to wash, more food to buy, not to mention the other things she needs. Do you think there is a penny from the old goat? You bet there isn't. He's off in pig heaven with his new wife, we hear. Now, it seems to me those who have kids should take care of them. The esteemed REVEREND never let a year go by without knocking my mother up. Of course, why should he worry about food? Everything we ate was donated by his congregation, and my mother was killing herself canning and baking to keep us going while he was off flirting with the matrons in the name of the Lord!" Helene stopped, flushed, while Bea assessed the depth of this woman's hatred for the man who had given her life.

"I see your point about the expense, and it seems your father hasn't realized that a young couple like you might like some private time too," said Bea. Helene nodded in agreement. "In fact, an idea is coming to me that might help us all out. Now, you know I never had another child after Johnny. Although he's a good boy, I don't have anyone to help me with the things a girl can do. How would you feel about your sister taking some of her meals with us? I never got out of the habit of cooking for three when Mr. Schott died, so I would be glad to be rid of the leftovers that are always stuffing my icebox. Anna can do a few chores for me and I'll pay her a bit. Maybe she can sew a little so you won't have to provide all her clothes. From what you said, I judge her father won't be needing her back right away unless it doesn't work out with the new lady."

"Well, I don't know," Helene began, the potential for free time playing on her mind. She wouldn't even have to mention it to Edwin at first. He never seemed to notice the girl anyway, he was so busy pawing and fawning over her when he got home. Then, after a few days he'd be off again, thinking Anna was there the whole time. Still, she didn't want to appear too eager.

"I could sure use her, I could, but if you can't spare her company, I will understand," Bea turned as if to leave. "That would leave you with a lot of time by yourself. I'd understand if you can't see your way to doing me this favor." Bea reached into her pocket and brought a pink, initialed handkerchief to her nose, watching Helene's reaction from behind it.

"Maybe I could, Mrs. Schott. You know I'd love to help a neighbor. Of course, I would have to talk to my husband about it, but I think we can help you out."

"That would be just fine, it would. I appreciate your consideration." With that, Bea stood up, tucked the handkerchief into her pocket, and picked up the untouched lemonade, not so frosty now. As she stepped down the porch stairs, the beginning of a satisfied smile was hidden from Helene's view. Up the street, she saw Anna, returning with a bag of groceries.

Chapter 9

Helene wasted no time getting the arrangement set up once the idea started to set in. It was true that Anna did a lot of work around the house, but she relished the time she'd have to herself if Anna was occupied elsewhere. She thought of Mick Levski, a leftover from her pre-marital days, and how hard it was to keep him out of sight since Anna had arrived. He was such a bull of a guy, a red-headed barbarian really; she could actually see him busting into the house if she didn't make some arrangements for them to be together more.

Helene had really intended to give Mick up when she got married. Mick, in fact, had proposed about the same time Edwin did, but she had to remind herself that Mick was not the kind of man you married. Christ, it would be worse than life with the Reverend—no money to speak of and a domineering hulk trying to keep you in your place all the time. No. Edwin was definitely the best route out of Paxon Ave, but Helene didn't find it as easy to cut her ties with Mick as she'd planned. The very things she despised about him for the long term made him oh-so-delicious for the short term. When Mick grabbed her and pulled her to him, she felt she had as much power as a twig in a windstorm. Mick never asked for sex—all Mamby-Pamby like Edwin did; he took her, throwing her on the bed, on the grass, in the back seat of the car—wherever they happened to be. One day, when she got out from under Papa's eye, she and Mick had driven to the next town. They were making their way down an alley that cut through to a Front Street hotel when Mick backed her up against a trash bin and reached up under her skirt, working his hand up the inside of her thigh. In anticipation of the hours to come, Helene had worn no panties at all, and when Mick's fingers discovered that fact, he went wild. His fingers were into her in a second, and while her mind registered the sounds of the restaurant workers just feet away, her body found their presence even more exciting and met his probing fingers with moist willingness. Mick was unzipped and into her in a moment, and Helene still got wet when she thought of the two of them beside that restaurant, pumping into each other in the dusk.

The fact that someone might come along made it more exciting than any of their previous meetings and there had been some competition. Mick was not one to hold himself back; in fact, she had to be careful that he didn't bruise her in places where Papa's eyes might see. If Papa got wind of her activities, she'd be Mrs. Mick Levski in no time flat. As much as Helene wanted to be out of the house, she planned her next move as a step up. That definitely eliminated Mick, a loader at the textile factory in Mayville. Besides, what would they do when they weren't in bed? She couldn't picture them out in places where people could see them. Along with that exciting masculinity, Mick exuded a sort of crudeness that was definitely not part of Helene's social plan for the future.

In fact, Mick was a factor in Helene's decision to marry Edwin. Because Mick's urges came on so strong, there often wasn't time to put on a rubber before they made love. Made love? Not exactly the term for it. It was just their bodies mating. Because Helene's own unexpected passion was almost as strong as Mick's, sometimes she didn't have her diaphragm in place either. Pregnancy was not something Helene welcomed at all, but unwed pregnancy was unthinkable. A girl lost all of her leverage when there was a brat on the way. Helene had seen girls stuck with real losers because of that. Therefore, when her period was nearly a week late, Helene became practical. Thinking over all the men she had recently dated, she found Edwin Lord her best candidate. Edwin was kind of skinny and a good fifteen years older than she was, but he had a real pretty house on Park Street and a healthy bank account. He'd spent that extra fifteen years getting himself into a real good position at the textile mill. Edwin spent a lot of time driving to Philly, driving to New York, driving to New Jersey, lining up contracts with sportswear companies for the woven material Mayville Textile was famous for. Another thing about Edwin was he was undemanding. Unlike her other men, Edwin had never pressed her beyond heavy petting. He was interested, all right, but she figured him for once or twice a week tops. The rest of the time she'd have the big house and money to spend while Edwin was out making money like a good husband should. That was fine with Helene. Generally, she didn't like sex that much; she'd found it a great tool to control and manipulate men, only putting out when there was something to be gained. That's why she couldn't figure Mick.

By the time her decision was final, her period had actually showed up, a fact that pleased her greatly. It didn't seem that a real lady got married knocked-up. She saw Mrs. Edwin Lord as a real lady.

She was fixing her hair and lipstick in a room Mick had borrowed from a friend when she gave him the news. He didn't say much; didn't ask her why she wasn't marrying him. He just scratched his head, looked at her with a suggestive grin, and half an hour later she had to fix her hair and lipstick all over again. Helene told herself she'd give him up as soon as she got married. She just had trouble following her own advice.

Her resolve lasted about a month after her wedding. She was dropping some records off at the mill for Edwin, who had to leave for New York before the office opened. Mick was behind the building, smoking during a break, when she started down the stairs from the office. Helene put on her Mrs. Edwin Lord face and nodded cordially at Mick, who'd kept his distance as she'd requested. Looking through her facade, Mick grabbed her by the hand and pulled her into a small alcove at the back of the building. Protesting feebly, Helene tottered on her high heels, smoothing her skirt. Mick reached down and lifted a trap door, then leaped down, pulling Helene with him. Inside the small space, surrounded with motor oil and tools, Mick pulled her to him with the same authority he always had. Helene had missed that. Today Helene was wearing panties, but they were part of her lacy trousseau, so Mick had them off in a moment. Even in the absolute dark, he knew his way around her body well enough that in minutes, with the rhythm of the machines as their music, they were making their own rhythm. Although not what Helene anticipated, it was just what she needed. Before Mick bounded out of the storage compartment to look out so Helene could leave without being seen, he knew when and how long Edwin would be gone as well as the fact that Helene slept with an open window. Helene started looking forward to Edwin's trips. It turned out Mick was better at keeping track of Edwin's schedule than she was at keeping track of Mick's shifts. He was always showing up to her surprise, striding out from behind bushes when she came out with her iced tea, slipping out from behind the dining room door as she passed through on the way to the living room, or—best of all—popping through her bedroom window, which he entered through the front porch roof. Helene had come to leave her window open no matter what the weather. More than once an erotic dream featuring Mick had been interrupted by an even better reality as his big body came down on hers. Mick had been there twice since Anna had arrived, and both times Helene had a fit, scared to death that Anna would hear since her window also opened onto the front porch roof where Mick entered. Actually, having Anna in the next room was a good route to multiple orgasms, but she did have her reputation to consider. She was, after all, Mrs. Edwin Lord.

This thing with Bea Schott could solve all her problems, particularly if Anna stayed overnight on any kind of regular basis. The night Bea spoke to her, Helene went to Anna's room and knocked on the door. She didn't think Anna was asleep, although she usually went to her room early. God knows what the kid did in there. Nothing fun, for sure. Anna opened the door, clearly surprised to see her sister who was reading one of those boring mythology stories again. They hadn't done a lot of chatting since Anna had arrived. What would they talk about? "I'd like to talk to you, Anna," Helene began.

"Of course," Anna said, stepping aside. "Is everything all right? Have you heard from Papa?"

"Everything is just peachy, but I wouldn't hold my breath waiting for the old man. You'll be lucky if you get a birthday card."

"Oh, I just thought maybe…" Anna's voice trailed off. She didn't want to appear ungrateful, but she couldn't get past the feeling that she was always in the way. She was pleasantly surprised that Helene remembered that her birthday was coming up.

Helene's eyes darted around the room and landed on Mama's nightgown, laid out on the bedside chair. "What are you doing with the beautiful gown, Anna? It is much too grown up for a young girl." Helene went to the chair and began to finger the fine lace. "My God, it's hot in here. Let's open the window, for crying out loud." She dropped the nightgown back in the chair, distracted by the heat or something else. "Actually, there is something else I wanted to talk to you about," Helene began, the nightgown forgotten. "Mrs. Schott across the street could use some help around the house, and she thinks you would be a good one to do it. You could go over there one or two days a week. She's even willing to pay you. Now, I would expect some of that for your room and board, of course, but maybe you could get some new clothes. Your clothing is beyond belief." Helene was sounding as excited about this as Anna was. Anna hadn't known anyone as kind as Mrs. Schott since Mama died. "Maybe you could take some of your meals over there too, and even stay over sometimes," Helene continued, pleased with Anna's reaction.

Anna tried to hide her delight. She bit the edge of her mouth to mask the smile she felt starting. She kept her voice even as she replied, “I’d be glad to help Mrs. Schott if that’s what you want.”

Both sisters felt that things could not have gone better.

Chapter 10

Once the plan was in the works, Helene wasted no time in implementing it. Within two weeks, Anna was knocking on Bea Schott's door with regularity. "Mrs. Schott, my sister told me she'd agreed to let me work for you today," Anna said, each time. So far, she had washed Mrs. Schott's good dishes, helped her arrange her beautiful linens in the buffet drawer, and cleaned the crystal prisms that hung from the chandelier in the dining room. Anna loved just handling the beautiful things Mrs. Schott owned. It hardly seemed like work. She was glad to be with Mrs. Schott, who was always so kind and full of stories of the anniversary when she got the crystal vase or the dinner at which she used the damask tablecloth. Anna did wish she looked better and had some stories of her own to share. Today Bea took Anna past the thick rugs and silver right to her sewing room off the kitchen.

"Now, the first thing we need to do is get a nice cup of tea into you, we do." Bea's pot was always steeping, and today it had an aromatic brew of Darjeeling, a tea Anna had never heard of. Bea swirled some honey into a large cup and passed it to Anna, now seated in a cozy chair. Filling another cup for herself, she sat down next to Anna. Anna felt deliciously wicked: no one before had ever suggested that her work time be spent sipping tea. Bea rose to her feet with surprising agility and returned with a box of arrowroot biscuits. "Now these are just the thing with tea, they are!" she proclaimed, passing the box to Anna.

"Mrs. Schott, I will burst right out of my dress," said Anna, on her third biscuit,

"Ah, my girl, speaking of that very thing, I thought we might do a bit of sewing today. I have some of Johnny's socks I have been putting off for ever so long. I do believe I have some material that might do to make you a dress that would fit you a bit better. Let's finish our tea and have a look."

Anna's breath caught when she saw the soft, fine pink material with happy white flowers on it. She couldn't believe something so beautiful and NEW was going to belong to her. It looked expensive. Anna hoped she'd make enough to pay Mrs. Schott for it. She was also nervous about sewing on something so fine. She'd helped Mama darn socks, but she was worried about ruining this beautiful material. Then she'd owe Mrs. Schott and still be wearing these worn hand-me-downs. While they darned the socks, Anna's eyes kept darting to the cotton, so smooth it might be silk. When Mrs. Schott left with the basket of darned socks, she returned with something that looked like tissue paper but it was much stronger. "Since my only child was a boy, we will have to make a pattern for you, Anna girl. You slip out of that dress and we will make you one to fit you right, we will." Anna undid the buttons on her dress. She didn't think it was possible to feel more uncomfortable. She vaguely remembered her older brothers digging in the back yard—a hole to China, they said. As her tattered slip emerged, Anna wished she could drop into that hole to a distant country. Bea didn't give a sign of noticing. She held the paper up to Anna's body, deftly making marks with a blue pencil. She measured the distance from Anna's neck to her waist and the length of her arm from her shoulder. In the front she folded the paper, marking the easement so the new dress would not pull as her present one did. All the while, she asked Anna questions. "Do you like the buttons in front? What kind of sleeves do you like best? How long would you like the skirt to be?" Anna's throat got tight as she was asked about the length. Since Mama's death, everything had been the length dictated by the depth of the hem. The dress would have a smart collar like the ones in Helene's magazines. The sleeves were just below the elbow. The waistband would come to a point in the front, ending in a skirt with just a bit of fullness. Something about Mrs. Schott made her forget her tattered slip. This dress was made just for her. She could wear it just below the knee like the girls in Helene's books. Anna didn't care if she had to work all year for this dress!

"Well, I guess there is a project going on here," Johnny's voice rang out as he stuck his head into the room. He jumped back when he saw Anna in her slip, blushing red as he backed out of the door, bumping into its frame. Johnny Schott was completely at home with accounts and ledgers of the bank, but the opposite sex had always made him feel foolish. If Anna hadn't been so embarrassed herself, she would have laughed at him—so stylishly dressed in a black business suit with matching vest, adorned with his father's gold watch fob—yet stumbling for all the world like a circus clown in oversized shoes. Anna, however, was fully occupied trying to cover her body with tissue paper.

“Johnny Schott, have you ever thought to knock before barging in, have you?” Mrs. Schott chided, amused by her awkward son. “Thanks to Anna, here, your socks are all mended, and you thank her by barging in while I am fitting her for a dress.” Bea’s words were harsh, but her face was soft with love for her only child.

“Gee…I’m sorry…uh…Anna…I didn’t mean…I thought Mom was in here…uh…I better change my clothes. Thanks for the socks.” With that he bolted from the room like an animal freed from a trap. His father had been no ladies’ man, but compared to Johnny, he’d been a virtual Cassanova.

Bea hadn’t thought of John Schott Sr. very much in the past year. In the first two years after his death, everything reminded her of him. When she looked at the claret overstuffed chair, she saw him sitting there for the last time clutching his chest. John had been troubled by indigestion for years so it wasn’t unusual to have him leave the bedroom at night to stride around downstairs where he wouldn’t bother her. That night was different. The “heartburn” wouldn’t pass. Bea had called the doctor but she’d known John was gone by the time the ambulance came.

Bea shook off the memory and smiled at the young girl before her. “I think it’s time to check the stew, I do. It would be about time to put the dumplings in. Why don’t you wash up, Anna? Helene said it was all right for you to take dinner with us.”

“Thank you, Mrs. Schott. I’d be pleased to stay.” Anna put her dress back and slipped into the worn cardigan she’d worn over it. In the pocket was the money Mrs. Schott had given her for yesterday’s work. It seemed to Anna that Mrs. Schott was doing more for her than she was giving, but she treasured the first money she’d ever had for herself. Someday, she’d trade some of it for something worthy of the purchase. She hadn’t decided what yet.

Bea Schott’s stew was a rival for anyone’s. Tender carrots and potatoes nestled among the brown meat in a succulent sauce, but the best part was the dumplings. Anna couldn’t imagine how they stayed so light and fluffy inside when the outside was moist and chewy with gravy. Anna and Johnny each ate two bowls, savoring the tasty mixture. The awkwardness of the sewing room disappeared in the comforting warmth of the kitchen, where the Schotts preferred to eat.

“The Old Sturbridge Building is finally sold on Center Street,” Johnny reported. “We’ll be handling the financing of the sale, and all signs are that the new owners have a viable renovation plan. They will put a barber shop on one side then rent the rest in two parcels. There is already interest in those. The rent from those two should handle the mortgage—a good investment as I see it. People have been reluctant to invest since the downturn, but this kind of boost to the downtown area gives them confidence again." Johnny was relaxed now. Never casual, his white shirt was unbuttoned at the neck and his sleeves were rolled up. His hands came together, each finger touching its twin on his other hand as he spoke. The hanging lamp reflected the golden hair on his arms. Not a man you'd call handsome, Johnny Schott at 30 was pleasant looking with his sandy brown hair already thinning but always so neatly combed. Anna felt his eyes were those of one you could always trust. "…so it gives the buyer some extra capital for unexpected expenses. A new investor always needs backup funds for expenses…" It was hard to reconcile this Johnny with the shy man he was in personal matters. As she finished her stew, Anna thought these people might be the best things in her life now that Mama was gone and Papa had seemed to have forgotten his youngest daughter.

Chapter 11

The decision came a few days later. Anna had kept Mrs. Schott's money in her pocket each day, reluctant to part with it, but her mind formed an image of herself having tea in a real honest-to-goodness restaurant for the first time. Tea seemed so grown up, so elegant. She pictured herself wearing a hat, swirling honey into the fragrant elixir. The image didn't include anything she presently had to wear, but it brought a smile to her lips.

On the chosen day, Helene was off shopping. It seemed to Anna that she was awfully concerned with how she looked, particularly the seams of her stockings. Before she left, she gave Anna her list of instructions. "Now be sure to polish all the furniture in the living room. Be sure the banister in the hall gleams—you know how important first impressions are. Oh, the windows in the hall. So streaked. We can't have that, can we?" Anna doubted that Helene would actually remember her assignments. She seemed more absorbed with her reflection in the mirror with glances at her watch. "If Edwin calls, be sure to let him know I'm shopping," she said as she whirled out the door.

Anna raced through her chores then bolted up the stairs to the bathroom. As usual, her hair was incorrigible as she vainly tried to arrange the errant curls with her brush. She smoothed her dress, reaching in the pocket of her sweater for the coins. They were still there and there was time to get to the Marcus Restaurant and have tea before Helene was back. Knowing she shouldn't, she crossed the hall to Helene's room. The aroma of jasmine permeated the air as if Helene was right there. Anna calmed herself and turned the switch of the vanity light. The lamp's crystal prisms sparkled in light that brought the room into view. There were Helene's movie magazines and more jewelry than Anna had ever seen before. Anna had no interest in bracelets and rings; instead, she picked up a pink hat with a crown of net, tossed aside in Helene's haste. Knowing she shouldn't, she put it on her head, stuffing as much of her hair as possible inside. Quickly, she scampered down the stairs, out the front door, and briskly walked down Park Street. Turn left to Market then two blocks to

Centre Street to number 24, the Marcus Cafe. As she approached the Cafe—the tearoom, as she liked to think of it, she slowed her pace—in keeping with what she imagined ladies did when they went to tea. Bells on the door jingled as she adjusted the brim of the pink hat and eased herself into the tearoom. She smiled at the blue checked tablecloths and the curtains that matched them. It was just as Mrs. Schott had described it. Each table had a number on it; two friends chatted at table 4. A blonde, plump waitress took their order—Coney Island hot dogs and lemonade. Anna sat at table 2 and the blonde waitress soon stopped by with her order pad. She could be anywhere from 20 to 40 years old. She had shiny blonde hair, but there were lines around her black rimmed eyes.

"Tea please. With lemon," Anna stated.

"Just tea, Honey? Or tea with honey?" the waitress snorted at her own joke.

"Tea with lemon and honey," said Anna, fingering the coins in her pocket.

"That will be twenty cents." Anna felt for a dime and two nickels, satisfied that she had enough. She adjusted wayward curls, pushing them under Helene's hat, noticing that there was someone alone at table 8 as well. It made her feel better. The blonde waitress returned with a teapot that looked like it belonged in Mrs. Schott's home. It had blue flowers and a graceful spout. A whole pot for herself. There was also a plate of lemon slices and a bowl of honey. Some day she would own such a pot and have tea every day. As she sipped her third cup, she envisioned the friends she would invite and the gleaming rooms in which they would drink it.

As the church bells chimed, Anna realized she'd stayed longer than she'd planned. She left her coins on the table and headed for the door where she hastened up Centre toward Market.

"Well, that was something," observed the blonde waitress to her co-worker. "She sits there nursing that tea for an hour then runs out without even leaving a tip!"

Breathless, Anna sprinted down Park Street. She headed for the back door, planning to use the back stairs to replace Helene's hat. As she got into the kitchen, however, she heard the sounds of a car pulling into the driveway. Helene's voice was sugary as she said goodbye. Anna took the hat off and scanned the kitchen for a place to stow it—in with the good dishes, she decided. Helene never set the table. Anna would think of how to get the hat upstairs later.

By the time Helene came inside, Anna had a polish cloth in her hand. Anna had been taught never to tell a lie, but if Helene concluded that she'd just finished the furniture, that would be a good thing. Helene, however, didn't even seem to notice. She had a funny smile on her face, making her look somehow softer and sweeter than usual. She had no packages at all. "Did Edwin call?" she asked, but her mind seemed elsewhere.

"I didn't hear the phone at all," Anna answered, sticking to the factual. Anna was starting to relax when Helene's voice rang out, "Anna, what in the hell were you doing in my room? Tell me, you little snoop. You come here right now!" Did Helene notice the missing hat? Anna didn't think she moved anything. Just then the phone rang. Helene picked it up, her voice cooing, "Edwin, I was hoping you'd call…me too, Honey, me too. Now you tell me about your day. Did you break any records? … That's just swell." As Helene went on, it was almost time for Anna to go to Mrs. Schott's and Anna gratefully slipped out the front door, wondering if she may have left the light on in Helene's room.

To Anna's surprise, the subject never came up when she returned that evening. Edwin had called to say he was coming home early, so Helene was focused on that. Helene's hat was still in the kitchen cupboard, but as the week went on, that turned out to be the least of Anna's problems.

Chapter 12

Weekday afternoons fell into a pattern at the Schott's as Anna learned to use the treadle sewing machine with some confidence. A dark skirt now hung in her closet, fitting her just right. The pink dress was taking shape to her amazement.

"Anna, is work all you ever do?" Johnny asked as she meticulously guided the fabric under the heavy foot of the machine. Johnny smiled, noticing that when she concentrated really hard, Anna bit the side of her cheek just a little.

"Oh, this isn't work, Johnny. The mending was done hours ago. This is my dress!" Her hand caressed the material. "Mrs. Sto…your mother is showing me how to do it. If it wasn't for her, I wouldn't have a thing to fit me." Johnny had seen the dress Anna was wearing and noticed that she wasn't the first to strain the seams. Now, however, it was covered up with one of his mother's aprons.

"How close are you to finishing it?" he asked.

"I have the front parts joined and the zipper is finally in place after taking it out three times. I need to join the shoulders and put the sleeves in. I'll need your mom's help with that. Then it's ready to hem."

"Are you ready to do the sleeves, Anna girl? Here I am willing and able. Here's some lemonade for the two of you." Bea's lemonade was special. Fresh strawberries floated in the tart liquid, and sprigs of mint adorned each glass. Johnny drank deeply from the red and blue ringed glass. He passed the glass from one hand to the other. It seemed he was about to say something, but he retreated to the icy drink. Finally, staring into his glass, he began, "Where do you think…" but neither Anna nor his mother heard him.

Anna looked at the nearly finished dress with amazement. "I never hoped to own something so pretty," she stated almost reverently. "How can I ever thank you?"

"You just wear it in good health, Anna girl," replied Bea. "Oh, and I have a few things in this bag I was going to return, but I couldn't find the sales slip.

I would be glad if you could take them off my hands, I would." Anna pulled a soft white sweater, some underwear and several pairs of socks from the bag Mrs. Schott dismissed so casually. How did she deserve this wonderful woman?

Johnny, sitting in the chair by the window, tried to appear disinterested. In fact, he had read the same line in the newspaper he held several times. "So where will you wear that fine dress, Anna?" he finally articulated. His voice caught a little, almost as if he had a cold.

"Where will I wear it?" Anna repeated, smoothing it against her body. "Nowhere I go is elegant enough for this dress. I guess I could wear it to church. Helene never goes to church. (Papa would have a fit) but I've been to the Community church at Centre and 4th Street. They are really nice and don't seem to mind that I'm not dressed up. Maybe I'll give them a treat this Sunday!"

"Maybe the first time out, that dress should go out to eat too. There is a pretty fair chicken and biscuit at the Simple Pleasure on Sunday. How would you two like to go there after church?" Johnny finished in a rush.

"That would be really something, Johnny, but I'm not sure I can afford it." Anna thought of the money in her pocket and all the things it was meant to buy.

"Oh, no," Johnny said, "I mean my treat—a kind of celebration."

"Oh my! That would give me something to shoot for. I think I can get it done by next Sunday," said Anna, now excited by the prospect,

"Yes," said Johnny very quietly, "It will give us both something to shoot for."

Chapter 13

The Sunday service at the community Church ended at 12:20 after the Rev Gernold admonished his parishioners for at least forty minutes regarding the rewards of a charitable life. To Anna, it seemed like an odd sermon. Back in Papa's church, she couldn't recall hearing anything other than the wages of sin. Papa's voice would boom through the nave, finding sin in almost any human activity. The members seemed glad to hear it, though. They nodded their heads strenuously, shook his hand firmly, thanked him abundantly for his inspiration, then went about their sinning again on Monday. Even Daniel Gruber, who was well known for spending time with women other than his wife, Lavinia, seemed determined to turn over a new leaf on Sundays.

But Anna didn't want to think about Papa now and spoil this beautiful day. She did feel nervous when she thought of how long it had been since she'd heard from Papa. He'd said he'd be back to get her soon, but soon—no matter how you measured it—was long past now. Anna couldn't imagine Helene wanting to have her around very long; in spite of all her efforts to be helpful, she'd sometimes find Helene watching her with a frown and frequent looks at the clock. Soon after, she often sent Anna over to Mrs. Schott's to see what she could do for her.

Anna, Johnny and Mrs. Schott shook hands with the Rev. Gernold, who commented on how pretty Anna looked. The new dress nipped in around Anna's waist, slipping over her hips to a swirl of flowers that swung when she walked. Underneath was a brand-new pair of underwear and Anna's socks exactly matched the pink of the dress. Anna felt so fine as she slid into the new car Johnny had "invested" in. As Mrs. Schott pushed her considerable bulk into the front seat, Anna was pushed tight against Johnny. She was afraid he couldn't work the shift with her so close, but he started the car up the hill with no problem at all, except that his face was a bit red.

The Simple Pleasure had big oak tables with white linen tablecloths and ruffled curtains at the window. Forest green napkins stood at attention at each place. When the waitress brought them glasses of water with lemon wedges, Anna thought she vaguely remembered her from school, but the girl's name didn't come to her. School seemed so long ago. They looked over their menus. Potato pancakes with applesauce sounded good, but she gave in to the broasted chicken with dumplings—a specialty of the restaurant. She wondered if it would be too bold to order a slice of the shoo-fly pie too. Big wedges of homemade bread and a dish of corn relish started the meal. As they chatted about the minister's blatant pitch for bigger pledges, the savory chicken arrived, with dumplings swimming in a rich gravy, reminding Anna of the meals her mother once cooked. Anna felt lucky indeed to be sharing this day with wonderful friends like the Schotts.

"How do you like the chicken, Anna?" Johnny asked.

"It's food for the Gods," she replied. "Better than ambrosia."

"Isn't ambrosia that fruit salad Mrs. Loftus brings to church suppers?" asked Bea.

"It was all the Greek Gods ate and they drank only nectar," Anna shared.

"Didn't they have meat sacrificed to them? I seem to remember stories about that," said Johnny.

"They did require sacrifices. In return they gave gifts to people. Poseidon gave them safety on the seas; Ares gave them swift journeys and protection from thieves; Athena gave them wisdom and cunning in battle, and Aphrodite gave them beauty and love."

"How do you know so much about Greek Gods?" asked Johnny.

"I love to read about them. Often, when I've finished my work for Helene, I reread one of the myths in my book."

"Well, you must have sacrificed some of your chicken to Aphrodite. You sure do look pretty today," declared Bea.

Snuggled between them in Johnny's new car, Anna heard Bea softly singing, "Let me call you sweetheart. I'm in love with you."

Anna joined in, "Let me hear you whisper that you love me too. Keep the love-light burning in your eyes so blue." Johnny joined them for the last line, "Let me call you sweetheart. I'm in love with you." As they slowed on Park Street, Anna didn't notice the unfamiliar car pulling out of the Lords' driveway.

Chapter 14

It was Monday and Helene didn't eat on Monday if she was one pound over her weight the previous Monday. As a result, all Anna had to prepare was broth for Helene and something for herself. Edwin was out of town. That made Monday a logical choice for heavy cleaning—not so much for Helene as for Anna. Helene, herself, was doing what she called "hand pressing," smoothing the clean clothes that didn't need ironing as they came off the line and folding them before Anna returned them to their drawers.

Anna finished scrubbing the kitchen and sun-porch floors then returned to the dining room where Helene was applying lotion to her hands, claiming exhaustion after finishing a pile of folded towels. "Have you heard anything from Papa?" Anna inquired of her sister. "When do you think he'll come back for me?" Anna herself had heard nothing.

"Roughly, never, I'd say, unless the witch dumps him. That old buzzard is definitely a man who prefers a woman in the kitchen and the bedroom to a cleaning girl. He has his hands full with the new Mrs. Hiram, I hear." Helene chuckled.

Anna regularly cleaned Helene's house from top to bottom, so she certainly "paid her keep" as Helene liked to put it. Now, with the time she spent at Schotts' she felt things were starting to go her way. She actually hoped Papa wouldn't come back and take her to a house that was certainly the new Mrs. Hiram's domain by this time.

Anna wondered who had done the work before she came. Writing letters, doing her nails, taking bubble baths, and reading movie magazines seemed to keep Helene very busy. When she was in a mood to talk, Helene could tell you about any movie star you could name. Betty Grable was her special favorite. Betty was married to a band leader named Harry James. She had beautiful legs that were actually insured for thousands of dollars. Helene often went to the movies—with Edwin if he was home or without him. She had never invited Anna to go so Anna had never been inside a movie theater. Anna would never bring it up since it didn't seem right to ask Helene to pay her way, and she had more pressing uses for the money Mrs. Schott paid her.

"Are you finished with those floors, Anna? If you are, the furniture could use some polishing." With that, she picked up an armload of towels. "Gee, I'm bushed. I think I'll take a bath and have a little rest."

Anna went to the cupboard to get the lemon oil. Helene's house had so much woodwork that she could polish until her next birthday and not be finished. She decided to polish the beautiful mahogany furniture in the dining room. She loved the way the rich wood gleamed, providing a striking background for the footed punch bowl. With long, smooth strokes, she applied the polish then rubbed it until she could see her own reflection in the tabletop. Although Helene often pointed out that she needed to get her hair cut it never happened, so her unruly curls were still pulled back into a thick braid, making her face all angles. Maybe she should ask Mrs. Schott about someone to cut her hair. Rampant freckles collided on her nose. No one would mistake her for Betty Grable, that's for sure!

With the top finished, she slipped under the table to polish its sloping Duncan Pfyfe legs. Helene must have decided against the bath. Anna heard her voice from the kitchen, and she seemed to be in a much better mood. From under the table, Anna heard another, deeper voice and Helene's responsive laugh. Anna couldn't make out much of what they said at first, but Helene's voice was lilting and the man's was deep and throaty. As they approached the dining room, Anna stayed motionless under the table. Helene would never believe she was just polishing under there, being firmly against "snooping around," as she called it.

"All those Mondays are paying off. That is one tight little body you have, Baby," said the man.

"Shhh. My sister is around here somewhere. The kid is under my feet all the time. I hardly have a minute to myself."

"I don't see her and good old Edwin is off making bucks, so what do you say to a little fun?"

"I told you…" there was a long silence and then Helene's staggered breath. "God, Mick, you sure do that good."

"There's some other things I can do if I haven't lost the touch. How does this feel?"

"Mick, get out of here before she comes back." Helene straightened her hair and rebuttoned her blouse.

"That is just a taste. I'll be back. Leave your window open tonight."

With no dinner, Anna didn't have to avoid Helene's eyes at dinner. After her bath, Helene wrapped herself in a soft robe and started working on her nails, which already looked perfect to Anna. Helene was not in the mood to talk so Anna went upstairs where she could hear Rosemary Clooney's voice wafting up from the living room. Anna looked at her own nails, split and ragged from the daily hours of housework, then looked at her reflection in the mirror. Maybe some make-up would help, she thought guiltily. Anna had heard Papa's diatribes to her older sisters on the subject of make-up. Painted women, he called them. Whores of Babylon. Babylon, she had been instructed, was a city in the Bible which had been destroyed because of wickedness. Make-up, perhaps, or even worse.

Anna quickly bathed, careful not to use too much water. She'd heard Helene complaining that the hot water bills had been out of sight since Anna had arrived. She dried her hair with the towel and returned to her room. Without the braid her hair curled around her face, framing the angles to a softness. *It looked better, probably because it hid part of her face,* she thought. She reached into her drawer for the filmy nightgown that had been her mother's. Tenderly, she draped it over the chair by her bed as she did each night. It had become the only link to a childhood that seemed ever more distant. Having it nearby made it seem as if part of Mama was still with her.

The shirt she had been wearing to bed had become too tight for comfort, so she slipped into the bed without it. Pulling the quilt under her arms, she reached for the copy of *Gone with the Wind.* Anna had never seen Helene read a book, and yet it had been on the Lords' bookshelf along with several other recent books. Edwin had told her she could help herself. She found it equal to the Greek myths she loved and enormously better than Helene's magazines. Scarlet was so spirited and strong. She reminded Anna of Hera, queen of the Gods. She was beautiful, but not helpless as beautiful women often seemed to be. Anna hoped to be more like that. She wondered if there were any real-life men like Ashley. As her eyes grew heavy, she wondered if she'd be more like Scarlet or Melanie if she ever had someone to love.

Chapter 15

Sometime later Anna was aware of a sound, just at the end of her consciousness—a scraping sound, as if a tree branch was rubbing the house. Her body tensed defensively, differentiating it from the familiar sounds of the night. The room was dark, although she didn't recall turning the lights out. Her book was back under her pillow, but a cool breeze wafted over her chilled, bare body. As she reached for the quilt, she heard the breathing to her left. There was a shadow between her and the window. Anna slowly and quietly groped the right side of the bed, trying to separate herself from the barely audible sound. As she pushed with her left arm a strong hand clamped her wrist. Another hand clamped down over her mouth. Around a large form, she could see that the window was open. Her exposed body shrank from the cold night air and whatever partially blocked it.

"Well, what do we have here?" The whispered voice was raspy but she recognized it as the one she heard when she was under the table earlier. The left side of the bed sank as he sat on it and her body rolled toward him in spite of her clutching fingers. A sour smell like the port wine Papa drank clung to him, mingling with the spice of his after-shave lotion. He shifted his weight, throwing his leg over her. His hand clamped her wrist like a manacle. Her mouth was briefly released, allowing her to gulp some air. "Now, you don't want to be making any noise, do you?" He lifted his hand in a threatening motion. Anna closed her eyes, willing him to disappear, but his weight stayed on her pinning her legs. and he roughly fondled her breasts. A blast of foul breath clouded her nostrils and then his mouth was on hers, working her lips. Then his tongue was in her mouth, making her want to gag. Anna felt sick and she knew she could choke on her own vomit since she couldn't free her face from his. His hands were pressing every part of her, up and down her body and between her legs which he pried open with his knee. Anna twisted her head, gasping for air, pummeling him with a free hand, but his shoulder pinned her to the bed and she could feel a new pressure between her spread legs as he shifted and adjusted his clothing. Sweat, cold and nausea co-mingled with a jolt of pain as he plowed into her body, rutting, pounding, and sending white-hot jolts of pain through her. Anna went limp, waiting for him to finish, tasting blood from her own lip as she prayed to die.

It was over. He was beside the bed pulling up his pants. Now accustomed to the dark, she could see him looking down at her. "You are a sexy little bitch," he said, his voice soft but guttural. She pulled her legs together as tight as she could, clenching an oozing wetness between them. "Now, you aren't going to want to be talking to your sister about this. She isn't so hot on having you here in the first place, let alone you teasing her friends with that body of yours. What is a guy to do when a hot little number like you comes on to him, huh? That's what I'll say. What good girl would be wearing a fancy nightgown like this if she didn't have something in mind? And it isn't torn a bit, so you must have been good and willing."

I wasn't wearing that nightgown, Anna thought, then she realized how that would sound. Of course Helene would know Mick did this, but she'd never give them away by saying so. Edwin, it seemed, would think whatever Helene told him to think. Anna buried her face in the pillow as Mick climbed out the window to the porch roof.

Anna examined the damage to her body-the tender places along her arms and wrists where he had held her down. There was a burning between her legs and on the sheet was blood mixed with something thick and white. Limping into the bathroom, she washed every place he had touched her and brushed her teeth over and over. In the dresser she found the clean strips of sheet she'd used for the bleeding before. Again, she wrapped them between her legs and around her body. Her face was brush-burned from his whiskers, but he hadn't hit her. She wasn't going to die from this. If Persephone could survive six months in the underworld with Hades, she could get through this. Clutching Mama's nightgown, she crawled back into bed and forced her mind, once again, back to her last afternoon with her mother in the front seat of their car.

Chapter 16

Edwin Lord pulled the maroon Packard convertible into the narrow driveway of his home on Park Street, careful not to touch the bushes Helene had growing near the front walk. That Helene was pretty picky, but she was some looker. He never took her anywhere without all the guys eyeing her up. He felt pretty pleased that she was his wife. In fact, he'd been darned surprised when he'd asked her out two years ago and she'd accepted. Edwin had been a success in his business, but his experience with girls was limited, and he would have bet that Helene would have gone for a faster guy. She had accepted, though, and they'd had a good time—dinner at the Armory Inn and a ride in the old Chevy he'd had at the time. Helene had asked him a lot of questions about his job, how long he'd been there, what he hoped to do in the future—a lot of stuff he wouldn't have thought she'd have been interested in. She was, though, and she let him kiss her good night when he brought her back to the Reverend Hiram's house. It had to be early, she said, since her father was so strict. In fact, the Reverend had propped a hammer up inside the door when his daughters were told to be in, and if he heard it drop, someone was in big trouble. Of the girls, only the rebellious Norma had been athletic enough to crawl in and out of the upstairs window by climbing the tree.

Edwin never deceived himself that he was the only man Helene was seeing, but she seemed to stay interested. It was not too much later, when they were walking down Center Street, that Helene pulled him over to show him the rings in Marston's Jewelry Store. The one she really liked was close to three months' salary. Edwin hadn't really thought about getting married before then, but once the idea settled in, it felt pretty good. Having a beauty like Helene waiting for him with dinner, putting her arms around him, sleeping next to him after they made love; it sounded too good to be true. It was.

By Christmas Helene was wearing that ring and telling Edwin what an old man car the Chevy was, so by their wedding day, June 26th, they were driving the Packard convertible. If Edwin was to be disappointed on his wedding night, at least he felt really fine when he saw Helene coming down the aisle, looking like a picture in one of her magazines, and no man was ever prouder than Edwin driving away in the Packard beside the most beautiful girl he'd ever seen in this town, or any other for that matter. His wife. Helene had told him she just had to have the pale pink suit from Bengers for their honeymoon. Of course, it just couldn't be worn without the matching hat, handbag and shoes! Edwin happily bought them all for her and pinned a corsage of pale pink orchids on the lapel before they headed off for Niagara Falls. She reached out a slender hand with fingernails painted the exact shade of the suit and patted his cheek. Her beautiful diamond engagement ring glittered next to the band of tiny diamonds on her wedding band as she declared the day was all she'd ever thought it could be.

Helene seemed made for love, so Edwin was surprised and disappointed when she seemed more interested in preserving her hairdo and arranging the folds of her chiffon nightgown than making love that night. New bride jitters, Edwin assumed when she responded to his kisses and caresses with admonitions to be careful about this and not to mess that, please. By the time their union was consummated, Edwin felt like a disgusting animal, participating in an act of lust all alone. He rolled over, feeling lonely, as Helene washed and douched and sprayed in the bathroom.

The next morning, Helene seemed happy as she could be, anxious to talk about their future together and the house they would live in. As they had breakfast in a restaurant overlooking the crashing Niagara, Edwin with the blue plate special: two eggs, two strips of bacon, home fried potatoes and toast, Helene with half of a grapefruit and black coffee, he agreed with her that they would have to buy a lot of furniture and new appliances so they could have a really up-to-date kitchen. Helene seemed so excited about their new life together that he felt sure their first night must have been just a slow start. Wishing on the tiny drops of spray that clung to the window and split into a prism of color, Edwin hoped that their love life would take off like their married life seemed to. Edwin was wrong.

After two years, Helene still loved to shop and seemed to enjoy the changes they made to their home, but there was always something wrong. The house was too much work, she'd said, pouting in a way he still found irresistible. *But now, with Anna here, that should be all right,* Edwin thought. At first, he'd been uncertain about having Helene's younger sister living with them, but

Helene's father really didn't give them much choice. He just showed up with Anna and left. Actually, Anna seemed to be a big help, always doing something around the house. The woodwork gleamed with polish and the floors were so clean, you almost felt bad walking on them. When Anna wasn't working for Helene, she was either over working for Bea Schott or up in her room reading—mostly myths it seemed. She seemed especially determined to stay out of their way lately.

Not that Helene would ever acknowledge any of this. To hear Helene, you'd think that Anna was a burden she had to bear, a guest she had to wait on. Well, Edwin was certainly not entering that arena. Don't make waves was a good policy with Helene.

Today, Anna was in the kitchen starting supper when he came in the back door. She looked like a little waif with her head bent over the vegetables in the sink as she peeled them. Edwin felt guilty. Her clothes looked shabby and outgrown. She should at least have some decent clothes after all the work she did for them. Edwin hated to bring it up to Helene, however. "Here comes the Lord of the manor," Edwin quipped, "and where is my lady?" Anna mumbled something, but the words got caught in her hair, hanging loosely by the side of her face. Edwin approached her and gently pulled the wayward curls back to hear her better. Anna tried to avert her eyes as mumbled, "Helene's in her room doing her nails," but Edwin saw the red rims around them anyway.

Awkwardly Edwin dropped his hand as the smile left his face. "Is something wrong, Anna?" he asked.

"Oh, no, Edwin. I was just peeling onions," Anna replied. Edwin saw no onions, only potatoes and carrots in the sink full of vegetables, but he decided to let it go.

"I'm sure it'll be delicious, Anna. You're a great cook." With that he went in search of his wife.

Chapter 17

In the ten weeks that had gone by since "that night" as Anna had labeled it in her mind, life had gone on undisturbed for everyone else, it seemed. Anna, however, felt as if she were in a plastic bubble, moving around in the world and yet separated from the rest, somehow gasping for breath as if she existed in rarefied air, just a bit short of oxygen. She continued to do Helene's housework but avoided contact with her sister otherwise, always wondering if her sister had found out what happened and blamed her for it. It seemed as if Helene was looking at her strangely at times. Where would she go if Helene made her leave? In all the time since her father had left her for her "visit" she had heard nothing from him. Even on the hottest of evenings the window to her room remained securely locked, but still Anna could never sleep soundly. The slightest sound in the night, even an innocent gust of wind on the shutter sent her into a panic of wakefulness. Since the day Edwin had spoken to her in the kitchen, she'd sometimes see him looking at her with concern, but she didn't see how he could know about her without knowing about Helene too. She was pretty sure he didn't.

Mick continued to show up when Edwin was out of town, and Anna found herself often hiding in the bathroom or out behind the storage shed in the back yard to escape an encounter with him. So far, she had been successful, except for one day when she was hanging clothes on the line and looked up to see his face in an upstairs window. Before she could duck behind the shed, he smiled a leering smile that seemed both predatory and conspiratorial. Anna turned, her face a bright red as if she had actually played a part in the secret they shared. How could she talk to anyone else about what happened when she somehow felt blamed for it?

And so Anna suffered alone. Her eyes took on dark rings from sleepless nights. Her face was drawn and her appetite was reduced to nothing, although it did nothing to eliminate the tightness of her outgrown clothes. The tops were especially tight, and Anna's breasts ached dully. Needles of pain shot through her when she bumped them accidentally. Mrs. Schott had given her an apron which is really like a dress with no back, which allowed her to unbutton some of the tight buttons, relieving the strain on the old dresses which she still wore beneath.

Even her time at the Schotts' was different. After all the measuring and calculation, her latest new dress, which seemed to fit just fine, was too tight around the waist and she had to let it out before she could wear it. Anna had taken the seams apart with Mrs. Schott's guidance, but seemed strangely disinterested in the reassembly. Bea Schott worried about the change in Anna. She was as polite and hard working as always, with little fleeting smiles when Bea teased her about her hair and her freckles, but there seemed to be no joy in the girl anymore. Her eyes often looked out past Bea's face as they talked, and Bea could swear there was a glimmer of fear in them. Anna, however, maintained that everything was fine.

One afternoon when Anna was washing beautiful crystal goblets that were way up on the top shelf of the cupboard, Bea—drying the beautiful footed glasses—reminisced "My mother gave these to me when I married my John. She saved up the whole time we were promised, she did, so we had twelve of them by our wedding day. You know, I don't think we ever used them. It seemed there wasn't a time special enough, but just owning them was enough, it was." Bea had tuned the radio to the Passion of Margot Malone. Now Bea didn't make a practice of listening to Margot's woes every day, but there certainly could be no harm in listening as you polished the crystal and put it away, she told Anna. Anna nodded and just kept washing the goblets, carefully placing them in the dish rack here Bea could retrieve them and polish them to glistening brilliance. As usual, Margot's bravado had gotten her into trouble. This time she was standing up to Buck, the neighborhood bully, that Margot felt sure had pushed her first love down the stairs to his death. Margot had ignored her current fiancé's advice to stay clear of Buck. Now he had her alone, and organ music swelled as he crossed the room toward her, torn between his need to eliminate the threat she posed and his interest in her heaving bosom. There was clearly nothing Margot could do as Buck, outweighing her by seventy pounds cornered her by the couch. He couldn't keep his hands from clutching her as she fell onto the couch, where he was quickly on top of her, pinning her fisted hands to her sides. A crescendo of organ music led to a Duz commercial, but not before a ragged sob filled the room.

Anna fell to her knees, dropping one of the precious goblets which broke on the floor as her soapy hands came to her face trying to quell the sobs which convulsed her body. As the glass disintegrated into fragments, Anna did too, all the pain she had been suppressing escaping in this unguarded moment. Bea took the sobbing girl in her arms, lifting her to her feet away from the glass shards. "Oh, Mrs. Schott, I am so sorry. Your beautiful glass; your wedding present." The rest of what Anna had to say was swallowed in gasping sobs.

"Now, Anna girl, don't you worry. There's not a thing that can't be replaced, but people are another thing, they are. There's something worse wrong with you than with that glass, and you are going to tell me right now." Anna clung to the older woman, releasing all the fears, doubts, guilt and agony she'd been carrying by herself. By the end of the avalanche, Bea Schott knew it all—the reason why Anna's dress no longer fit and the source of the desperation and despair she'd seen in the girl.

Chapter 18

Edwin Lord was barely home from a lengthy business trip to Boston, when he knew that something was up. Helene came sauntering out of the back door to greet him, sending the white pleats of her skirt swinging back and forth. It reminded him of the early days of their dating and that sweet period just after he'd agreed to her choice of a diamond. She smiled up at him, reaching to run her finger through the hair just above his ear. He put his arm tentatively around her, but he didn't feel the familiar stiffening he'd come to expect since their marriage. Encouraged, he leaned toward her lips, but she averted his kiss. "Edwin, honey, I just put fresh lipstick on, and just for you," she pouted prettily. "Would you like something to drink?" she asked. This, too, was a surprise as Helene was usually on the porch or in the parlor when he returned, waiting for him to bring her a drink as he passed through the house. He followed her into the kitchen and she opened the refrigerator, taking out a pitcher of martinis she'd already mixed. Helene had her modern kitchen with its new range and a refrigerator that put the old ones to shame. Small appliances of all kinds gleamed on the yellow counter. Some had probably never been used since Helene was dieting more often than not. It did pay off. Nobody looked better in a pair of shorts, or a pleated skirt, for that matter, than Helene did.

"Where's Anna?" Edwin asked.

"Oh, she's over at the Schotts'. She'll have dinner with Bea and Johnny tonight. She's in another of her moods," Helene replied. "Tonight is just the two of us. I have everything ready."

Edwin tried not to show his shock that Helene had made dinner. It was hard to recall the last time she had. If she wasn't dieting, then Anna cooked or Helene wanted to go out to dinner. He sipped his martini and took the cold chicken salad plate she was handing him. She led the way to the dining room where the table was set with his mother's good china. A tall glass flute was filled with fruit at each of their places and a basket of sweet rolls was between the two place settings. "This looks great, Helene. You didn't do this all by yourself did you?"

"Well, no, Silly, but I did make the chicken salad after Anna cooked the chicken breasts. Look here; it has celery and nuts, even grapes in it. The rolls came from McGrooders' Bakery. Don't they look swell? Here, pull up your chair." She smiled and held out her martini glass, now half empty. "Here is to our future and our family." A smile played around Helene's mouth.

Enjoying himself immensely, Edwin couldn't help but wonder what Helene was up to. These spurts of domestic dedication always preceded the need for some rather large investment in the house or Helene's personal needs. Edwin waited to find out what it would be. It didn't take long. As soon as she finished the little bit of chicken salad, she allowed herself, Helene moved her chair closer to his.

"Edwin, how long have we been married?"

"Well, it feels like about six months."

"No, silly, I mean really. We had our two-year anniversary. Let's see." She counted on her immaculately manicured lavender tipped fingers, "June, July, August, September, we're married two years and four months." Edwin wondered what purchase was called for at two and a third years, but he enjoyed her enthusiasm. "Do you ever think about a family, Edwin?"

"Well, I always thought I'd like to be a family man someday, but you always said that childbirth was not for you, and I can live with that. I would be a very happy man if you changed your mind, though. Is that it? Helene, do you want to have a baby?"

"You know I couldn't do that, Edwin, not with my small bones and all. Having a baby would kill me. Plus you know what childbirth does to your body. Why, I'd never be the same. I have felt that I'd like a child, however. It's so lonely here when you're away. A baby would give me someone to play with and I could dress it so cute. It would be my little doll. As it happens there is a girl in the family way who will need someone, a good, married family, to adopt her baby. Her family won't accept her with a child. We could help her out. What do you think, Edwin?" It didn't actually matter what Edwin thought, and he knew it. The Lords were going to be parents.

Chapter 19

As Anna put the last of her few clothes in the suitcase, her mind was on the day at the Schott home when she accepted the truth of her situation.

When she'd burst into tears with Mrs. Schott, the older woman felt sure that the girl was about to have a baby. "Now, now, Anna girl. It's not your fault, it isn't," she had cooed. Anna herself had fallen into stunned disbelief. A baby? How could she have a baby? She didn't feel at all like a grown-up herself. It was true, however, that her clothes were becoming tight. But how could what Mick did to her, ever result in a baby? He had hurt her, torn her. There would never be any babies if that was the way it happened. A baby? HIS baby! It seemed beyond Anna's grasp. Yet she knew it was true as Mrs. Schott held her with her calming words. Since that day Anna had stumbled through the reality of her situation like one in a deep fog, without purpose or direction. After her outburst, a few weeks ago, she'd withdrawn into a kind of distanced presence, impervious to Mrs. Schott's attempts to draw her out.

Certainly, the family would take care of her, Mrs. Schott had decided. Mrs. Schott offered to talk to Helene for her, but Anna refused. She knew Helene would do anything to keep her relationship with Mick a secret, no matter what it meant for Anna.

It was just one week ago when Helene had burst into the bathroom, startling Anna as she was getting out of the tub. Anna had clutched the towel around her naked body, but Helene had torn it from her, looking at her once flat belly and the blue veins that traveled her breasts.

"I thought so!" hissed Helene. "You're knocked up, aren't you? Look at that belly and look at those tits." Helene's nose dilated in distaste as if she could smell the pregnancy.

"Helene, I wanted to tell you," Anna began, "he came—"

Helene wouldn't let her finish. "I'll bet you wanted to tell me. Fifteen years old and sleeping around. You little tramp! I'll tell you; I can't have you in my house, bringing disgrace to the Lords. Edwin won't put up with this! We give you a home, food to eat, and what do you do? You get knocked up!" She spotted Anna's book of myths on the table, and picked it up with a sneer. "You better hope there is a goddess of bastards in this thing!" She tossed Anna's precious book to the bathroom floor.

Anna reached for the end of the towel, but Helene jerked it away, leaving Anna trying to cover herself with crossed arms as she backed into the corner. She suddenly felt like a giant, her body filling the room with enormous blue-veined breasts. Her face lit with shame as if she'd actually been responsible as Helene was suggesting. She couldn't say anything about Mick. Of course Helene wouldn't even acknowledge that Mick had ever been in the house. Helene tossed the towel to the floor and Anna lunged for it, clutching it to her disgusting body.

"What exactly do you think you'll do with the little bastard? Girls like you go to the Overton home and the baby will be put in the orphanage. Too bad more of those kids don't survive," Helene added, arching her eyebrows and measuring Anna's reaction. "And of course, no decent man would want you when he finds out you had a kid already. You have already played a girl's trump card. No man worth having wants a girl like that. Damaged goods!"

Helene stopped as if a new idea had just occurred to her. "Now, wait a minute. Maybe there is something we could do. Of course, we have to get you out of here right away, before you show any more. We can't have anyone suspecting what you've been up to, for Christ's sake. But maybe, just maybe we can find a nice married couple to adopt the baby. No one would have to know. Maybe you could go up to Buffalo with Norma until you had the kid."

Anna, clutching the towel and shivering from a cold that came deep within her, felt like she was in a dark, windowless tunnel. In the far distance, the sound of an enormous engine came relentlessly closer as she searched for any way out. Then, suddenly, there was a crack of light as a door she'd not seen opened the tiniest bit. What was on the other side? She didn't know, but she did know the train was coming and she had to go somewhere.

Within two days it was arranged. Norma was an unknown commodity, like all of Anna's older siblings. She'd escaped Papa's rules at the earliest opportunity while Anna was still a child. Anna could recall her mother shaking her head and saying, "Oh that Norma!" when the high-spirited older sister had escaped her room by climbing out of her bedroom window and down the tree to meet her boyfriend, Al. Norma's barbed comments to Papa lingered in the air as legend long after she'd taken off for Buffalo, NY with Al. Anna couldn't imagine life with Norma being worse than with Helene. At least there would be no Mick. And this way she could save her baby from Overton, where so many babies died.

Yesterday she had broken her silence as she spent her last day at the Schotts' house, sobbing in Bea's arms. "It's not your fault, Anna girl," Mrs. Schott had crooned, rocking her back and forth. "You're a good girl and God will bless you yet, he will." As Anna left the Schott home, she felt she was leaving the only person in the world who really cared about her.

Anna was wrong. Standing on the porch as she came downstairs from her packing was Johnny Schott. He looked miserable as he passed his hat from hand to hand, torturing its brim with his nervous fingers. "Anna, I need to speak to you. Will you come and walk with me a bit?" he asked. Normally, Anna would have been worried about doing anything without asking Helene. In view of the current situation, however, an unauthorized walk seemed insignificant. Anna followed Johnny down the steps.

"I hear from my mother that you're leaving soon," Johnny began.

"Yes, I was finishing my packing. I'll go to my sister's place in Buffalo tomorrow," Anna replied.

"And you're to be a mother too?"

"Yes," Anna acknowledged, lowering her head. "Helene is going to arrange for a couple to adopt the baby."

"Is that what you want, Anna?"

Anna kept her gaze averted. "It's better than Overton. With the baby adopted, I'll know it has good parents and is being taken care of, being loved..." Anna's voice disappeared in a stifled sob. Johnny reached out and took her hand.

"Anna, you do have another choice, and I'm here to give it to you. I propose to marry you and take care of you and the little one. I know many would say I am much too old for you, but I have some money saved, and my mother already loves you like a daughter. I'm no handsome Romeo, but I'm steady and I would always be good to you."

Anna turned to Johnny, amazed by the longest, most eloquent thing she'd ever heard him say. Squeezing his hand in both of hers, she looked at him through blurred eyes. "Johnny, I can't express how you've touched my heart. You and your mother are the two best people on this earth. To be part of your family – it would be such an honor.” Anna looked into Johnny’s bashful eyes, and suddenly she felt she was the older of the two.

“That’s why I can’t marry you, Johnny. Out there somewhere is a girl who will love you with all her heart, without the burden of a child that isn’t yours. You must wait for that girl, Johnny, because you deserve nothing less.”

The next day, Anna was on the train to Buffalo.

Chapter 20

The train came into Buffalo late, but for Anna it had been the travel adventure of her life. It was almost enough to make her forget the reason for her trip for a little while. The train had seemed to fly through the hills that Anna had only seen in the distance through cities that Anna had only heard about. When the train crossed into New York, somewhere north of Scranton, it was the first time Anna had been in any state but Pennsylvania. The clustered mining towns that had brought Anna's grandparents to Pennsylvania gave way to broad fields of black and white Jersey cattle and green, rolling hills where they chewed slowly on the rich clover and low grasses. They passed Schenectady where shoe factories dominated the landscape. Anna didn't know it, because they weren't originally bought new for her, but the very shoes on her feet were made in a city in the shadows of the engine's shriek.

The best part was the dining car. Anna had no bed to sleep in. Helene had said those reclining seats were comfortable enough, although there were people on the train who spent the night in a regular bed with a curtain over the entrance to it. Helene had encouraged Anna to take meals in the dining car. Since the fate of Anna's baby had been decided, Helene was forever stuffing Anna with milk, with vegetables, with fruit, with meat. "We have to be sure that the baby is born healthy. You are eating for two now." As the trip commenced, Helene had given Anna an envelope with money for meals, reminding her once again to drink lots of milk. Anna was astonished at the number of bills in the envelope, as Helene had never before given her any money. At times it almost seemed as if Helene was concerned about her. It was a good feeling Anna had not experienced since Mama's death. When Anna saw the prices on the menu, she realized that she could actually order anything she wanted for the first time. Remembering Helene's dictum, she ordered chicken, green beans, baked potato and a glass of milk.

"Will that be all?" the waiter asked. He stood tall with a towel around his arm. "We have a number of delicious specials today. If you like chicken, you will enjoy our Chicken Oscar, I think. Would the young lady like to try that?" Anna would and she did. Wickedly she changed the milk to chocolate milk too. The only chocolate Anna had ever had was in her stocking at Christmas—well at least up until recently—even though she lived a short distance from Hershey which supplied the whole country with foil-wrapped kisses and brown wrapped chocolate bars. Anna let the delicious milk roll over her tongue feeling the creamy silkiness of the chocolate flavor. The chicken came with a creamy sauce and another meat on top of it. It was Anna's first taste of crab and she found it immediately delicious. The beans came with almonds in them, making them something she was eating for her own pleasure, not just on Helene's instructions. Anna didn't know what had happened to the baked potato. It was already open and it seemed that someone had made mashed potatoes and put them inside the baked one. They were delicious. As she was finishing the last bit of the wonderful meal, the waiter reappeared with a tray containing more desserts than Anna had ever seen. There was apple pie like Mama used to make but quite unlike Anna's attempts. There was a chocolate cake with a lot of skinny layers, but the waiter called it a torte. A dish of pudding was heaped with cream and a red sauce. Anna decided on something called a moose. It too was heaped with cream and Anna thought that was close enough to milk to be good for the baby, so she ordered the Moose, which, by the way, had no resemblance to the animal although Anna kept thinking of the huge, antler burdened beast as she ate it and she had to laugh to herself. Anna felt like she'd been born to wealth as she finished every bit of the Moose and paid for the bill, adding some extra for the waiter as she had seen Johnny do at the Plain and Fancy. Anna leaned back, resting her hand on her full stomach. Only then did she remember the reason for this extravagant journey and by the time they had approached the first of the Finger Lakes, Anna was too worried to notice the beautiful towns with Indian names that surrounded them.

By the time the train arrived in Buffalo, she'd combed her hair, and straightened her now-wrinkled new dress. Since two buttons wouldn't close, in spite of her alterations, her beautiful new dress tended to hang in an awkward and unflattering pleat. She wondered what her sister Norma had been told about her and now the future seemed as scary as the past. She briefly thought of Johnny Schott and what her life would be like if she had accepted his proposal, but she brushed the thought away hastily as an unfair solution to her problem. Most men, Anna knew, would never make such an offer. Once made, however, most girls would snap it up in a second. To be married was to be safe, it seemed, but Anna still dreamed, though probably in vain now, for something more. Yes, love, a drawing together of two people that went farther than convenience. Anna hoped that it was not a child's dream.

As the train pulled into the station, Anna clutched the old suitcase with Mama's name still on it. The porter had offered to take care of her luggage, but she didn't want to let the case with her precious mythology books and Mama's nightgown out of her sight. It was cooler in Buffalo and Anna wrapped herself in the blue-green sweater Mrs. Schott had given her. Anna was not sure who to look for as it had been years since Norma left her family home never to return. No pictures arrived at the Reverend Hiram's home, even when the news came through the grapevine that Norma had a child. If they did, they were never shared or displayed, so Anna had no image whatsoever of her sister. She went into the station, greeted by the largest bronze Buffalo she'd ever seen. There was an enormous clock high up on the tiled wall, telling Anna that her train was two hours late. She wondered if Norma knew this, or if she stayed around in any event. She'd made about 320 degrees of her 360-degree turn when she heard her voice being called. "Anna, is that you?" Anna spotted a woman barely five feet tall who seemed intent on expanding her girth to match her height. Norma strode with surprising agility toward her young sister, holding her at arms' length to get a better look.

"Well, will you look at what the cat dragged in," Norma exclaimed to her companion, a man as tall and thin as she was short and round. "This must be the prodigal sister, bun in the oven and all." Norma laughed with genuine mirth and there was something Anna liked about her at once, in spite of the fact that the laughter was at her expense. The tall companion said nothing, but tipped his hat at Anna. She thought the ends of his mouth may have curved up slightly in a smile, but she couldn't be sure. "What do you think of the last of the Hirams, Charley? She was just a squirt when I took off."

"Lo, Anna," Charley said in a low-pitched rumble. Anna felt sure that Norma's husband's name was Al, but she didn't want to say anything, so she just assumed her best company manners and said, "I am glad to finally meet Norma's husband. Thank you for having me, Charley."

Norma broke out into laughter. "You're thinking of Al—Oh my God. He's long-gone. What a fool, but he got me away from that hell they called home. No, honey, this is the latest model—Charley."

Blushing, Anna extended her hand again.

"Welcome to Buffalo, Anna," Norma said, wrapping her arm around her younger sister, "and welcome to the bitch that is a woman's life."

Chapter 21

If Bea Schott had realized what was going on inside the Lord house, perhaps she would not have waited so long to go over. For one thing, the weather had turned cold very early, keeping Bea inside and Helene off the porch. That being the case, when Bea saw Helene getting into the car two months later, she couldn't believe what she saw. At first, catching her out of the corner of her eye, she didn't think it was Helene at all. When she recognized her young neighbor, she strained for a closer look. Edwin held Helene's elbow solicitously as he eased her into the car.

If Bea had been inside the house, she would have seen the nursery start to emerge in the room where Anna had slept when she was with Helene and Edwin. The walls had been painted a light yellow and white daisies made of felt were blossoming on the walls. A padded changing table flanked a crib of deep mahogany, skirted with yellow and white checks. On a bureau was a lamp that looked like a rocking horse, complete with yarn mane. The drawers of the bureau were already filled with tiny shirts, diapers, and receiving blankets. The Venetian blinds on the window provided shade for naps or bright sun with a pull of the chord. A white rocking chair was padded with yellow fabric and a mobile of butterflies swirled in front of the window. Helene had spared no expense for the new arrival. Perhaps this room would have prepared Bea for Helene's appearance that day. The day was cold, for sure, but in spite of the heavy coat, it was clear that Helene was no longer the slim woman she had been. Her loose hanging dress was pushed out beyond her unbuttoned coat in a noticeable swell.

Is Helene pregnant too? Bea wondered. "And whose baby would it be?" she speculated. Unable to contain her curiosity, Bea made it a point to visit the Lords on the next day. It was true that she could not be called close to Helene, but she could certainly ask about Anna, she could. Helene couldn't know that she'd determined where Anna was going in Buffalo and had sent her several notes to let Anna know that she wasn't alone. She hadn't received anything-back from Anna, but that didn't deter Bea from reaching out with support and encouragement every week.

Johnny seemed interested in Anna's situation too, although an interest in any girl was certainly not Johnny's style. Bea had confided to Johnny that Anna was pregnant and the circumstances under which it had happened just after Anna had lost control of her secret all those weeks ago. Bea had never thought of her son as an emotional man; her own John seemed demonstrative by comparison, but his kind face had clouded and he looked angrier than she had ever seen him. His hands had clenched as if they were intent on connecting with the man who had done this to Anna. Bea didn't think she'd ever seen that in her son before. She knew that he'd gone over to say goodbye to Anna, but she doubted that he'd let her know that he was aware of her situation.

The wind had picked up the next day when Bea made her visit to the Lord house. Bea was wishing she'd put a heavier coat on as she stood on the wide, front porch. She pulled her sweater around her and pressed the bell for a second time. She was sure she had seen someone moving beyond the curtains on the oval plate-glass window. Still, no one opened the door. She pressed the bell again, twice this time and after another cold minute the lace was pulled aside and Helene peered out. "Just a moment Mrs. Schott," she mouthed, releasing the curtain quickly while Bea shivered on the porch. Less quickly, she came back to the door and turned the lock, allowing Bea into the Lords' front hall.

"I wasn't dressed, Mrs. Schott," Helene said, but Bea noticed that she wasn't dressed even as they spoke. Helene wore an oversized chenille bathrobe, which spanned her considerable girth even though her hair was immaculately arranged and her makeup seemed to be perfect. The robe didn't hide nylons and high heels. Bea rubbed her hands made cold by the brisk wind.

"I don't mean to bother you, I don't. It is just that I hadn't seen you for some time and I meant to call and see how it is with your family. It seems that I have picked the coldest day to do so."

"Is it really so cold? I haven't been out at all today. You see, I am not feeling so well." With this, Helene patted the round at her waist. "I am expecting a baby."

Bea feigned surprise. "Well you don't say. The very best to you and your husband. And when will the little one be coming along?"

"A few more months. I'll tell you; I can't wait."

“I’m sure you can’t. I remember how I longed for my little Johnny. Oh, a baby is one of the great blessings of life, it is.”

“Well I, for one, can’t wait to get out of these shapeless bags I have to wear. They have about as much style as a burlap bag. And I can’t tell you how I hate looking like a walking blimp. Why, no one gives you a second look.” Helene’s face changed, softening as she continued, “Well, I guess it is worth it. Babies sure are cute, aren’t they?”

“They are the most precious things in the world, they are. You are a lucky woman, that is for sure. I will be glad to give you a hand should you need it. You need to conserve your strength, you do.”

“After the baby is born, I will have some help. Anna will be coming back to assist me. I can’t take care of a baby and a house all by myself.”

“It is a big job, it is. And how is Anna.; I miss her, I do.”

“Oh, she’s off in Buffalo with our sister, Norma. She’s taking it easy up there.”

Bea was still for a moment, processing this new information, then she said, “Give Anna my best when you talk to her. Tell her I miss her.” With that Bea left.

Chapter 22

Anna looked down past the swell of her breasts to her now nearly-flat stomach. This, like everything else since the baby girl had been born, seemed to be viewed through several layers of glass that not only separated her from the happenings around her, but blurred the sounds too. To Anna, people's speech resembled a phonograph record, played at a too-slow speed. She no longer felt any pain, although it seemed to her that she must have. She had to be cut to take the baby after twenty hours of labor failed to push the baby from her body. She vaguely remembered the pain, but it seemed to be something she had been told about rather than something her body had experienced.

She had been told a lot. As her pregnancy had advanced Norma shared the experience of her own pregnancy with graphic detail.

"It's no picnic, I 'll tell you," Norma had instructed. "The men have their fun then it's up to us to stretch our skin enough to insert a watermelon under it then push it out through a hole no bigger than a corn cob. And then you've no sooner had the thing then they're back at you to lie on your back and get in the family way again before the parts that ripped are even healed." Norma shot a sour look at her present consort. "Well, you can think again if you ever have any of those thoughts. No more brats for me." Junie, at 13 and Norma's only child, had heard enough versions of this conversation that she didn't even take it personally any more.

"The one you have is more than enough," Charley said. "Junie's okay, you know, but you and me, we have more fun without any more of them kids."

Norma, of course, was recalling Al, still legally her husband. She'd stayed with him until she had support payments lined up after Junie's birth, freeing her to resume a life that she considered more fun. What she didn't remember or care to share was the fact that she had cursed him up and down as they made their way to the hospital when her contractions were still eight minutes apart. The doctor had told her that she didn't have to come in yet, it being a first child and all, but Norma got her packed suitcase out of the closet and demanded that

Al take her then and there. While Al was filling out the paperwork, Norma was already demanding anesthesia.

"Too soon," the obstetric nurse told her, and the doctor wasn't even there yet, but Norma bellowed until drugs were administered—more for the other women who were starting to be frightened by Norma's howls. Essentially, Norma's request, "Wake me up when it is over," was pretty much what happened. Nevertheless, she had details of birth to share with Anna. Alternately, she told Anna of the cutting or the tearing of her genitals. ("You will never enjoy sex again") following the pressing of the baby's feet on the uterus until the membranes ruptured, bathing the birth canal with blood. According to Norma, she could never have another child without putting her life in jeopardy. None of these details had come from the doctor, although Norma had requested so many drugs that labor was quite prolonged. Norma's excess weight might have added to the difficulty too, since she was exceptionally fond of hot fudge sundaes and like to tell anyone who might question her appetites, "I've caught my train, Sweetie. Mind your own business." Al, the train that she had caught, was informed of the extraordinary birth difficulties and made well aware of his financial responsibilities as a father within an hour of Norma's awakening. He had other responsibilities as well. It was Al who got up at night to feed Junie, what with Norma being still so sore and all. As months went by, Al realized that although his responsibilities had increased fourfold, his rights as a husband had gotten lost along the way.

"Not tonight, Al. I am so tired from the baby."

"I have to go to the bathroom, Al."

"My God, not now. I might get pregnant. I couldn't stand that again."

"For crying out loud. Is that thing all you think about?"

Al eventually stopped asking, then he stopped coming home after work. Then he moved in with a woman he had met at the bar where he spent time. No one could say that Al was in love; he just needed a place where he didn't feel like a culprit. Now he stopped by on payday to see Junie and drop off money for Norma, who was still legally his wife. The lesson in the hospital recovery room had stuck.

Anna's delivery was somewhat different from Norma's. The first feelings of labor were in her back, feeling like a pressure on her bowels. It wasn't what she'd been told to expect, so she said nothing to Norma or Junie as she waited for the feeling of knives cutting her insides apart that Norma had told her about. It hurt, but she was able to endure it, so she knew she would have a long time before real labor even began. Several times Anna went to the bathroom but her bowels would not move and she still had the feeling that they would soon. She didn't want to be a problem already since she knew she had such worse agony to go, so she went to her room and strode the four steps that took her from one side of the room to the other over and over, stopping to clutch the bed when the pressure made her break out in perspiration. She thought it must be what was called false labor since she felt none of the tearing that Norma had told her about. Charley had come over in the afternoon, so Norma was not really paying much attention, but late in the afternoon, Junie came into the bedroom to find Anna on her knees clutching the mahogany pineapple that graced the top of the bedpost with white fingers. Anna made no sound, but she was unable to get up until the pressure was over, and it lasted for a long time. Junie was able to say Anna's name four times, each time waiting in vain for Anna to respond to her. The fourth time, Anna seemed unaware that Junie was even there. Finally, she turned her head, strove for focus, and asked Junie, "What do you want?"

"You couldn't even hear me, Anna. I am going to get Norma." Norma had always preferred that Junie call her by her first name since they were so close in age anyway. Now that Junie was looking more grown-up, Norma liked to take her along to the movies and if a couple of guys should show some interest—well, there was nothing wrong with that.

"Oh, no Junie. This is nothing, I am sure. This baby won't be born this easily." Junie had been alarmed, however, and when she brought Norma in, they timed the contractions and found they were already a minute and thirty seconds apart. They lasted several seconds.

"Charley, we have to get her to the hospital. God, girl, are you planning to have the kid on my living room rug?" Anna didn't answer, being in the throes of another contraction. Charley pulled the car up while Norma called the doctor and they got Anna down the stairs and into the car only by stopping five or six times along the way when Anna's knees threatened to buckle. At the hospital, Anna was transferred to a wheelchair and whisked to the maternity ward as soon as they got into the building.

"We need to examine you to see how far you are along," the resident doctor said, and the nurse helped Anna onto a flat, rolling cart after cutting away her panties. There was blood in the panties and Anna was reminded of that first blood back in Papa's house after Mama's death. She started crying and the nurse thought it was because of the pain. Then, another contraction took control of her body and she remembered nothing more. A splash of liquid sprayed from between her legs onto the doctor who was getting in position to examine her. She could see that there were small white pieces of curd-like substance on his glasses. "The baby's a breech. Get an IV into her, now," the doctor ordered, handing his glasses to the nurse to clean. "And give me a towel. Her water just broke." The nurse scurried around, following the doctor's orders and dabbing at him with a towel. Anna was just about to apologize for the mess she had made, when the drugs in her arm started taking effect. Little by little, she felt her heavy body grow light and part-by-part, she became numb until she drifted in a sleep.

And now, almost four weeks later, it was as if the drugs had never quite worn off. Gratefully Anna floated above the shame of her situation and her need to know about her child like a balloon floating above a sharp object that would surely pierce its fragile existence.

Chapter 23

In the weeks following the baby's birth Norma had become bored with Charley. Al still showed up on paydays, but they seemed to have nothing else to do with each other. Norma seemed to feel that she should be around more now that Anna was in the house, but she really didn't know how to deal with Anna's deep, quiet sadness or her "sour puss" as she named it. Anna was grateful to stay home by herself when Norma and Junie finally boarded the bus and headed for downtown Buffalo. She would lose herself in an insulated bubble where no memories could touch her. Sometimes they asked her to come along, but Anna always said no. Norma figured that the Cesarean section Anna had might have even rivaled her own agonizing experience, so she looked at Anna through narrowed eyes in disbelief, but she tossed her head as if to say "Suits me," and sailed through the door.

One evening after they had been gone all day, Anna heard the apartment door open and Junie peeked in at her. Anna thought of pretending to be asleep, but she wasn't fast enough and Junie came in and crossed the hardwood floor to the small bed. Pausing for a moment, Junie sat down on the edge of the yellow roses on the quilt. Junie was getting quite heavy and her weight caused Anna to roll involuntarily closer to her exposing her reddened eyes.

"Are you okay, Anna?" Junie asked. As usual, she was chewing her fingernails as she sat on the edge of the bed. Anna saw the ragged edges.

"I'm okay, Junie," Anna replied, her voice drifting from that far place where she kept her emotions locked up. "Thanks for asking. What did you do today? Did you see a movie?"

"We rode down to the Grants' store first, then we were going to go up to the Lafayette Theater. Esther Williams has a new movie up there, but I didn't see it." Anna had never seen Esther Williams, but Junie had told her before about the beautiful aquatic scenes in which Esther would descend from the sky like an angel on a floral swing while thirty or thirty-five slim swimmers made intricate, coordinated patterns in the water beneath her. Esther and all of the other women had their hair drawn back with flowers so even the graceful dives where the water lapped their pointed toes never seemed to disturb its perfection. Junie would often stay to see the feature a second time if Norma joined someone during the show.

"Why didn't you see the movie?" Anna asked.

"Well, Norma came upon this man as we were going past the bus station. For a while I stayed with them, but then he wanted to take her into Laube's so he gave me some money to walk up to the White House and have a sundae. Actually, I had two. He gave me quite a bit. His name is Ralph."

"Did Norma know him before?"

"I don't think so. I 've never seen him before. He does have a great car, but it's a roadster and only two people fit into it. Ralph said he'd give me a ride soon."

"So you were alone in the coffee shop all day?"

"Not really all day. We did go to Grants'," Junie hung her head. "Well, I guess it was most of the day. The chocolate fudge sundaes were the best, though. The fudge was rich and thick with the biggest mound of whipped cream you ever saw." The tip of Junie's tongue rounded the corner of her mouth in recollection.

"Junie, doesn't it bother you when she leaves you by yourself all day like that? Aren't you afraid?"

Junie paused, and then manufactured a broad smile, which made her round face almost pretty. "Nobody wants any sad sacks. Our downtown days are to have fun and there are no fellas who like a long puss." She parroted, looking convinced of her own words. "Oh, and yeah, we're going on a trip. You are going too Anna. Ralph is borrowing a bigger car and taking us to Pennsylvania. We might even go to Atlantic City. Won't that be fun?"

Anna imagined that this was just another tale Norma told Junie. They were always going somewhere—New York, Philadelphia, Washington D.C.

Anna, of course, had been to none of these places, and it seemed that Junie and Norma never really got there either, based on what Anna had seen.

In Ralph, however, Norma had found a man of action and when Norma passed Al's money to Mrs. Brennan, the landlady, at the beginning of the month, Anna heard her saying that they'd be leaving at the end of the month and gone indefinitely. Norma's apartment was furnished, so the multitude of various prints; gladiolus on the sofa, soldiers on the armchair, vines on the wallpaper, and large roses on the carpet would be left for someone else to enjoy. Norma packed her own dishes and household belongings in boxes that went to a storage warehouse "for safe keeping" as she liked to say. Their clothes were stuffed into the suitcases. Since Anna had so few clothes herself, some of Junie's clothes were added to Mama's old suitcase until it could barely be closed and they all climbed into the large sedan Ralph had come up with.

They cut through back roads Anna didn't know, heading south. There was a heavy mist in the air, nearly fog, as they left New York and entered Pennsylvania. *Now I have been in two states*, Anna thought to herself. Next to her in the back seat Junie snacked on the Tastykakes Norma had brought along. "Would you like one?" Junie asked. "There is a chocolate with cream filling and a lemon one with lemon frosting left."

"Thanks, Junie," Anna replied. "I think I will read for a while." In truth, Anna was alarmed by the sudden curves that seemed to emerge unannounced out of the mist. Ralph's attention was divided between the winding road and Norma. His right hand strayed into her lap prompting an illegible murmur from Norma. Anna, knowing there was nothing she could do about it anyway, opened her *Greek Myths and Legends*. As Ralph planted sloppy kisses on Norma in the front seat, Anna thought that Artemis would have turned him into a stag right on the spot and shot him with her bow and arrow. Somehow, she liked the idea. The way the Greeks saw it a god or goddess could be dabbling in your life almost any time. Arachne, for instance, ended up being turned into a spider mostly because Athena was jealous of her skill as a weaver. That kind of God might be cruel, but at least you knew what to expect from them. Anna wondered about Papa's God. Was he vengeful like Zeus or just negligent? Anna couldn't imagine why any god would take her mother away, take her father away then put her in Mick's way. Anna remembered that according to Papa's sermons they were all sinners from the day they were born, but Anna couldn't rightly recall doing so many sinful things that would make God that angry at her.

Anna wasn't aware of falling asleep, but the next thing she knew the car was creeping up a narrow, bricked street that angled itself sharply up toward the sky. Both sides of the street were lined with porches, terraced up the hill with each a few feet higher than the next. Some had gliders, but the one Norma pointed to had a porch swing, hanging from two hooks in the ceiling with metal chains. "There it is," said Norma, pointing to a porch that clung to the sidewalk under a black and white canvas awning. "We're here." Norma turned to the back seat. "Get your things, Junie, and for God's sake, wipe those cake crumbs off your dress. You're going to be visiting your cousin, Mae for a while." A frown appeared on Junie's wide, good-natured face, but she obediently brushed the chocolate and lemon crumbs from her ample chest and started to crawl from the back seat.

"Not in this car, for crying out loud," Ralph protested as he saw the mess in the back seat. He looked at Norma in irritation as he went to the trunk to remove Junie's small green suitcase. Norma, however, was already halfway up the walk to her sister's house. Edith was a shorter, fairer version of Norma, Anna noticed. Something about her reminded her of Mama, but she couldn't exactly say which feature. Anna didn't remember Edith since she had been gone from the house for so long. She did remember her cousin Mae coming for a visit when Anna was five or so, but Mae was older than Junie was now, so they had had little to say beyond hello. Although Edith didn't have the same reputation Norma did, she too had escaped Papa's tyranny at a young age, marrying a phone company worker when she was 18. It was hard to imagine this matronly, aproned woman being her sister or ever being 18. Junie clutched the suitcase's white handle and followed Norma up the walk. Her rumpled dress wouldn't respond to her attempts to smooth it.

"Some of Junie's clothes are in my suitcase," Anna told Ralph who was waiting impatiently by the car. Anna saw smears of Norma's pancake makeup on his shirt. At the same time Junie must have had the same thought. She caught up with her mother. "I put some things in Anna's suitcase, Norma. I think my nightgown is in there and some of my skirts."

"For crying out loud, Junie. What did you do that for? We don't have all day, you know." She nudged her daughter toward the door, glancing back at Ralph.

"There wasn't room in my suitcase and Anna had lots of room in hers. I thought we were all going to Atlantic City." Junie's voice was pitiful.

"Oh, Junie, don't be a sour puss. Your stuff will be right here in town. Now get inside. Ralph and I have to drop Anna off." She gave her daughter a shove in the door then sped back to the car with a wave over her shoulder. It seemed to Anna that Norma may not have even said hello to her sister, but she guessed she must have.

"It's about time," Ralph complained.

“Yeah, yeah, we’ll be on our way in no time,” Norma replied. “One more to drop off.” Anna wondered where she was being dropped off. *So much for Atlantic City,* Anna thought, looking at Junie’s betrayed face as they pulled away.

Chapter 24

Getting the mail from her mailbox, Bea Schott looked across the street as Edwin Lord pushed his front screen door open on an unseasonably warm day. Pink blankets cascaded from his arm and he looked tenderly at the tiny being in his arms. He stepped aside, avoiding the swinging door and walked carefully down the three steps to the waiting carriage. A British perambulator, all rubbed with linseed oil, waited at the bottom of the steps. He balanced the baby on his arm, pulling the mosquito netting aside, then laid the child into the carriage, placing a kiss on her forehead as he did. He looked every inch the proud father, but Bea still wondered.

In the months after Bea's first visit, Helene was regularly seen wearing maternity clothes. She had enough of them, she did. To each event she would appear with another flowing dress or flouncy top over her slacks. It was more like a fashion show than anything else. It just seemed to come so suddenly with no gradual thickening of Helene's waist before it. And she didn't walk like a pregnant woman. She continued wearing the highest heels, right up until the baby's birth. It seemed to Bea, as long as it had been since Johnny's birth, that your feet didn't put up with that when you were nine months pregnant.

Edwin started down Park Street, pushing the carriage. A little girl, she was, and a pretty little one too. She wanted for nothing. Bea had seen that fancy British carriage, just like the ones nannies preferred, being delivered. She saw the truck from Clayton's Furniture too—with a Jenny Lind crib, a chest of drawers, and a lovely rocking chair. The ladies' guild at the church had a shower for Helene even though she rarely set foot in the church. Edwin's family, the Lords, had been members of the church as long as anyone could remember, and it seemed only right that Edwin's first child should get a shower, no matter who he had married. While Helene was opening a yellow sweater set at the shower, one of her earrings fell to the floor. Before Cassie Lewis, who was sitting next to Helene and writing down who gave what, could get it for her, Helene swept down in such a way as to flatten the swelling on her lap. Bea didn't think anyone else noticed, but she sure did. Of course, the thing that made her wonder most of all was that as soon as Edwin was out of town, that same familiar car would be in the driveway—often all night. She guessed she wasn't supposed to notice.

Edwin was hardly down the street when a big, unfamiliar Ford pulled up in front of the Lord's. A loud woman in the front, barking orders, seemed to be in a big rush. As she directed the driver to the trunk, the back door opened and the girl Bea had last seen eight months ago emerged. Anna looked tiny, almost frail. The clothes that had been too tight on her now hung on her slender frame. She seemed a lot older. Bea thought it was the way she held herself. Anna had once darted forward as if anxious to engage life, but now there was a weariness about her—an awareness of life's hurts. She walked slowly up the front steps, clutching her small suitcase, as if she was marching to the guillotine.

Ever since they had left Edith's house, Anna felt sure of where she would be dropped off. By the time they turned onto Park Street, Anna retreated into that now familiar place of calm where you cannot be hurt. When the car stopped in front of Helene and Edwin Lord's house, she opened the door and emerged with resignation, just as she had left without complaint eight months ago. She avoided looking at the window where Mick had entered. She didn't think about how long she would be staying here. Papa had clearly abandoned her, and she had no doubt Norma would do the same if things worked out with Ralph. She didn't want to think about what would happen to Junie. She could hear Norma telling Ralph, "Hold your horses. We'll be out of here in a minute." Helene came out to the porch looking lovely as always. Her hair was a little longer, curled around her face. Her perfect nails matched her lipstick exactly and a slim skirt was cinched by a wide belt around her slender waist. She was Helene.

'"Anna, Norma, please come in," her voice seeming breathless with the effort of the greeting. "Will you have some tea? Edwin just made a fresh pot before he went on a walk."

"I'd like to, Sis, but we have to hit the road. You know how guys are."

"Not as well as you do, I'm sure." Helene responded icily. "How about you, Anna. Would you like some tea? It's right in the kitchen. You know where that is. And would you be a love and bring me a cup too?"

Anna mutely entered the house with her suitcase. She sat it in the front hall and headed for the kitchen. The parlor looked just as she remembered it. Overstuffed chairs clustered in conversational groupings for conversations that never happened. The mahogany tables from Edwin's family were polished. *Who?* Anna wondered. She couldn't picture Helene doing it. In the dining room she passed the table and remembered hiding under it when she first realized who Mick was and what he was to Helene. The memory made her throat catch. The kitchen, never overused, was immaculate. She automatically reached for the cups in the upper left cupboard then opened the refrigerator to get some lemon. There she saw it. A line of formula bottles just under the tiny freezer. Helene and Edwin were the "good family" who would give her child a "good home." *Helene as a mother. Edwin gone all the time. Mick lurking around.* Anna stiffened at the thought. She looked around for other signs of the baby. There were none. No blankets, no toys, no concession to this small being at all. And it was quiet. Was her baby sleeping-perhaps in the same room where her life had begun? Anna poured the tea and headed for the parlor.

"Well, that took a long time, didn't it?" Helene cajoled. "Did you forget where to find things? Norma had to go. Her stud was in a hurry, it seems."

"The formula in the refrigerator…" Anna began.

"Yes, we have a baby now," Helene declared.

"You adopted my baby?"

"I think it is best we not think of it that way. Everyone thinks I am the mother and it will not do you or Peggy any good to have anyone think otherwise. Honestly, I am relieved to have you here. Edwin and I have gotten NO sleep since Peggy arrived. The bags under my eyes are down to my waist." Helene laughed and pointed to the non-existent blemishes. "Not to mention what a child does to your nails." She inspected one perfect hand.

"Where is she? Peggy, my baby?" Anna stammered.

"She is out for a walk with her daddy. In fact, they should be back any time now. Oh, and Anna, did you see anything in the refrigerator for supper? I have just been so busy with the baby. I cannot tell you."

Anna processed what she had just learned, her emotions churning. Her first thought had been that Helene was exactly the worst type of mother for her child…but if she would be here to watch over her, take care of her, love her…well, that would be different. For the first time, she was glad to be back at Helene's house. Her heart thumped as she saw Edwin pushing the buggy up the walk. It seemed it took him hours as Anna crept to the window, straining to get a peek. He reached in and lifted a pink bundle of blankets. Anna closed her eyes for a moment, unable to predict her own emotions. When they opened, she saw a tiny pink face surrounded by a fuzzy pink bonnet. A fringe of dark hair framed the bonnet. Her lips were puckered into a small bow. A tiny nose was tipped up as if she'd detected a wonderful smell. Anna smiled.

"Would you like to hold her, Anna? I need to warm a bottle. The buggy always puts her to sleep, but she doesn't like to miss a meal," Edwin said. His face lit up as he looked down at the baby…Peggy was her name. Anna tried not to think what she would have named her if she'd gotten to choose. As she took the baby from Edwin, she felt a tugging deep within her as if her body remembered having this child inside. Peggy's eyes fluttered open for just a second. They were a soft brown. For Anna, it was like looking in the mirror. She was lighter than Anna expected, but warm in her blanket.

Did her look say, "Why did you leave me?" Perhaps one day she would be able to…No, she mustn't think of that. Helene was right. It was best for Peggy that people think she was Helene and Edwin's child. Her little body started and she reached out with one hand. Anna extended a finger and the baby clutched it, closing miniature fingers around it. Her eyes opened again, and this time Anna detected no accusation.

"Almost ready," Edwin said. "We'll take her upstairs and change her. She usually falls asleep after she eats." Anna carefully navigated the stairs trying almost superstitiously not to dislodge the tiny fist clinging to her finger.

"I'll just stay down here," Helene called. "Too many people in the room at once." In Anna's former room a crib now stood at the very window where Mick had entered. Today streams of light bounced off the ornamental balls atop the headboard. The big rocker was next to the crib and a changing table stored a stack of clean diapers. Anna lay the baby on the table as Edwin peeled her blankets away. On her soft jumper pink lambs gamboled. She wore booties with bows at the ankles. Her legs each bent to the side and her feet met between as contrite hands in prayer. Anna felt her soft skin as she undid the snaps.

"Do you want me to do that?" Edwin asked as she revealed the wet diaper. "Helene hates changing diapers. She says it is disgusting."

"No, I want to do it," said Anna, bent over the baby. "Just show me how to do it right."

“Here are the cotton balls. You can wipe her with baby oil then sprinkle her with powder. The really messy ones need soap and water too, but this isn’t bad. I’ll rinse it out in the bathroom then we’ll put it in the diaper pail.” Edwin seemed incapable of looking directly at her.

Anna slipped a fresh diaper under Peggy’s tiny bottom and started to secure it with large pins. Her first try was too loose, but Peggy was awake now and interested so Anna re-pinned for a snug fit. “Here’s her bottle,” Edwin said, “She needs to be burped every two ounces then she’ll go into her crib. This rocking chair is great for this part.” Anna nodded her head. Something made it impossible for her to speak as she cradled her little girl, watching her latch eagerly onto the nipple of the bottle as the sunlight revealed the red highlights in her hair.

Chapter 25

Anna adapted to the new routine as if she'd never been away. The gray fog that had enveloped her since the birth disappeared. She slept in the same room with Peggy, so it was Anna who rose in the night as the baby cried, Anna who held her in her arms and rocked her to sleep after she'd had her bottle. At times Anna thought her own body might provide the needed milk, so painful was the pressure in her breasts when the baby cried. Once Anna instinctively pulled her nightgown up and cradled Peggy to her throbbing breast. The little girl latched on, but too much time had gone by and her body had given up producing the needed milk. Despairing, Anna warmed a bottle for her daughter and fed her, studying her long eyelashes and turned up lips long after the baby had gone back to sleep.

It was Anna who lulled her to sleep in the moonlight. It was Anna who rose in the pre-dawn hours to answer the little girl's cry. Anna washed Peggy and dressed her. Except when Edwin was home, it was Anna who put her into her perambulator and walked her into the sunshine.

On one early-dawn hour—she hadn't checked the clock—Anna lifted the hungry baby from her crib, laid her on the bed and changed her wet diaper while softly singing "*Tura lura lura*" which Peggy seemed to like. Anna wasn't quite sure why she spoke and sang in a hushed voice. Helene never seemed to wake to Peggy's cry. Anna worried about the time before she had come. Now, Anna and Peggy went down to the kitchen. As always in the dark times when she was alone, she scanned the backyard and the driveway next to the house while she made sure the doors were locked and the windows were secured. As far as she knew Mick was still in town and although she hadn't seen him at the house, she was pretty sure Helene met him somewhere else. Satisfied that they were alone, Anna went to the refrigerator, but this morning, if you could call quarter to six morning, there was no bottle waiting in the refrigerator. "How could I go to bed without checking?" Anna scolded herself. Peggy's whimpers crescendoed to cries, and Anna bounced her harder on her hip, moving things in the refrigerator until she found one hidden bottle. Putting the bottle in its warmer, Anna heard the rattle of bottles outside the side door. Balancing Peggy on her hip, she scurried down the three steps to the latched compartment where the milk bottles were deposited. She removed one of the two newly delivered bottles when the outside door re-opened and she was looking through it into the most remarkable hazel eyes she had ever seen. A young man looked through at her, a smile playing on his bow shaped lips. His hair was such a dark brown that you could almost think it black in the early morning half-light. Now, why was she noticing all of this? Anna blushed just as he said, "Well, good morning. I never expected anyone would be up at this time." He tipped the white hat advertising the Belkauf Dairy and smiled at Anna through the milk box.

"Oh, I'm often up with the baby," Anna replied. "She thinks this is the perfect time for breakfast." He smiled at her. For some reason Anna had no fear of this man. She even thought of inviting him to come to the door to see the baby. What was she thinking? She wasn't even dressed-still in her nightgown. "Thank you," Anna said, lowering her eyes and, retrieving the other quart of milk, she closed and locked the milk compartment. She heard the outside door close as well. Putting the bottles on the counter, Anna tested Peggy's bottle. The milk felt neither cold nor hot on the inside of Anna's wrist, which meant it was ready for the hungry baby. Peggy eagerly latched onto the bottle.

Anna felt drawn to the dining room window as he made his way out the driveway with the two empty glass milk bottles in his carrier. He was quite tall—about six feet Anna thought, and on the slim side. There was something about his walk that suggested energy and a kind of grace. He strode rather than walked and when he stepped up into the milk truck, it looked effortless, as if some unseen force was lifting him. The baby started crying again, and Anna lifted her to her shoulder, forcing a burp with gentle pats on her back. Peggy's eyes closed as she rhythmically sucked on the nipple and fifteen minutes she'd returned to sleep. Anna, however, was fully awake. After she put Peggy back in her crib, she tried to read one of her favorite myths, the story of the nymph Daphne and her pursuit by Apollo, but Anna found her attention drifting back to the man with the white uniform rather than the nymph with the green hair.

Later that afternoon, Bea Schott got her first chance to talk with Anna since she had returned. In the weeks that had passed, there was no suggestion that

Anna should return to work in the Schott home, and Bea could see that Anna was busy full time taking care of the baby. Edwin clearly doted on her, but he was often away on business and Helene seemed to be gone a lot too, although she did seem to enjoy showing off the beautifully dressed sleeping infant when someone would stop at the Lord porch to look at her. Anna emerged from the door with a pink-blanketed bundle in her arms. Bea waved but Anna 's eyes were glued to the little one. She shifted the diaper bag hanging over her shoulder and leaned to pull back the netting that covered the beautiful navy-blue perambulator. From across the street Bea could see a smile on Anna's face for the first time since her return. She was wearing clothing that fit her for a change. Bea waved again and called, "Anna, girl, how are you?" Anna looked up and her smile widened as she spotted Bea waving to her. Carefully she lowered the buggy down the front steps and looked both ways before crossing to the Schott house. Bea's arms went around her and Anna relaxed into her embrace. It had been so long since anyone had held her. Probably Bea. And before that, Mama. Anna thought it was. Bea's face beamed the steadfast support she'd expressed to Anna with her notes. Plenty of people blamed the girl in a case like this but not Bea Schott. "Anna, Anna girl," Mrs. Schott clucked in that way she had. "And this is the wee one," Bea beamed, pulling the netting aside slightly to get a better look. "And she's a beauty, she is. Peggy, you call her?"

"Helene and Edwin named her Peggy. It's a nice name, isn't it?"

"Any name is a nice one when it's bein' worn by one you love," Mrs. Schott replied. "And you are taking care of her, you are? And how is that for you, Anna girl?"

Anna felt the tears starting in her eyes. "Oh, Mrs. Schott, I just love her so. I don't think I could bear to be parted from her again." Anna got control of her emotions and looked at the woman who had become like a mother to her. "How are you, Mrs. Schott, and how is Johnny?"

"Well, Anna girl, I am how I am and that's good enough, it is. Johnny…well he's another story. He's doing well at the bank, but I wish he had things other than work in his life. He won't talk to me about it, but something is wrong these last few months. Maybe you can get it out of him now that you're back. He always had a soft spot for you Anna, he did."

Anna realized that Johnny apparently hadn't shared his offer to marry her with his mother.

Chapter 26

Although life at the Wilson house was hectic with the four boys between 17 and 22, Marion ran a tight ship. She had to since Abram had died of the black lung when Allan, the youngest, was only eight years old. They'd come from Wales, to Petersville where the mines seemed full of unlimited coal, but that had turned out to be an empty promise. The only thing that was without limit was the fine dust that eventually shortened the life of most of the miners, both here in Petersville as well as Wales. Marion wasn't one to complain. When she found herself a widow in her early 40s with five children to feed, she took in ironing and baked her famous pies to sell on Fridays to make ends meet. Gladys, her only daughter, helped with these jobs and Henry and Russ got a paper route, uncomplainingly handing the money they made over to their mother.

It had been hard at the start, but now they were doing better money-wise. Henry had taken a job in the factory and Russell was a deliveryman for Belkauf Dairy. Gladys was engaged to a young man from the factory, so her future was taken care of, but of course when she left, Marion would have to cut down on either the ironing or the baking. Thomas wanted to go to college to be an accountant, but for now he had to help out with the books at the Leady Brewery and take night courses. Allan was slated to graduate high school in the spring, if he could just get through his math classes with Thomas' help. Marion was bound and determined that all her children would be high school graduates, and Allan was going to fall in with that plan whether he wanted to or not.

Over all, things were pretty good, Marion thought as she scooped large servings of fried scrapple with syrup on plates for the boys. Gladys, thinking of her wedding day, would not eat what she considered to be disgusting food—pork and cornmeal boiled into a lump and then fried-ugh. Instead, she nibbled on a biscuit and several cups from the large teapot Marion always had steeping. According to Marion, the teapot was the source of all delight and the answer to all problems so she forgave Gladys for her "pickiness." This morning's flavor was Earl Grey, Gladys' favorite, although she liked the Indian Darjeeling too. Contrasting her own considerable girth to Gladys' tiny waist, Marion allowed that she might do with a little less scrapple too.

Allan had almost finished his plate, and was ready for more. Russ had been on the delivery route for hours already and would be home soon for breakfast before returning to the dairy to stock tomorrow's trucks. "Henry, Thomas, breakfast is ready. Get yourself down here before Allan eats it all." Almost before the words were out of her mouth, Henry appeared, washed up with his hair slicked to one side in an even part. Henry was in line for a foreman's position at the factory, which made Marion proud. He had certainly been her rock when Abram died. She smiled at her eldest son and slid a steaming plate of scrapple toward him. She poured hot Earl Grey into a large mug. No dainty teacups for Henry. "Thomas, are you coming?" Marion called.

Just then the outside door opened and Russ stepped in, removing his Belkauf Dairy hat as he entered, placing a glass bottle of milk on the cupboard. *With that wavy, dark hair, he should never wear a hat,* Marion thought. There were plenty of girls who noticed that hair too, not to mention the hazel eyes that had caught everyone's attention since he was a baby. There didn't seem to be any special girl in Russ' life, but he had a lot of different girls at the skating rink. Since his dairy work was mostly so early in the day, Russ' evenings were available and he was the skate master at Roller Matic. Maybe all that skating was what kept him so slim. His waist had never been over a 30 although his shoulders were quite broad. It surely wasn't for the lack of an appetite, Marion grinned as Russ dropped to a chair with a smile and dug into the plate of steaming food. "Today isn't our day for milk, is it Russell?" Marion inquired, digging into her own plate with her usual hearty appetite. *She'd cut back on the scrapple tomorrow,* she thought.

"It's a gift from the Schoeppels, Ma," Russ said, washing his scrapple down with a big gulp of Earl Grey. "I went to deliver them this morning and there was a note with their payment in the box. They said they had to head off to help Rita's mother out and give today's milk delivery to someone who could use it. I figured we could use it. Any chance of turning that into a custard pie, Ma?" Russ grinned his slightly lop-sided grin and Marion was already planning to add another pie to the orders she would be filling tomorrow.

"Anything Russ wants, Russ gets," Allan interjected, wiping his mouth with the napkin Marion forced on him.

"Well, you don't say," said Russ, ready to take his little brother on. "In that case, from you I will take a new Ford sedan. And maybe a high school graduation with honors from you this spring." He kept his gaze on Allan who avoided his older brother's eyes, as he suddenly had to get ready for school.

"How was the Belkauf route today?" Henry asked his brother, giving Allan a chance to escape.

"Finished it in three hours, seventeen minutes!" Russ proclaimed. It was Russ' habit to race against his own record, presently three hours, fifteen and a half minutes. "The note at the Schoppels slowed me down some and at the Lord's someone was actually up. I had just put the milk in the door when I heard the inside one open. I looked inside and there she was—a girl—and she had the Lord's baby."

"I heard that Helene Lord had had a baby, but I can't say I see her about with it. Now Edwin you will see, walking around with that fancy English buggy."

"Who is the girl? Does she work for them?" Russ asked.

"You interested, Russ?" asked Henry.

"She is sort of pretty, but more than that there is this hurt look in her eyes. I don't know…and a sort of hope that she won't get hurt again." Russ struggled with the words.

"All of this from one look through the milk door?" Marion declared, taking a long look at her son. Russ had always been so oblivious to girls, even the ones who fawned all over him. He was like a piece of slippery soap as far as girls went, skating with one than another at the rink. From what she heard they were happy to be the chosen one even for one song.

"Who is she?" Henry asked. He also seemed to notice the change in Russ.

"She's Helene Lord's sister," Marion told him. "Their father just dumped her off at Lords last year, then the first thing you know she was off with another sister somewhere else, and now she's back again. Bea Schott says Helene uses her like an unpaid servant. And the poor thing still believes her father will come back and get her. Bea says he's forgotten all about her, most likely. Her mother died and he has himself a new wife now. And he should know better; he's a minister."

"What is her name?" Russ asked, his food forgotten for the moment.

"I think it's Anne…no, it's Anna. I'm sure that's what Bea said."

"Anna," Russ repeated, and he seemed to linger on the syllables as if they were an object that he cradled in his hands, turning it this way and that to get a better look at it.

Chapter 27

"Dammit, you reneged back two plays ago. Spades are trump and you played a club off. NOW you come up with a spade," Bob Bedwin shouted at his wife Edith as she trumped a play, she shouldn't have had trump for any more. It was true that she had misplayed, but it was also true that she had seldom played pinochle and she was always nervous when she did anything with her sister Helene and her husband Edwin Lord. In fact, the two sisters rarely saw each other although they lived in the same town, but Junie had been staying with Edith ever since Norma dropped her off "for a while" on the way to Atlantic City and that had been weeks ago-no, it had actually turned into months. Junie had been asking to see Anna, and actually Edith was anxious to see her younger sister too, but not at the price of spending time with Helene.

"I'm sorry Bob. It won't happen again," Edith said, now not sure what to do with the trump card she had just played.

"Sorry is as sorry does, Edie," said Bob in a milder voice. "But the trick is ours, for sure. Watch those cards."

"What do you mean the trick is yours?" asked Helene, now more interested in the game. "If she hadn't taken this trick, she would have taken one before."

"And you know that, I'm sure, being the great card player you are, Helene," said Bob. He liked his sister-in-law even less than Edie did. Damn ice queen was what she seemed like to him. In spite of the fact that she was the best looking of Edie's sisters, he couldn't imagine how Edwin put up with her. Working out of town a lot probably helped.

"Well, you can have it this time, but keep an eye on those cards, Edith," said Edwin. Wishy-washy Edwin. You could count on him to never ruffle the waters. Bob started the next trick as if they had taken the one before.

"Hey wait just a minute," Helene chimed in. "That was our trick."

"Yeah, yeah, yeah. And the Pope is Presbyterian," Bob said, withdrawing his card. This night was a bust anyway. At least Junie and Anna seemed to be glad to see each other. They were in each other's arms the moment they pulled up to Park Street. God knows how long Junie would be with them. Norma was off with her latest—to Atlantic City Bob thought Edie said. Well, Junie was no trouble. She was like a little mouse—no, a fairly large mouse. She had put on even more weight since she'd arrived at his house and she'd started off pretty big as it was.

"Are you ever going to play, Bob?" Helene asked in that whiny voice she had.

"Just for you, Honey, just for you," Bob replied sarcastically as he trumped her trick.

The baby was finally asleep. Anna had fed her and both she and Junie had given her a bath. Peggy loved the water and she kicked her chubby legs in delight as the girls soaped her pink body and washed the reddish-brown curls that spread out in the water as she rested securely on Anna's hand. Next, she had a bottle and then Anna and Junie took turns rocking her until she was drowsy. Anna loved the feel of her soft skin and the freshly washed smell of the top of her head. Now she was in her crib soundly asleep. If anything, she was more beautiful than ever. Her skin had taken on a pinkish hue that made her look very "girlie" as Anna thought of it. She also had a new range of noises, mostly coos and squeals that she emitted with obvious delight when someone she knew was nearby. It seemed to Anna that she was especially communicative when she was around. *Did babies have some sense of who their real mothers were?* she wondered. Based on the pattern of the last few weeks Peggy was likely to remain asleep until the early morning. Both girls stood over the crib just looking at her in the dim light. "She's beautiful, Anna," Junie said. Anna just nodded, swallowing to dislodge the tightness in her throat.

Anna and Junie could hear the two couples arguing as they played cards downstairs. Anna couldn't imagine why anyone would find that fun. Then again there was a lot about Helene and Edwin that she didn't understand. She and Junie tiptoed from the room, although it probably wasn't necessary since Peggy slept quite soundly now. "Should we go for a walk? Peggy won't wake up for a long time now, and I sure don't want to let Helene see me or she'll think up some job for me to do."

Usually Junie wasn't very interested in walking, but she knew that the Lords didn't live very far from the roller rink. Junie had heard all about it from Mae, who was on a date there that very night. Since they'd been living together the two cousins had had a pleasant but not very close relationship. But in this case, Mae had told Junie all about the music, the skate-dance competitions, and the wonderful skaters who took the center area to twirl and do figures as the more conventional skaters formed a moving oval around them. Mae herself was learning to do a figure 8, she told Junie. The skate master was helping her complete the move since Jake, the fellow she'd been dating, was only skilled enough to be part of the moving frame around the perimeter. "Let's walk over to the skating rink," Junie said. "Mae is over there tonight. She's out with her boyfriend, Jake. She thinks they will get married someday soon." Junie reported.

"How close is the rink?" Anna asked. "I can't go too far just in case Peggy wakes up."

"Oh, it's not far. Just up to Centre and down two blocks. Let's go. I really want to see it and Edith and Bob live too far away. It is supposed to be swell. They change the lights every ten minutes or so. I 'd like to see all – blue lights. Blue is my favorite color." Junie was more excited than Anna had ever seen her. They left the house by the front hall and closed the door behind them, erasing the sound of the arguing couples. It took longer to get to Centre than Anna thought. Junie was a slow walker and they had to stop twice for her to catch her breath. When they turned off Centre, Anna saw what Junie meant. The doors were open in the warm fall evening and the lights – yellow right now – reached out like golden roads inviting you to travel them. Just as they approached the lights turned to blue. "Oh look," Junie sighed, "blue, just like I wished for." As they approached the door, Anna saw the skaters bathed in the soft, blue light as if they were visitors from a distant fairyland. The skaters around the outside were steady, rhythmic with only an occasional awkward beginner crashing into the wall or stumbling. For the most part they were smooth, even, like a moving wall protecting the skaters in the center. Mae wasn't practicing her figure 8 right now but several skaters were skating backward, jumping into twirls or even doing flips. One beautiful couple was skating hand in hand when he lifted her over his head and turned her slowly as he skated on. As he lifted her so lightly to her feet, Anna saw his face. It was a face she knew and she pictured it under a Belkauf Dairy hat. He was so powerful and the girl he skated with was so beautiful. Anna wondered if she was his girlfriend. They made a wonderful couple. Just then the girl skated away and he blew a whistle, hanging around his neck. The lights turned to green and the skaters on the periphery slowed then turned and started skating in the opposite direction. The skate-master joined the skaters on the outside, patting an occasional child or taking an uncertain girl's hand for part of the way while she blushed. Sometimes he skated around the outside backward, smiling at the others while weaving through them effortlessly. That was what he was doing as he passed Anna, who was just inside the door. His eyes flashed in recognition and it almost seemed that he tipped his hat, except that he wasn't wearing a hat. Anna flushed and smiled back at him. He beckoned for her to come in, but she shook her head, pointing to the door. Then he was gone and Anna looked for Junie. At first, she didn't see her but then she spotted her by the candy stand getting some licorice. "Come on, Junie, we have to get back." Anna gasped. Her breath was short as if she had been skating. She looked back as they slipped from the lights, now blue again.

Anna never saw the red headed man outside the side door who watched her with such unabashed interest as he took a drag on his cigarette. With a smile still on her face, she turned and slipped her arm through Junie's as they headed back to Helene and Edwin's house.

Chapter 28

Russ Wilson's alarm rang at 2:30 just as it did every working morning. In an hour he'd be at the dairy with the truck loaded up and by 4, he'd be out on his route. He donned his white Belkauf Dairy uniform, freshly pressed by his mother, Marion, and combed his nearly black hair, coaxing the wave that wanted to fall across his forehead up to fit under the cap. Russ didn't know it but that errant wave was the very thing that turned so many of the girls at the skating rink where he was skate-master into melting chocolate as they looked at him. Once they were close enough, his eyes finished them off. The color could be described as hazel, but the reality went beyond that. There were tiny flecks of both brown and blue in a field of steel gray that seemed both electrified and magnetic. Russ' slim body had been molded by the years on skates and his arms were well muscled, both from lifting his partners in doubles skating and hauling cases of milk at the dairy. The most attractive thing about him, however, was that he seemed unaware of the effect he had upon women. He was friendly and charming to all the girls, flirting with many of them, but Russ had never been in love in spite of the many opportunities he barely seemed to notice.

With the wave in check under his hat, he headed off toward the dairy, stopping off in the kitchen for the breakfast Marion had laid out for him. The old green Chevy that had belonged to his father before he died was in the driveway, but Thomas had farther to go to work so Russ generally walked to the dairy. Once the truck was loaded, he headed up Main Street to Maple then turned down Woodcrest. For the last several weeks he'd been altering his established route in this way. His route had included an immediate turn down Park at this point, but since the morning he'd been running late because of some problems with the truck's battery, he'd been saving Park for the end of his route. That morning he'd seen that girl. He now knew her name was Anna, but that morning all he knew as he looked at her through the milk door was that he was experiencing something new to him. She was holding a baby and at first, he'd thought she was married, although she looked awfully young. He was surprised by how much that seemed to matter to him. He didn't even know her. Since then, he'd found out that the baby was her sister's—Helene Lord. Russ had always hated collecting at the Lords since Helene would keep him there waiting endlessly while she strutted around "looking for her cash" week after week, stopping to arrange her "messy hair" in the mirror with a pose and giving him ample views of her cleavage as she bent over, looking up at him through lowered eyelashes. Russ recognized it for what it was, and he wasn't interested. Helene Lord was not only married, but her bold gestures seemed more about her than him anyway. He remained businesslike and pleasant, waiting as long as he needed to, while counting the minutes until he could collect her money and move onto the next customer.

Anna. According to his mother (He'd heard her talking to friends about it. He'd been careful not to reveal any interest) was staying with the Lords since her father, a minister for crying out loud, had abandoned her nearly two years ago. She'd been gone for a while-off with another sister, the ladies gossip chain determined, and now she was back helping Helene with her new baby. Since that morning, Russ had changed the route of his deliveries, arriving at the Lord house at the same time he'd been there that day, hoping to see Anna again. He never had. Then one night she was suddenly at the skating rink, near the door, but before he could get around the rink again, she was gone.

Just last week he'd found out that Mae Bedwin, his friend Jake's girlfriend, was Anna's niece. It always seemed odd to him when the niece was older than the aunt. Russ had been helping Mae with her figure 8s and had taken the opportunity to learn a bit more about the girl he couldn't get out of his mind.

"So how's it going with your family, Mae?"

"Oh, pretty good. You know my cousin Junie is staying with us. My aunt Norma is off with another of her guys. Junie's no trouble though. She's actually a lot of help around the house. Gives me more time with Jake," she smiled, her dark eyes glistening.

"Your Aunt Helene has company too. The Lords are on my route with Belkauf."

"That would be Anna. She's my mother's youngest sister—younger than me, even."

"How old is she, this Anna? She's your aunt too, right?"

"She is, but that seems funny. I think she's only sixteen—maybe seventeen. I don't see much of her. My mom and Aunt Helene don't get along very well. The only thing they have in common is they both hate my grandfather."

"The minister?"

"Yes. I guess he was so mean to them that each of the girls left home as soon as she could. Norma, Junie's mother, was first. My mom says she climbed down the tree outside her window to meet the man she ran away with. My mother married young too—and Helene. He drove them out."

"What about Anna?" Mae jerked on her skates as she cut into her turn. No, not like that, Mae. Keep your weight on the inside, like this. Russ demonstrated effortlessly and Mae regained her stability. "What about Anna?" Russ repeated.

Mae looked at him steadily. This had moved beyond idle talk. "Well, Anna was just a girl when Grandmother died and for a while Grandfather—the Reverend," she said sarcastically, "needed her. She took care of that big house and cooked for my uncles who were still at home. She even had to drop out of school. My mom says she was a very good student, but he didn't care. All he wanted was someone to do the work. Then he met another woman, married her, and deposited Anna here. I can't even remember what his second wife's name is. Anna thought he'd be back for her, but my mom says no."

"So the Lords took her in?"

"Well, yes, they did, but my mom says Helene just uses Anna as a servant too. Anna was up with Aunt Norma and Junie for a while too. She lived near Buffalo in Western New York. Something happened there, I think. I don't just know what it is, but I heard my mom and Aunt Helene fighting about it just before Anna left. That was when I met Jake so I wasn't around that much and my mom and dad always clammed up as soon as they knew I was around so I never really found out what it was all about. Some night when I'm alone with Junie, I'll get it out of her." With this Mae leaned into the turn for a perfect 8. "I did it!"

"You sure did. Nice work. Now, try it again, and this time lean even more into the turn." Mae did, her brown curls bouncing as she gained confidence in the move.

“Hey, there’s Jake. Jake, c’mon over. Look at what Russ taught me.” Mae moved into the figure again. She ended and beamed at the stolid young blonde-haired man who moved toward them uncertainly on his skates.

“Jeez, Russ, how do you handle these things? If God had wanted me to have wheels, he would have made me a Studebaker.”

Russ smiled at his friend who surely looked more comfortable on a football field than a roller rink. Jake would do anything for Mae. As she skated to him gracefully, he broke into a wide grin, reaching out to take her hand as they joined the stream of bodies circling the rink.

Chapter 29

Helene opened the milk box to retrieve the two quarts of milk delivered earlier that morning. A piece of paper under the glass bottles caught her attention. After she'd freed her hands by putting the two quarts of milk into the refrigerator, she went back to the milk box and picked it up, closing the inside door after her. "Blue Moon Skating Rink?" Helene mused. "What is this all about? Those damn business men aren't satisfied with just filling the mail with advertising, now they had invaded the milk delivery too. The nerve of them." Looking closer, Helene saw that it was a free pass to the Blue Moon. One Free Pass, Good for One Night of Skating at the Blue Moon Skating Rink, the ticket said. "Well, I don't know what we would ever do with this, wherever it came from." With that, Helene threw the ticket into the wastebasket and craned her neck toward the front hall. She thought she heard something from upstairs. Anna, who was usually up for hours by this time, was still upstairs after a wakeful night with Peggy. *Whenever something was bothering her, she surely kept everyone up*, Helene thought peevishly. Why last night alone, she'd been awakened twice when Anna's rocking couldn't coax the baby back to sleep. Of course, she could be awfully cute too. Helene loved to see her in the frilly, smocked dresses she loved to buy for her. But now Anna and Peggy slept while Helene had to make her own coffee and put the milk away. Helene sighed.

Helene poured her coffee and dusted it with sweetener before heading for the stairs. *Thank the heavens there were no calories in coffee,* she thought. At least there was one thing a girl could have without worrying about her figure. As she passed the hall mirror, Helene hesitated, pulling her shoulders back and sucking her already flat stomach in. She leaned forward and examined a bluish shadow on her cheek. Almost invisible. In a few days she could stop applying makeup. Mick had become increasingly more physical in recent months; last week his hand had sent her reeling during one of their more athletic encounters. An accident, he assured her. He'd fallen on his knees begging her forgiveness and soon he was kissing her toes, and then he was kissing her knees, and then he was kissing her thighs, and then that led to a whole hour of him proving to her just how sorry he was. There was no doubt that the brute strength of him was a big part of what kept her coming back, but she wondered, not sure herself just how it had happened.

Oh, well, it was almost gone. She smiled her most beguiling smile and tossed her head back as she balanced her coffee cup and climbed the stairs to her boudoir. She really had to come up with a dress for next weekend. Edith's daughter Mae was getting married with virtually no notice. Helene snorted knowingly. *You always knew what that meant. Another kid born prematurely.* Helene hadn't seen Edith since several weeks ago when she and her husband, Bob had been over to play pinochle. Bob was always such a sore loser. You'd think cards were the most important thing in the world. She hadn't heard from Edith since then either until yesterday when she was suddenly at the other end when the phone rang.

"Helene, how are you doing today?" Edith had said, as if they called each other all the time. In fact, they never did. Helene knew something was up.

Helene decided not to make the call easier for Edith. "I'm fine." She waited, checking a chip in her left index finger nail while a wrinkle crept across her brow. She quickly reversed it. No use inviting frown lines. They came soon enough anyway.

Edith plunged ahead, fighting the awkwardness of the call. "I'm calling because Mae has moved her wedding up."

"Oh, really," Helene commented, prolonging her sister's agony.

"Yes, she thought she and Jake could have it real soon while Junie is still here and Anna too," said Edith.

"Oh, is Mae engaged?" Helene inquired innocently, enjoying the conversation immensely.

"Of course, everyone knows she and Jake are getting married; they just hadn't decided on a date yet."

"Is Junie going to be leaving soon? I know Anna is planning to stay for the foreseeable future. When will Mae be getting married.?"

"We have decided on the twenty sixth."

"The 26th of this month? Why, that's a week from Saturday."

"That's the date. Four o' clock with a reception at the church hall afterward. We hope you and Edwin can come. Please invite Anna for us too.

Bea Schott says she will be pleased to watch Peggy that day. Well, I have to go. Lots to do as you can imagine." With that, the call ended as Helene smiled.

Remembering the conversation, Helene put her coffee cup on the dressing table and went to her closet. She pulled blue chiffon with a dropped shoulder then decided it was too light for the chill this time of year could bring. A gold knit would look wonderful, but it was far too dressy for an afternoon reception at the church, for crying out loud. Then she thought of another dress in the closet next door, and she entered the room where Anna and Peggy slept. They were both on Anna's bed, the baby cradled in Anna's embrace. Helene's eyes narrowed with annoyance. Anna woke as Helene came in. "Oh, I hope I didn't disturb you," Helene said nonchalantly, breezing over to the closet. She extracted a royal blue suit with silver piping around the neck and sleeves. Perfect. Helene held it up to herself and turned to Anna. "What do you think?" she asked.

"It's beautiful," Anna said sleepily. She'd only had two hours sleep. Peggy had been restless all night. Maybe her first tooth was coming in.

"You will need something too. It seems that Mae is marrying that fellow she has been seeing, and it will be next week. Bea Schott says she will watch Peggy so you can go to the wedding too," said Helene.

"Oh, that's wonderful." Anna was now rising from her drowsiness. "Junie says Mae is terribly in love with Jake. Her smile broadened. And I have never been to a wedding. I think I can wear the dress Mrs. Schott helped me make."

Peggy started to stir and Anna got up, slightly bleary eyed but happy to have something to look forward to.

Chapter 30

The organ played *I Love you Truly* very softly as the guests filed into the church. Anna felt thrilled to be at her first wedding ever. Mae was marrying Jake after almost four years of dating and each year had brought them closer together. It was true, as Helene had assumed, that Mae was expecting a child, but it was nothing but a source of joy to the young parents to be married here today. Jake waited at the front of the church as Anna sat down with Helene in a row close enough to be reserved for family. Jake's hair was parted in an uncharacteristically straight part to a shiny smoothness, and he wore a proud smile as he looked forward to becoming Mae's husband today. He didn't own a dress suit. Every bit of money had to be saved for the life they would begin together today, so he wore a suit a bit too tight at the shoulders and waist, which he borrowed from his best man's brother.

Anna's breath caught as she saw the man who stood up with Jake during the wedding. The lean form that made him a noticeable figure on the skating rink was complemented by the navy-blue pinstripe suit. A crisp white shirt and a boutonniere on his lapel completed a picture that could have been in one of Helene's fashion magazines. Anna's face flushed as her eyes rose to the handsome face beaming at his friend. An errant wave fell over his forehead above hazel eyes she had memorized while seeing them through the milk box over two weeks ago.

Anna hardly noticed her sister Edith, wearing a new powder blue lace dress, as she was led to her seat at the right front of the church. A second usher led a short, solid woman with gray hair braided around her head to the other side of the front. The organ music changed from the romantic serenade to a pontifical march with heavy base chords, and Junie, who had been both thrilled and terrified by Mae's invitation to be her maiden of honor, shuffled up the aisle in a deep burgundy dress that molded her considerable bulk pleasingly. She clutched a bouquet of lilies like a life rope, her face flushed nearly to the hue of her dress, her blue eyes glittering with excitement. Soon she was walking with more confidence, nearly to the beat of the music. Norma was seated two rows behind Helene, Edwin and Anna. She had returned from Atlantic City with a different man, this one named Tim or Jim. According to Norma, he was giving her and Junie a ride back up to Buffalo after the wedding. Anna was sorry Junie would be leaving. Although she didn't see her a lot, with Junie she felt a sense of total acceptance. She was one of the few people who knew all about her past and with Junie, Anna felt sure that knowledge was secure.

The music changed again, and every gaze except Anna's shifted to the back of the church as all the guests rose to their feet. Mae started up the aisle on her father's arm. Bob Bedwin supported Mae's hand as if she were a china doll. Indeed, she looked like a figurine of Dresden or porcelain, too pretty to be real in an ivory dress with a sweeping hemline. Mae wore no veil, inappropriate as that would be in her situation, but a crown of camellias nestled in her dark curls. Anna turned to see the intensity of Mae's view as she proceeded down the aisle. Her glistening eyes never left Jake's face, as his never left hers. The connection between them was so strong it seemed they floated toward each other, suspended by the strength of their love for each other.

Anna felt she was witnessing something she had never even known of before. A swirl of emotion made her only barely conscious of the ceremony as Jake and Mae eagerly took the vows that would bind them together for the rest of their lives. As drawn as she was to the obvious chemistry between the bride and groom, she couldn't help but keep stealing looks at the handsome best man. Did he spot her in the congregation too? Certainly she had imagined that.

Before she knew it, the beaming couple led them all downstairs to the church hall where the church women had prepared dainty sandwiches cut into triangles with the crusts meticulously trimmed off. Mae's bouquet was lying on the table next to a large cut glass punch bowl, which Anna remembered seeing on Edith's buffet on a long-ago visit. It looked elegant on the white tablecloth, surrounded by crisp, paper napkins with Jake and Mae's names hand written on them.

"Would everyone please take a cup of punch and we will toast the bride and groom," a clear, strong voice called out. When everyone was served, Russ Wilson led his friend Jake and his new bride to the front of the hall. "You know, some strange things happen when you are not paying attention," Russ began. "Jake and I have been friends forever, and we weren't always everyone's favorite two-some." A laugh passed over the assembled guests. "I had a different speech in mind before the wedding, but a funny thing happened. There was this poem that our junior year English teacher made us memorize that had been composed for her wedding. I know Jake will remember it, because he spent two nights after school before he gave up and memorized it." Again, the crowd laughed in appreciation, but soon they were still. "Today, as I watched my best friend marry the woman he's worshiped for so long, I realized what that poem really means. In honor of Jake and Mae, I will share it with you now."

Let me express my happiness
As much as I'm adept
As love and your commitment
Take another crucial step.
A partner is a lovely gift
Now you are man and wife,
Perhaps the greatest gift of all
Of many in your life.
And last, I wish the two of you
A marriage of your own
That has the joy of two-in-one
As one that I have known.

"Thank you, my friend, for bringing me to an understanding of that poem. Here is to you and the woman you love. To Jake and Mae. To Love." With this Russ raised his glass to the bride and groom then brought it to his lips.

The room was absolutely silent for a few seconds. Then there was a clinking of glasses, and spoken toasts, first murmured then rising to hearty cheers.

"To Jake and Mae."

"To Love!" Anna didn't realize she was holding her breath until it was time to sip her punch. She didn't notice the dapper fellow approach her.

"Anna, I have a cup of punch for you." Anna turned to face Johnny Schott, complete with his three-piece suit. "How are you, Anna? I'm so happy to see you. You are looking awfully pretty in that new dress."

"Johnny, how nice of you. I already have some punch. It's good to see you though. How are things at the bank? Oh, and your mother. How is she? I miss her so. I loved being at your house."

Johnny gulped, wishing that it had been himself that Anna had missed, but he wasn't about to let that on. He clung to the two punch cups awkwardly. "Oh, Mom is herself, all right. She wanted to make sure you got to come to Mae's wedding; she figured Helene would leave you at home with Peggy, so she called Helene and offered to baby-sit. At least that is what she said. I think she might have just looked forward to some time with the baby, myself." Johnny astonished himself with the length of this discourse, none of which had to do with bank business. He flushed pink around the neck of his stiff, white collar. He retreated to comfortable ground. "The bank is making a good recovery. I am in the mortgage department now." Johnny said with modesty. In fact, he WAS the mortgage department now. "We have worked out a system to avoid the defaults so many banks have been absorbing. People are pleased to have an arrangement where they can avoid losing their homes. It is pretty simple. The bank is better off with smaller payments for a longer time than with no money at all, so everyone is happy. In fact, I have been asked to go up to Wilkes-Barre and help them set up a similar program."

Anna never ceased to be amazed at the change in Johnny when he started to talk about the bank. It was as if he donned an invisible cloak that gave him unlimited confidence. She wished she could hug him and congratulate him, but she knew he would misinterpret her actions in a way that would hurt him. "That's wonderful, Johnny. They must be so glad to have you."

"Mom says she has missed you too. She told me to ask you to stop by when you could. Bring the baby, too." With this return to the personal, Johnny reverted to an awkward schoolboy, spilling punch on his trousers with a quick turn. "Excuse me, Anna, I need to dab this punch or it will be with me always, it will." In his distress he reverted to the cadence of his mother. Anna swelled with happiness. She so valued Mrs. Schott as a true friend. No. Friend wasn't enough. It was almost as if Mrs. Schott was her second mother. With a tinge of regret, Anna wished she could return Johnny's feelings. She watched him fondly, as he hurried to the men's room.

Mae and Jake made their way from group to group, thanking them for sharing their wedding and distributing flowers from the basket Mae carried. When Anna felt the touch at her elbow, she turned expecting to see the bride and groom. "I left you a pass for the skating rink last week," Russ smiled. "I guess you were too busy to come."

Anna frowned, not sure what he meant. "A pass to the skating rink? You left it for me?"

"I put it in with the milk. I saw you at the rink one night, and I was hoping you would come back again," said Russ.

"I was at the rink one night. I walked up with Junie when she was visiting. Junie is the maiden of honor, you know…" Anna paused, laughing at herself. "Of course you know. You're the best man."

"I met her during the rehearsal last night. She seemed so nervous. I'm glad she got down the aisle without a spill," Russ laughed. Anna smiled back, appreciating his slightly crooked smile. "Junie was thrilled to be in the wedding, but terrified too. She's been staying with the Bedwins for the last few months. How did you get to be best man?"

"Jake and I are friends from way back in elementary school. That's what comes from staying in the town you grew up in. You end up with some real long-term friends."

"I guess I don't know what that would be like. I've lost track of my friends from school since I had to leave."

"Where did you move from?" Russ already knew about this part of Anna's history, but somehow, he wanted to hear it from her. In fact, he found himself wanting to hear anything she had to say.

"My father is a minister in Strykersville, but since my mother died I've lived with two of my sisters Helene—you know her—and Junie's mother Norma, when they were living in Buffalo, New York."

"Well, you've traveled more than I have. I have been in one town my whole life. Would you like some more punch?" he asked.

"No, I have enough, but thank you," Anna hastily added.

"So why didn't you come to the rink?"

"I meant it when I said I never got the pass. Usually I get the milk in the morning, but if the baby is up a lot during the night, sometimes Helene does."

"Doesn't Helene get up with her baby at night? She makes you do it?"

"Oh, I don't mind. I love Peggy. We sleep in the same room, so if she's restless during the night, I am the one to hear her," Anna explained. "I did enjoy watching you at the skating rink, though. You and the girl you skated with looked just terrific together," Anna said hesitantly.

"That's Joy. She and I are going to enter some competitions together. There are pretty good cash prizes if you can come in first or second. I have a steady job at the dairy and my skating job too, but Joy is getting married next year and she just got laid off at the factory, so she could really use the money. She's good, and she makes me look good. We might have a chance if we get enough practice in."

Anna smiled with a thrill of relief she didn't expect to feel. Why should she care what went on between this man and his skating partner? Yet, she was undeniably happy to hear that she was about to marry someone else. As they talked, the time seemed to disappear and soon Edwin crossed the hall to let her know they'd be leaving soon.

"Anna, I 'd like to see you again. Can I call on you at the Lords?" Russ asked.

Anna hesitated. She wanted nothing more, but she was certainly not the carefree teenager he guessed she was.

Russ jumped on her hesitation. "I know. Come with me to the horning bee. Next Monday. It will be a gas. We give the new husband and wife two nights alone then we gang up on them at bedtime, honking horns and whistles until they give up and let us in. Come with me. I'm off the skating rink that night. We will start at about 8:30."

"I'll try to," Anna said, hurrying to follow Edwin's beckoning call. "I'll leave a note for you in the milk box that morning." She had no idea how she could make that happen, but she knew she wanted to.

Chapter 31

Ten months later, Anna stood at the sink washing dishes, most of which didn't match since they had been gathered hastily from leftovers in friends' cupboards. A smile played on her lips. The yellow cup with the blue cornflower garland really didn't look bad with the red plates—and there were three of those that matched one another—when you looked at them in a certain way. Anna's smile widened as she heard footsteps behind her.

"The baby is sound asleep," said Russ, encircling her with his arms from behind.

"Do you remember the first night we ever went out together?" asked Anna, relaxing into the comfort of his embrace. She reached into the soapy water and pulled out a silvery green dessert dish. Russ stepped beside her and took a towel from the cupboard, wiping the dish as he replied.

"The horning bee, you mean? Right after Mae and Jake got married?"

"Did you ever think we would be together now?" she asked.

"I think I knew that when I first saw you that morning at your sister's," Russ answered, looking down at her intently. "At least, I knew that day that I had to see you again." Anna flushed at his gaze, which she felt without even looking up at him. Feeling around the sink, she retrieved the last spoon. With it washed, she released the soapy water and wiped the sink. Russ was rifling through the cupboard. "Where do Jake and Mae keep these things?" he said, opening yet another drawer.

"It's hard to tell. They don't own very much that matches…but I don't think they mind a bit."

Anyone who thought Mae and Jake's hasty marriage ten months ago was unwelcome could not have been more wrong. Of course, they were both crazy about their little three-month-old Jeanette, finally asleep now in the nook of their bedroom. The apartment was tight, but it was all they could afford right now with Mae not working. Russ was a frequent visitor and sometimes babysitter, giving Jake and Mae scraps of time to themselves. Usually, they ran out to the grocery store or took a quick walk around the park, returning with anxious questions about how the baby had been. Recently, since Anna had begun joining Russ, they had started to go out when she was still awake. Together, Anna and Russ bathed the baby, washing her little fringe of hair, and rocking her to sleep as she finished her bottle. Mae had left creamy rice pudding for them, which they had taken turns eating as little Jeanette drifted off. Bedtime had been accomplished at the expense of the dishes, leaving that task for now.

Anna smiled as she returned to his embrace. "I had to sneak out that first night," she recalled. Anna remembered her nervousness as she told Helene she was going to Mrs. Schott's house. There had been many more lies since then and Anna had long since stopped feeling guilty. Lately she even told Helene that she was going to Mae's. Helene didn't really seem to care where she went as long as she was available to take care of Peggy, giving her complete freedom from the chores of motherhood. Peggy was Anna's first priority too, so there was no conflict there. Once Peggy was asleep at 7:30, she generally slept through the night, so all Anna needed to be sure of was that Helene or Stan would be home and she found herself free.

Russ found Anna's devotion to Peggy sweet but puzzling. It seemed to him that Anna was more interested in Peggy than her own mother was. Sensing his confusion, Anna had been on the verge of telling Russ the truth of Peggy's birth a few times, but she'd always backed down, sure that it would spell the end of their relationship. It was something she just couldn't give up right now. Here, in Mae and Jake's tiny apartment with a little girl asleep in the next room, it was almost as if they were a family. The attraction they both felt was still there – stronger than ever—but there was something else too—a sense of comfort and safety. They didn't have to do anything special to make their time together special. Sometimes they just took a walk. Anna made sure their route was well beyond Helene's notice. Walking, with her hand in his, everything took on a new look. She felt like a whole new person who had never been abandoned by her father or abused by Mick. "You are a pretty cheap date," Russ had teased her one night. Only one source of disagreement kept surfacing. "Why can't I just pick you up at the house for Christ's sake?" Russ complained. "It's about time that sister of yours released her grip."

"No, it's better this way. She says I can't date until I'm 18. If she finds out she won't let us be together at all. She might even send me back to Norma's in

Buffalo." Anna twisted inside at the thought of being separated from her daughter. Peggy now held her arms out each time Anna entered the room. As Anna woke in the morning, Peggy would often be playing in her crib. When she saw Anna's waking movement, she held her chubby arms out, her face lit with happiness as she called "Na-na-na" her name for Anna.

"We can't build anything worthwhile on lies," Russ said, Anna was silent. She knew that was true and his words cut her conscience deeply.

Nevertheless, Russ agreed to drop Anna off at the end of Park Street on nights like this. At the intersection he cut the engine and turned to gather her into his arms. Anna tipped her head back and inhaled the fresh scrubbed smell of him. She wished she could stay here forever. His lips on hers were soft and inviting. Without meaning to, she leaned further and further into the core of him until the warmth became a kind of heat. It was Russ who pulled away. "Anna, we need to…"

"I know," she replied. She really didn't know what his next words would be, but she knew several things they needed to do. The first one was getting back into her room at the Lords'. It was later than she usually got back. She got out of his car in a haze. Her head swam with her feelings for him. She couldn't imagine losing him now. If only she'd told him about Peggy sooner, when his leaving wouldn't hurt so much. But that seemed wrong too, as if she was presuming their relationship was more than it was. You didn't tell a thing like that to just anyone. In her turmoil, she didn't notice the other car parked just up from Helene's house.

As she always did, Anna slipped around the side of the house, hurrying down the empty, narrow driveway. Stan was off somewhere tonight. The only light in the house was a faint light in Helene's boudoir. She had disappeared there shortly after dinner with a headache. Anna carried Peggy in for a good night kiss, and Helene had given the little girl a pristine peck on the cheek, stepping back so Peggy wouldn't touch the folds of the peach chiffon peignoir she wore. Anna had brought up the idea of babysitting for Mae and to her surprise Helene thought it was a great idea. "As long as you get Peggy to bed first," she had qualified. Anna ran her finger along the door ledge, reaching for the key. It wasn't there. She tried the knob softly, and to her surprise, the door was open. It was unlike Helene not to lock the door…but she'd gone upstairs early…still, Anna had thought the door was locked…in the midst of these thoughts, and with the flush of Russ' kisses still on her lips, Anna didn't see him until it was too late. The door was closed and the lock was turned. She smelled him before she saw him—a mixture of tobacco and some kind of liquor mixed with another scent Anna had only smelled once before brought back another night she wanted to blot from her memory. Mick was in the kitchen. When he spoke, his voice was huskier than the one that filled her nightmares.

"Well, if it ain't the little sister," he said slowly. "Where would you be coming from? Is there another tramp in the family?" Anna didn't even really hear him. Her mind darted between various ways she could get past him and where she would go from there. Before she could take any action, his hands were on her breasts. "You've become quite the little woman since our last time. I like it. It's about time we had a second round." Mick's hands were suddenly everywhere, under her skirt, ripping at her underwear. His heavy body pushed at her, cornering her where the kitchen met the hallway. She looked desperately at the locked door. Even if she could get free, he'd be on her again before she got it open. His face pushed at hers but it was not a kiss. His unshaven jaw continued to her neck and she heard her blouse being ripped apart. He leaned into her and she felt the hard pressure that had hurt her so brutally before. She couldn't wait any longer.

"Helene!!!!" she screamed, her eyes opening wide. Mick hesitated just long enough to turn in the direction of her eyes. Anna brought her knee up between his legs. He stepped back into the darkness with a growl. Anna 's hand slid across the counter next to her, making contact with something—a pan—a fairly large one from the feel of it. Grasping the handle, she swung it wildly, hearing it connect with Mick's grunt of pain. She bolted. With no idea of what kind of shape he was in, she headed for the dining room, through the parlor and into the front hall. "Please let it be open," she whispered in a soft prayer, trying to ignore the sounds behind her. Her hand found the door knob and it turned, allowing her to flee the house. She never stopped on the porch; afraid Mick would overtake her. She had run half way down the street when a car pulled up beside her.

"Anna, Anna! Get in, What's the matter?" It was Russ and she gratefully scrambled into the car, her chest heaving as she clutched her torn clothes together.

"I need to get out of here," she sobbed. "Anywhere."

Chapter 32

Anna sipped her second cup of tea, after gulping the first one Marion Wilson provided for her. A large hanging light with hand painted roses brightened the kitchen as Russ sat across the table, holding her hand. Her breathing finally took on a regular pattern, after half an hour of sobbing. Anna didn't know what caused her to gasp more—the fact that she was nearly attacked again by the same man who fathered her child, or by the fact that she would surely lose Russ when he learned the truth about her. A robe, belonging to Russ' sister Gladys was around her shoulders covering the torn top of her blouse as she took her tea and unloaded the secrets she'd been keeping for so long to Russ and his mother.

Marion Wilson shook her head in sadness. "You never told the Lords how it happened?"

Anna looked earnestly into Russ' hazel eyes. She felt how important it was to make him understand. "I couldn't. I didn't have anywhere else to go, and Helene…well, she still sees him. He said he could make it look like it was my fault. Anna averted her eyes as she continued. I was sleeping without anything on when he broke into my bedroom. I don't own a nightgown, but he saw one of my mother's that I kept after she died. I put it on the chair when I go to sleep every night. He said it would prove that I hadn't been attacked since it wasn't torn. And Edwin. Edwin would be so hurt if he knew about Mick and Helene. He's been kind to me – better than my own sister." As she spoke it sounded foolish, even to herself. She should have called the police. Maybe they would have forced Papa to take her back in. But then she would have the baby all by herself—or worse with her father and his new wife. Anna choked back a ragged sob.

Marion moved closer to her and put her arm around the desolate girl. "There, there," she crooned. "It will be alright." She patted Anna gently. "There was talk when Helene had that baby. A lot of people have thought there was something peculiar going on there." Marion's head bobbed knowingly.

Russ had released Anna's hand as the painful pieces of her story filled the space between them. His face took on a hardness she had never seen there before. The hazel eyes looked dark, almost black. One hand, the one that had held hers just minutes before, made a fist and punched his other hand. His eyes bored into some indefinable spot far away.

"Mick Levski. Mick Levski!" I had hoped to never hear that name again. His mouth made a hard line that transformed him into someone Anna didn't even recognize. He wouldn't look at her. Anna didn't blame him. "Do you remember Elaine Margine?" he asked his mother.

Marion paused and a cloud came over her face. "Of course I do. Nothing worse has ever happened in this town. Elaine was in my Sunday school class. Very shy, but one of the sweetest children I'd ever known." She looked back at Russ. "She was only fourteen when it happened, wasn't she?"

"Fourteen years old," Russ nodded. "Hangs herself in her father's garage with an old rope. Henry Margine will never be the same after finding her that morning."

"They found out she was expecting a child—and her just a child herself. She'd never had any boyfriends that her parents or her friends had known about, but they all said she'd cut herself off from them in the last few months."

"I knew her from the skating rink. She was just a beautiful kid, fooling around with other kids. She had everything to live for. And I saw him—Levski—over by the side, watching her, smoking his cigarettes. He looked like an animal on the hunt. It wasn't anything that could be proved, but a man knows that look, and he often left right after she and her friends did." His fist tightened. "That bastard's not getting away with it again."

Russ pushed his chair back, nearly knocking it over and strode to the stairs, taking them two at a time. Anna could hear the sounds of him waking his brothers from their sleep and soon the three of them came down the stairs on heavy feet. Russ still didn't look at Anna. He addressed his mother as the three of them strode across the kitchen to the door. "We are paying Mr. Levski a visit!" After that was only the sound of the car starting and roaring away.

Chapter 33

It was two o'clock in the morning before Russ and his brothers returned. Henry looked pale and Allan flushed by the encounter. Russ' face was dark and unforgiving. Looking at him, Anna could hardly recognize the kind, understanding face of the man she'd spent so much time with. His hard mouth didn't speak to her and his beautiful eyes, now nearly black didn't even look at her as he strode into the room. He was clearly finished with her. She contracted her arms, her shoulders, her whole body, wishing she could disappear.

Russ strode back and forth in front of the door. "We convinced him that preying on young girls is not in his best interest. For now he is scared, but there is something in a guy like him that will not stop him for long. Anna, come outside with me. I need to talk to you." Was his tone softer, or did she just wish it was? She started toward the door, slowly, pushing her new, smaller self to a place it didn't want to go. Anna knew this was the end between them. And the thing was she didn't even blame him. Just like Helene said, she was damaged goods. Russ deserved something better. There would be no shortage of available girls from what she had seen. He reached down and took her hand, pulling her outside the door. She noticed a long, bloody line on his knuckles. When it was closed, he turned to her and said, "We need to get you out of here." Anna wasn't sure what Russ meant. Where could she go? And what about Peggy? She looked at Russ with questioning eyes.

"I'm sorry it can't be more romantic, Anna, but we need to leave Petersville before Mick comes around, meaner than he was before. I want to marry you, Anna. I had hoped it would be in a church with bridesmaids and everyone we know, but now it will have to be a justice of the peace in a new town. Will you marry me?"

"I love you, Russ, but what about Peggy? I can't leave her," Anna blurted, unable to believe what she was hearing.

"Anna, Peggy legally belongs to Helene and Edwin. You gave up your rights to her when she was adopted. Don't think she will ever be yours again. You know Helene too well." Anna knew he was right, but leaving Peggy was something she couldn't imagine. She also couldn't imagine returning to the Lord house on Park Street where Mick would surely show up again.

Anna could barely see Russ through the tears in her eyes. He actually wanted her. He loved her in spite of everything. With Russ, she would be safe from Mick. With Russ, people like Mick wouldn't even exist. Could she just leave? Other than Mrs. Schott and Johnny, she wasn't even sure that anyone would miss her. Would Peggy even remember her when she grew up? Perhaps it was better that she didn't. "Russ, are you sure? Can you live with this? I love you, too. I am so sorry I didn't tell you about it before, but…"

Russ folded her in his arms. "I'm sorry you couldn't tell me too, but I guess I can see why. Anna, come be my wife and we will never speak of Mick again, as long as we both shall live." It was a strange kind of wedding vow, but one Anna could embrace as she began to relax in Russ' arms. "We'll head north. Your sister is in Buffalo. Maybe she will know of some jobs up there. I'll finish up at the dairy this morning and we'll be on the way to Buffalo right after I go to the bank. Let's go in and tell Mom. You can stay here with her while I take care of things."

Full of misgivings, Anna followed Russ into the kitchen. His brothers waited expectantly at the table with mugs of steaming tea in front of them. Anna was afraid to look at Marion Wilson as her son announced that they would be marrying and moving north. There was the briefest of pauses before Marion rose to her feet and took the both of them in her arms. "I have known that you were the girl to make Russ happy, Anna, and that makes me happy too. I hate to see you leave, but I see you must. Can you get married here before you go, so I can see you two become man and wife?"

"We don't have a license. We will have to wait a few days for that," said Russ.

"I think I can work that out. My cousin, Arthur, is a Justice of the Peace in Barona, and I think he might get you an application for a license then post-date your marriage certificate when it comes through. Let me get to work on that."

Anna couldn't believe that the Wilsons were rallying around her. As first one then another of Russ' brothers hugged her, she counted herself blessed that she was to have the man she loved and this wonderful group of people as her family.

Ignoring the early hour, Marion made the call to her cousin Arthur, who said he'd take care of the paperwork and would look for them as soon as they could get there. Russ had left for his last day on the milk route and his two brothers were showering and dressing upstairs. Anna made herself useful by washing the teacups and wiping the table. She was going to be married today. She would be Mrs. Russell Wilson. She suddenly realized that she didn't even know Russ' middle name. Oh, well, there would be a lifetime of days to learn all the things they didn't know about each other. The best thing was that he knew the worst thing about her and he still loved her. He loved her! Anna couldn't believe her good fortune. In her present state of mind Mick didn't even exist, and Peggy was a thought Anna pushed far to the back of her mind. In her heart she knew Russ was right. She had already lost Peggy.

For the first time Anna realized that she had nothing to wear. She couldn't become Russ' wife in his sister's bathrobe. The few things she owned were in the drawer back at the Lord house. Marion was way ahead of her. "Anna, you come upstairs with me. Gladys left some clothing behind that you could make use of, I believe, until Russ has a chance to get you some things. And if you would care to, I would be so pleased if you would wear my wedding dress. I've kept it all these years, never knowing what for. You can hardly imagine it now," she chuckled, patting her substantial middle, "but I was about your size when I married Abram." She took Anna upstairs and opened a long closet. Two dresses were pulled from the farthest corner and one had a matching sweater. "I'll be glad for the closet space," said Marion. Then she reached even farther into the closet and retrieved the most beautiful dress Anna had ever seen. It was no longer a pure white, but its lace bodice had faded to a beautiful creamy color and the soft folds of a gossamer fabric fell to the ankle. Satin gloves, turned by time to the same creamy shade were fastened to the hanger. Anna inhaled slowly.

"You would let me wear this?" she said reverently.

"I would be so happy if you did," said Marion.

Chapter 34

In their Buffalo apartment, Anna brushed the overstuffed mohair chair vigorously with a stiff brush, then arranged the white cloth on the back of the chair until it was perfectly smooth. Now the carpet sweeper. She moved each piece of furniture as she swept the whole room, although she had just done it yesterday. Past the freshly waxed floor, a pot of beef, rice, and tomato bubbled on the stove, filling the apartment with its savory aroma. She stepped back and smiled. It was so much fun doing such things in your own home. Nothing was too much trouble for Anna now that she and Russ had their own place. The things she had done at Helene's house out of duty were now done out of love. They had been lucky to find such a nice apartment right here on South Park Avenue, just up the street from the coffee shop and the Botanical Gardens. Anna had discovered that on Tuesdays, the gardens changed their exhibits and there were piles of nearly fresh flowers behind the greenhouses for the taking. As a result, the Wilson apartment always had flowers, even if its furnishings were sparse. The mohair chair had been secured at a second-hand shop farther down South Park. A bed had been obtained from Norma, who had returned to the Buffalo area from her latest jaunt with her most recent man with an urge to redecorate. Anna wondered how Al could take her back, but he did. In the kitchen a very nice table and chairs had been retrieved from a neighbor's trash. One of the leaves didn't pull out, but the other one did and the chrome legs had shined up very well with a little steel wool and a lot of work. A treadle sewing machine served as a table in the living room when Anna wasn't busily constructing curtains or a bedspread. A short bus ride took her to The Rag Shop, a fabric store with discontinued bolts of all kinds of cloth. Anna's trips back from the shop usually included a bundle that she had picked up for next to nothing, so nearly all the windows had curtains on them now and the bed had a new rose-colored bedspread. In the kitchen cupboard an Aunt Jemima cookie jar, only slightly chipped, was stuffed with coins and dollar bills after only six months as Anna proudly saved everything extra at the end of Russ' two-week check for a house they would someday have. At least once a month they would open the cookie jar and count the money, progressing ever closer to that precious down payment.

In the bedroom closet hung Anna's clothes and Russ' work clothes, freshly laundered and ironed. Mrs. Brennan, their landlady, allowed Anna to use her clothes washer, which was conveniently located in the garage right under the apartment. Anna hung the clothes on the line to dry in the fresh air or on racks in the spare bedroom when the weather didn't allow.

The suit Russ had worn for their wedding hung there too, as well as Marion Wilson's beautiful wedding dress. Anna had felt like a queen wearing that dress as she and Russ exchanged their vows. The fitted bodice seemed to be made for her and the years of mellowing to a cream color only made it more beautiful. The filmy skirt swished as she walked. Marion had kept her satin shoes too, but Anna's feet were smaller, so she had to stuff the toes with tissue paper to keep them on. Anna wore the long, satin gloves that Marion had kept with the dress, and Russ had returned with three creamy, yellow roses surrounded by fragrant freesia for her to carry. He looked handsome in his pin striped suit once again. Marion thought that her wedding dress might stay with Anna "for posterity" as she put it. The justice of the peace had said he'd never seen a better-looking couple, and he produced fluted glasses of champagne, Anna's first, for Russ, Anna, and Henry and Marion who stood up for them, as they all hugged each other at the end of the ceremony. That night as Marion bid them goodbye at the train station, Anna realized how blessed she was to have this new family in her life. She saw Henry hand Russ a piece of paper, which he read and pocketed, hugging his brother before they boarded the train. Anna wore a suit of Gladys', which Marion said she would need for the cold, winter winds in Buffalo. There were many better paying jobs in Buffalo according to Norma's husband Al, and no Mick Levski, so the young couple decided to start their life together there. Anna cried real tears as she hugged Marion goodbye. She had a real mother again, and now she was moving away just as life brought them together.

"You'll come and visit us?" Anna implored her mother-in-law.

"You couldn't keep me away," Marion maintained, but Anna knew that Marion had never been more than 50 miles from Petersville since she arrived there from Wales.

The train whistle blew and Russ took Anna's hand, leading her gently onto the train and into their future. A final blow of the whistle found them sliding into their seats as the train took off. Anna clung to Russ' hand as she looked out the window Russ' mother and brother as the train slowly started to move. "Come over here and wave at them," she told Russ, and she rose up to let him slide behind her. The train lurched and Anna was deposited on Russ' lap as he made his way behind her. He put his arms around her and kissed her right behind her ear. Anna felt tingles that went up to the top of her scalp and down her back as he kissed her again. The movement of the train pushed her harder against him and she could feel the rising pressure under her skirt. With no one in the seat beside him or her, they were hidden by the high seat backs making a private den in which only the two of them existed. As the lights dimmed, Russ' hands slipped up under her jacket, making slow circles. Anna's breath escaped in a gasp. She and Russ had kissed and snuggled, often totally alone in Mae and Jake's apartment, but Russ had always stopped while she still would have liked more, sometimes going out to take a walk "to clear his head" as he said. Mick Levski had never been mentioned, and Russ treated Anna like a treasure he could not tarnish. She certainly hadn't expected to feel this rush of warmth spreading from so many areas of her body. She relaxed into the feeling and wiggled slightly on Russ' lap. The pressure under her increased and she felt her own body swelling downward in response. Russ groaned ever so softly and the sound touched off wetness beneath her legs and a longing to get so close to him that they were one person.

Anna could see the porter coming down the aisle and she wiggled to the side, but Russ held onto her. "I'm going to be very embarrassed if you get up," he whispered in her ear. The feeling of his breath stirred her further, but she attempted to smooth her skirt and look proper as the porter collected the tickets with a wink at Russ. When he disappeared from view Anna relaxed again, feeling Russ' lips on the back of her neck. She felt as if her hair must be standing on end as her nerve endings tingled with the light touch of his lips. His hands slipped slowly under her jacket and teased her breasts lightly sending a surge of feeling that made her squirm. the tingling and the warmth that was spreading all through her body was beyond anything she had experienced even in their most ardent evenings. There was looseness to the trunk of her body that made it feel almost liquid and each time Russ touched her, ever so lightly, it was as if a tiny point of fireworks had gone off in the area of his touch. She could feel a swelling and a pressure between her legs and at this point it was hard to know whether it came from her or Russ. Anna let out a ragged sigh, clamping her hand over her mouth as she realized how loud it was. She opened her closed eyes to see if the people in the seat in front of them had turned around, but the rhythmic sound of the tracks had lulled them into a doze, and the lights in the car had dimmed for the overnight ride. Russ slid his right hand from under her jacket and pulled the paper John had given him from his pocket. "John treated us to a berth," he told Anna, "but we should eat dinner first. Are you hungry?" Anna shook her head from side to side, unable to speak as the swelling and the warmth increased. Russ' arms tightened around her. "The sleeping car is the one behind us. You have me so worked up I'm going to have to carry my jacket in front of me to get our bag from the luggage bin."

Anna smiled, still dealing with the semi-solidity of her body. "I hope I can stand up. My legs feel a lot like rubber bands right now." Russ started to reach for her again, but he thought better of it, working his suit jacket off instead.

"Well, Mrs. Wilson, it is time to head out," he said as his jacket was loose. Anna clung to the armrest as she entered the aisle, surprised her legs would hold her. Russ got out of his seat and stood so close behind her that she swore she could feel the heat of his body even through the jacket he held in front of himself. In a moment he had their overnight bag and they shuffled like a pair of guilty robbers up the aisle and through the door to the sleeper car. Russ located the berth and threw the bag inside. Anna slipped her shoes off and ducked in between the curtains. Russ followed and they sat in the dim glow of the night-light in a small cave of their new world. "Do you want me to leave while you undress?" Russ asked, a catch in his throat.

"No," Anna whispered, and she started to unbutton her jacket. Slowly, as if in a trance, her eyes focused on her reflection in Russ' eyes. In the dim light, she removed her jacket, undid the snaps of her skirt, sliding the zipper down so she could twist her way out of it. She pulled her slip up, bending her head so she could pull it over her hair. She handed each garment to Russ like a gift and he slowly folded each one lovingly, embracing her with his eyes. "Will you help me?" she murmured. His hands lingered on her shoulders and slid down to unfasten her garters. Patiently, he slid the nylons down her legs, kissing each knee as he passed it. As Anna slipped out of her panties, Russ removed the trousers and the shirt he still wore. The haste of the train car was past. A liquid glow enveloped the newlyweds as they sunk into the softness of the berth. *Never had she felt so loved*, Anna thought, as Russ made slow, worshipful love to her and her body responded. Only the distant memory of a baby's cry intruded on the splendor of their union.

Anna snapped from her reverie as she heard Russ coming up the stairs. She smoothed her hair and dropped her apron on the hook in the red and white kitchen as she headed for the stairs. She had barely opened the door when two arms, encased in cold, hound's-tooth wool encircled her and warm lips found hers. Russ swung her around the kitchen in an arc as she relaxed in the cocoon of his arms.

"Hum, something smells good," he said, sniffing the air and putting her down to slip out of his coat. "What's for supper?"

"Porcupines," Anna announced proudly. She had found a cookbook with 100 ways to fix ground beef and it served as a bible for their menu.

"And what, may I ask, are porcupines?" Russ asked, kissing her again.

"You cook the ground beef and rice in a tomato sauce and the rice pops out like porcupine quills." Anna lifted the lid of the fry pan to show him the simmering meatballs with their protruding rice. Neither one of them minded that the same ingredients had been presented as Spanish rice just last night.

"And what is for dessert?" Russ smirked. It was their joke since in months since their marriage they had never once stayed in the kitchen long enough for dessert. After their basic hunger for food was sated, another hunger took precedence and they moved to the bedroom for "dessert." Russ' arm slid around her waist as she scooped the porcupines from their pan and put them on two of their matching plates. Anna always made sure the plates they ate their supper on matched. It seemed like it would be bad luck if they didn't. She plucked two baked potatoes from the oven and placed them next to the meat on the plates and poured cups of steaming coffee as Russ took the plates to the shiny table with today's flowers, a perky bouquet of daffodils retrieved upon the breakdown of the current floral show at the botanical gardens.

"How did it go at work today?" Anna inquired, digging into her baked potato.

"There were some guys coming around during the break, telling everyone we're gonna have a work slowdown so they can deal a better contract."

“A work slow-down?” The concept of working less than you could was a foreign one to Anna.

“They want us all to drag our feet on the lines, just to show we’re together in this.”

“Do you think it’s right?”

“Well, on one hand, I really like Mr. Helpen. He gave me a chance and he’s a great boss. On the other hand, I wouldn’t hate making more money. We could get that house faster.” Anna nodded, sipping her coffee. Just as she was about to respond, the doorbell rang.

Russ got up, wiping the tomato sauce with the bright cloth Anna had sewed into a napkin. Anna could hear him at the door. “Yes, Mrs. Anna Wilson is here.” Then he called up the stairs, “Anna, come here. It’s Western Union for you. They need you to sign.” Anna had never before received a telegram and couldn’t imagine who was sending her one now. Was it about Peggy? Her stomach tightened into a hard ball, ending her appetite as she made her way down the stairs. The young man smiled and handed her a pen. Signing for the message, she opened it while Russ searched his pockets in vain for some coins to tip the delivery fellow.

“What is it?” Russ asked.

“It’s my father,” Anna replied, feeling a curious mixture of guilt and relief. “He died.”

Chapter 35

This time the train's rumbling sounded like a snarl instead of a sensuous murmur to Anna as she checked her watch again. Three more hours to Petersville and Papa's funeral. No one could say that her father had given Anna any love or support in the last several years. In truth he had abandoned her after she no longer served the purpose he'd used her for after Mama's death, and yet a sadness flooded her in spite of it all. She had no parents now. Anna spent the rest of the trip trying to focus on the good times when the family was whole and Mama's presence made it work.

Russ had offered to come with her, but with the money they would have to spend for two train fares plus the pay Russ would lose by taking time off from the plant, it seemed better that she should go alone and not put such a big dent in their cookie jar savings. For better or worse, Anna would be surrounded by family during this brief stay. Norma was off on another trip, visiting their brother Quentin in Virginia, so she and Junie would be coming to the funeral from the South. As the train pulled into the station, Anna gratefully saw Edith waiting by the platform. Anna craned close to the window and waved at her older sister who squinted into the setting sun while she scanned the passing windows of the slowing train. She was truly coming home.

"Anna, Anna!" Edith called, unaware that Anna had spotted her from the train. "You look just swell. Look at you. All grown up!" She took Anna in her arms, admiring her slim figure and the way the mass of curls now softened around her face. She had never seen Anna in clothing not worn or worn out by an older sister.

"How are Mae and Jake? And little Jeanette? Mae owes me a letter," Anna exclaimed.

"Oh, she and Jake are doing just fine. In fact they are moving to a bigger apartment this month. That's probably why she hasn't written. Well, that and she hasn't felt so good. She's expecting again. Just found out."

"I guess that's why they need a bigger place. A little brother or sister for Jeanette. That is great! I'm so happy for her. Will she be there tonight?"

"I expect she will."

The wake would begin at the Artine Funeral Home at 7 in the evening. Tonight was for family only. Anna swallowed as she wondered whether Helene and Edwin would bring Peggy.

Edith helped Anna load the luggage into the car and they were headed down Depot Street in a matter of minutes. "Would you like to go by the house?" Edith asked. Pausing for a minute, Anna said she would.

A new minister would be sought within the month, but for now the house stood empty. Ruth had moved out when the Reverend had gone into the hospital and it appeared she had no intention of ever returning. The empty windows, stripped of their curtains, peered out like startled eyes in the wake of devastation. More carnage became obvious when they entered the front parlor. Any wonder the front door was unlocked. There was not a thing in the house that anyone would want. The parlor contained only a broken plant stand. A lightened rectangle betrayed the spot where the Oriental rug had once been. The dining room, without its enormous oak table with butterfly leaves, looked like a ballroom. The built-in sideboard held none of Mama's hand painted dishes. It seemed like Ruth's daughters had them now just as she had promised them. The punch bowl that stood on the gate leg table—who had that now?

"Where did everything go?" Anna inquired.

"You know Ruth. She didn't waste a minute removing everything that had any value," Edith answered.

"I'm just going to go upstairs for a minute," Anna told Edith. She started toward the stairs. At the top was her old room. In her mind she heard the pumps as Mama's body lay there after her death. Passing her old room, she took one last look into her parents' bedroom. The wallpaper with violets had been chosen by Mama. Anna was almost glad that the bedroom set was gone. She couldn't stand to see the bed her father had shared with Mama and Ruth. Retracing her steps, Anna returned to the head of the stairs stopping outside her former room. How small it looked. How could she have shared this tiny room with Helene? Gathering her courage, Anna crossed the room and looked out the window at the apple trees beside the house. Apple blossoms and rosy fruit had measured her life. Thirteen seasons in this house. The room was empty except for a wardrobe where she and Helene had kept their clothes. The bed where her mother's body had lain was no longer there to haunt her. On impulse, Anna opened the wardrobe door for the last time. She wasn't sure why. It had been nearly empty when she was still in this room months, no, it was years ago now. At first glance, it seemed empty, but in the far corner was a small box with ANNA written in her mother's handwriting. Anna stooped and lifted the package almost reverently. Had Ruth had the decency to leave it for her, or had she simply missed it when emptying the house's contents? The box looked old and the paper inside, as she opened the lid, was dry with age. Under the tissue was a tiny cradle containing a doll with china arms and legs on its soft body. The china head, painted with black hair, had a worn spot over the brow where Anna had rubbed the little doll in her childhood, as she fell asleep beside it. For a moment Anna was back in a cozy bed where worries were a distant unknown. "Bitsy," she whispered to the doll. Tenderly, she placed Bitsy back in the cradle, returned it to the box, and left the room with it. Thank heavens she had the courage to come in.

"Edith, look what I found. From Mama." Anna showed her sister the doll and cradle.

"At least you got something. Ruth didn't miss much." She put her arm around Anna and they left the house for the last time.

The lights were dim that night in the Repose Room. Artine, the funeral director, had finally gotten his way and Papa lay in the largest room the funeral home had, as Mama should have. A bright light would have shown the same maroon brocade upholstery, and the Fleur de Lis rug, now more worn. If business was good, Mr. Artine wasn't reinvesting it in the place. There were already several people there when Anna and Edith arrived. Anna looked around like a guest at an unfamiliar party for faces she knew. Could these people all be related to her? Tonight was just for family, so they had to be. She was, after all, one of ten surviving children. In fact, many of them had been married and gone before she'd been thought of. None had returned, except in times of obligation, like this one. As she paused, Edith took her hand and squeezed it. "Quite a bunch, huh," Edith confided to her. Anna didn't really know.

Mae wove her way through the older people with a big grin on her face, totally inappropriate for the occasion, as the look on her mother's face indicated. “Anna, Anna. It’s really you. I’ve missed you so.” Her arms went around Anna’s neck, and Anna too found herself smiling.

“Mae, you look wonderful. I heard about the new apartment…and your other news too.” Anna wasn’t exactly sure she should bring it up, but Mae bubbled over with her good news, in typical style.

“Yes, Jeanette will have a brother or sister. We are so happy. Jake wants a boy, or so he says, but the truth is we will be happy with a healthy baby, no matter what.” Mae’s sparkling eyes announced her happiness more than any words could. She whispered conspiratorially to Anna, “Have you met the mob? Have you viewed the monster?” The last was directed at the body on view at the far end of the Repose Room. The answer was a decided no. Anna hadn’t seen Papa for years now, on the day she’d been deposited and left at her sister’s. Mae pulled her across the room toward the casket, surrounded by flowers. Usually Anna loved flowers, but these seemed to combine in a sickly-sweet aroma that brought a nauseous feeling to her throat; her eyes ventured a look at her father’s body. With astonishment, she couldn’t believe how small he looked, how harmless. His small mustache was trimmed over lips that lacked the tightness they almost always wore in life. The judgmental eyes were closed, giving his face a repose she didn’t recognize. Still, Anna didn’t hate him the way most of the people in the room did. He was simply someone who was no longer in her life. All of this came to her as she stood there, and it was as if a weight was lifted from her. She had a new life now, and this man, who had given her life, was part of another life. Anna turned, ready to meet anyone in the room except the Lords and Peggy. She was someone Anna knew she could never completely relegate to the past, although she felt it would be best for Peggy if she pretended to.

That night Anna met her brothers Earl and Fred, the two oldest of her brothers—total strangers to her. They must have been at Mama’s funeral, but Anna had no recollection. Earl was tall and thin, unlike most of the Hirams. He had gone to Chicago to become a stockbroker. His wife was a tall brunette, wearing a beautiful wool suit. Anna felt she was meeting royalty. Fred was a clerk somewhere near Indianapolis. They might have come from Mars, as much as Anna knew about their part of the country. She had three nieces and a nephew she’d never seen. They hadn’t come along, and Fred’s wife stayed home with them. Anna’s sister Rachel had come with her triplets. Her husband was having heart problems-two heart attacks in the last five months—so Rachel was going through a difficult time. Norma arrived with Junie in tow.

With Junie and Mae, Anna felt like she was really with family. Quentin and Ham, both now located in Virginia, came over to Anna, hardly able to recognize their grown-up little sister. They had no way of knowing this young woman, so their remarks were limited to, "Well, Anna, have you learned to bake a pie yet?" Anna smiled, but she couldn't help wondering why these brothers, whom she had waited on during the years in their childhood had done nothing to help her. She dismissed the thought. Joseph, the third oldest, who had married into wealth, showed up in his Cadillac with his wife, Veronica. He now was running the sportswear factory Veronica's father had started before his untimely death. Anna kept wondering, where were these people when she was Papa's slave? When he left her in bondage with Helene? Helene finally arrived, alone, looking like a movie star. Anna could imagine all the time that had gone into the selection of her navy-blue wool suit and its matching shoes. With great sighs, she would tell anyone who listened about how difficult a child was without any help at all. Anna's meeting with her might have been between two slight acquaintances rather than sisters who shared a child. Helene dismissed Anna as if she were beneath her notice. Anna didn't know if she was relieved or disappointed that Edwin had stayed home with Peggy. What she did know was after tomorrow, when she was back on the train home, apart from Junie and Mae, she would miss no one here.

Chapter 36

Dearest Peggy,

My sweet girl, I've learned that I am about to have another baby. This time I will have the blessing of a husband who loves me and wants to take care of both of us. How I wish that your birth had been different than it was. Although I hated your father, I couldn't help but love you. If I had had any way of taking care of you, I never would have let you go, but I was so young and giving you to someone else seemed the only thing I could do. Looking at you, holding you, loving you came so easily to me. You almost seemed to know that I was something more than your Aunt Anna. The hardest thing in my life was leaving you, even though you didn't ever know you were mine.

And now I am pregnant. I remember so well how I felt when you were about to be born. I can't picture any other child than you. Will it be a girl? Will she look like you, Peggy?

Let me promise you that as I take care of this new child, it will never replace you. As I sing it to sleep, I sing to you too. As I kiss its tiny hands, they are your hands I kiss too. As I feed it from my body, I will finally share my milk with you. The love I give to this new child will be your love too.

I will never be able to tell you these things, but my written record of my feelings is my pledge to you, my very special first child.

Your mother

Finishing her letter, Anna creased it both ways and slipped it into the red satin candy box Russ had given her full of chocolates on Valentine's Day. The wet spots on the page blurred the ink in places. Anna knew it didn't really matter. Peggy would never read the words she had written. They were for her. She and Russ hadn't talked about it, but Anna's thoughts had been more and more with Peggy since she'd learned she was pregnant again a few months after returning from her father's funeral in Pennsylvania. She pictured the little girl in her sister's house. Was her hair still dark? Were there still dimples on her hands? Did Helene have the patience to deal with messy fingers and toilet training? Somehow, she couldn't picture it. Did Peggy get hugged and loved when Edwin was away working? Anna forced herself to shake herself loose of those thoughts. Peggy wasn't hers anymore, but this baby was, and she would dedicate herself to being the best mother a child ever had. It would be for this baby and Peggy.

Anna's maternity dress hung, tent like, over her ballooning midsection. From time to time, the baby moved and a lump, visible if Anna was seated, made its way across her midsection. Russ placed his hand on her with anticipation, but she noticed that he blanched at the same time. This time, Anna was determined to have a local anesthetic to see her baby born, although Doctor Dees told her that most mothers were still opting for a general anesthetic. There was research now that showed that babies born with local anesthetic were easier to rouse, feeding better and sooner. Anna read everything she could get her hands on and talked it all over with the doctor. Anna's dress rolled again as she smiled at the thought of Russ as a father. Russ would happily stride in from the father's waiting room with a bouquet of too expensive flowers. Twice, he had stopped at the Once Upon a Child shop on his way home from work, buying things he felt the baby would need. The first was a high chair, which now sat in the corner of the kitchen. Anna hadn't told him that the baby wouldn't even be able to sit up until it was six months old. It was just nice that he was thinking of its arrival, so she put her arms around him, getting as close as she could and told him what a great daddy he would be. Together they had bought tiny shirts and a mountain of snowy, white diapers, along with king sized packages of Ivory Snow, which was the recommended detergent for baby clothes. On another day, Russ came home with a store-wrapped package in silver paper with the Haley's logo on it. He presented it to Anna as she shook her head in disbelief. "Haley's, Russ. Can we afford anything from Haley's?" Her hands trembled as she separated the paper, determined not to tear it.

"I saved for it from my work allowance," Russ said proudly. "I had three fewer smokes since you got pregnant, and now I am down to six less. I'm going to cut back on the drinks too. I'm going to quit altogether and save the money for our little one to go to school."

“Of course, she will go to school. You don’t have to give up your cigarettes for that.” Everyone smoked. Most people felt nude without a cigarette in their hand. The only reason Anna didn’t was that she had never had the money to do so. The Reverend Hiram dictated the official policy that Hiram girls should not smoke, but other than Helene, who preferred to spend her money on cosmetics, clothes and movie magazines, all the girls did as soon as they worked their way out of the house’s walls. Anna didn’t comment on the drinking. Anna was overwhelmed by Russ’ offer and the fact that she’d just expressed her certainty that the baby would be a girl. Now that he had a second job, bartending at the Amvets’ Hall on weekends, having a smoke with the guys during his break was the only social life Russ had. Anna opened the top of the unwrapped box, separating filmy pink tissue with silver stars on it (a trademark of Haley’s) to reveal an exquisite, silver piggy bank.

“I don’t just mean high school,” Russ clarified. “I mean college. Our baby will know that from the time before it was born, we were planning for college. We may not be able to put too much in until after we get our house, but my cigarette money will get the fund going.” Russ beamed with the idea, innocent of how hard it was going to be. Anna put the bank tenderly on the shelf before she turned to her wonderful husband, who folded her as far into his arms as he could as their baby rolled between them.

Chapter 37

Again, the night was dark and rain pelted on the window like icy shards hitting its surface. The curtain started to rustle as the window slowly opened, letting the cruel night invade the warm house. The curtain fluttered uncertainly, then billowed out in a chilling gust as a muscular torso inched its way through the opening. Nearly invisible in the dark night, he intruded the open space insidiously. Suddenly, the cold, wet air was blocked momentarily as a dark form worked its way into the total obscurity of the house. Inside, it inched the window closed, turned toward Anna. It seemed to move toward her, and yet left no wet footprints on the carpet. The chill that trailed down Anna's body transcended the weather. She clutched the blanketed baby to her, willing her not to cry. She was rooted to the spot. The dark form turned slowly. Anna refused to look at him. He would surely kill her if she could identify him. His hair was covered with a dark cap; she couldn't even tell what color his hair was. She willed herself not to look. There was something in his hand, Anna couldn't tell just what. He seemed to be passing it back and forth between gloved hands. As he stood, he blocked the entire window, snuffing the last bit of light. His body seemed to expand, filling the whole room and using all the oxygen in it as Anna gasped for air.

"Honey, Anna, wake up. It's all right," Russ crooned. He held Anna in their bed and rocked her as he always did when the nightmares came. Anna's hands flailed then settled as she realized she was safe in her own apartment with Russ. Tears of relief formed in her eyes. Russ kissed her eyelids. "Shhh, shhh. Don't cry, Anna." As relieved as he was to have her soothed for tonight, Russ worried that the nightmares still came after all this time. "It's all right," he crooned as he rocked her.

"The baby," Anna gasped.

"She's just fine," Russ said, but he knew that Anna was dreaming of the phantom baby and not their own six-month-old Claire, sleeping contentedly in the nursery. Claire would be up soon. The morning light was just sending small ribbons through the Venetian blinds on the window. When she quieted, he held her away slightly, "Was it the same?" he asked. "The man through the window?" Anna nodded, snuggling deeper against him. Russ looked at their second story window as if to check that it was secure in spite of how foolish it was.

Anna beat down the tyranny of her nightmare once again, and woke to a new day. Her own apartment, her own husband who loved her. Why had the nightmares, which had tortured her right after Peggy's birth, returned? It had been years since she'd seen Mick Levski, and by all accounts he was in another state. Claire's birth had been uncomplicated and the little girl was healthy and happy. Anna was relieved to see that she didn't look just like Peggy. Claire's hair was much darker, curling into ringlets when it was damp, as it probably was now in the morning. Claire had long eyelashes, framing eyes that copied a trace of Russ'. Anna smiled in spite of herself as she thought of her girl, and the nightmare started to evaporate like evil mist.

Anna and Russ had spent the last few Sundays at open-houses, but they hadn't found the right one in their price range yet. They were finding that the down payment they'd scraped together was not going to go far in the real estate market. If the house was affordable, the neighborhood was questionable. Anna was interested in some of the doubles they had looked at. "We could rent one apartment and let it help us pay the mortgage," she told Russ, who remained unconvinced.

"I want our house to be OUR house," Russ said. "Nobody else messing up the place and in the way all the time." Anna could see what he meant, plus Russ wasn't really a handyman. She just wasn't sure they could afford a single house. Russ had left the Salem Steel Plant when the strike seemed to be imminent. They just couldn't afford to be out of work at this time. Now, he worked at the Ford plant, which was good in a lot of ways, but quite a trip from their apartment. Since they didn't have a car, Russ found some guys to ride with and paid for gas and some beers on the stop on the way home. It made a longer day for him, and Anna was frankly thinking that a nearby neighbor in an apartment they owned wouldn't be a bad thing at all.

A few weeks later, Anna, and Russ boarded yet another bus for yet another house for sale. Claire beamed from her yellow bonnet, her eyes dancing in pleasure—the bus was fun with its entire bevy of people to look at. Anna smiled at the happy child, kissing her forehead as she switched hips and bounced her in the way Claire loved. Anna took a seat near the front and Russ stood near them, holding onto a strap on the ceiling of the bus. When they got to their stop, Russ took Claire and they walked hopefully past the delicatessen to the latest prospect. They looked at one another with surprise when they reached 679 Electric Ave. It was painted recently, an inoffensive beige. The windows were all intact and the porch was free of debris. They had seen the worst of the worst since they had been looking and this was very hopeful.

"Are you sure this is the right address?" Anna asked.

"Six seventy-nine; yeah, this is it. Even the lawn is mowed. What can be wrong with it?" Just then the real estate man pulled up and got out of a recent model car.

"Are you the Wilsons?" he asked. "I am Herb Manzia of Cedar Woods Realty. We talked yesterday." He held his hand out and Russ shifted Claire so he could shake it. Anna smiled hopefully, and Claire was delighted just as she had been with all the dismal places they'd seen already. "Now, I must tell you about the place before we go inside. It belonged to an elderly lady, Mrs. Vacineck, and when she died, about a year ago her son decided to rent it. I'm afraid although Mr. Vacineck kept up with the outside; the tenants were not so kind to the inside."

It can't be so bad, Anna thought. She was wrong. The devastation started in the front hall. The lighting fixtures had all been removed. The smell of smoke was heavy in the living room although there was no fireplace. A dark burn in the middle of the hardwood floor marked the spot where someone had started a fire. Pieces of wet ceiling tile dangled where the firemen had put the fire out. Stepping around the debris, they entered a kitchen that might have been bright before it had been stripped of every appliance and fixture. Even before they encountered the smell in the bedroom from the adjoining bathroom Anna and Russ realized they didn't have enough money to make this place livable in a reasonable amount of time. They looked at one another in despair.

"Mr. Manzia, I don't…" Russ began.

"Call me Herb. I know this place is a real fixer-upper."

"We really are looking for a place to fix up. Anna and I don't mind any amount of elbow grease, but this is beyond us. Thanks anyway."

As they walked back to the bus stop, even Claire was not smiling. Of course in her case, it was because she was ready to eat. To Anna this was the worst one yet—it had seemed so possible. "I don't know what we're going to do. Anything we can afford; we can't afford the repairs. If they don't need repairs, they are too expensive. And, of course, we have to stay where you can catch your ride."

"I've been thinking about that," said Russ as they stepped back on the bus. "What if we got a car? Then we could look out beyond the plant. It gets rural pretty fast and real estate is much less expensive."

That was how they bought the car that would change their lives. They were both smiling as they thought about it, but they wouldn't be if they could see into the future.

Chapter 38

The car was several years old, but it was in good shape; maybe a little rumble when you tried to get away with lower octane gas, but overall, very reliable. Russ was delighted as he took a turn driving out to the plant. Anna wondered why they didn't get home sooner since Russ didn't need to buy drinks for his part any more, but the stops at the bar had become routine.

The car also gave Anna, Russ and Claire a new weekend activity. For the price of a dollar's worth of gas, they could take drives in the country, unexplored territory for all of them. Nine-month-old Claire cooed in her seat between her parents as the trees flew by and she experienced the delight of a random piece of gum wrapper or a cigarette box. Anna kept pushing her foot to the floor as the trees flew by a bit too fast, she thought, especially on this winding country road, beautiful as it was. *Maybe it was just because she didn't drive herself,* she thought, biting her tongue to keep from saying anything to ruin the beautiful day. Softly, she started humming a familiar song to curb her nervousness. Soon Russ, recognizing the song she hummed, was singing along in his warm baritone and Anna joined in, forgetting the unease she had been feeling just moments ago. "I Want a Girl, just like the Girl who married Dear old Dad," they sang, smiling at one another in the sun of the beautiful Sunday afternoon.

A favorite ride took them out along the Lake Erie shore. Tucked back from the view of the common man were summer homes that hinted at the luxury of the turn of the century magnates. Anna craned her neck as they would their way along the shore, trying to get a peek at the mansions. Anna held Claire who was just finishing nursing and drifting off to sleep.

"I think that is where the Darwin Martins spent their summers," she said, pointing to an amber-colored home deep to their right.

"And who were the Darwin Martins, if I may ask?" Russ said.

"They were only one of the most influential families in Buffalo at the time," Anna said, trying to remember the magazine article that made her aware of Buffalo's former elite. "He was really important in one of the big companies-the Larkin Company, I think it was."

"The Larkin company—they sold soap powder, didn't they? With dishes inside?"

"How ever did you know that?"

"My mother has dishes that came in boxes of soap powder. The trick was finding the pieces you needed. I think she never got a sugar bowl and she was short two cups too."

Further up the narrow road, two large pillars flanking an enormous driveway marked the entrance to West Lake Park. A quick turn into the driveway brought them to the unmanned ticket gate since it was late in the season. "It looks like we have the place to ourselves, My Lady." Russ jumped out of the car and came around to open the door for Anna lifting Claire in his arms. "Can you handle the blanket and the picnic basket?" Claire's eyes opened for a moment, but soon she fell right back to sleep as Russ carried her through the sandy path that led to the water. Soon Anna took her shoes off, loving the feel of the warm sand. The rolling sound of the lake invited them through a tunnel that went through the sand dune to the beach beyond. In the distance two late season boats plowed through a smooth blend of blue/gray; it was hard to see where the water ended and the sky began.

"Oh, Russ. It's just beautiful. And look at this." There was a tiny alcove, surrounded by young trees providing one last shady oasis before the sunny expanse of glistening sand. Flagstone steps wound in a circle up the dune, disappearing into the shrubbery that somehow managed to take root on the sand. Russ gently deposited Claire on one side of the spread blanket. In the picnic basket were cuts of their favorite cheeses, a sausage that reminded them of the summer sausage from Pennsylvania, a loaf of rye bread and their beverages—soda for Anna and beer for Russ.

Claire was fast asleep again, so Anna had to find out what was at the top of the steps. Returning, she was breathless. "You will never believe it—what's up there." Anna's eyes sparkled and her cheeks were flushed under the sprinkling of freckles. He pulled her down onto his lap.

"So what did you find?" He grinned down at her, pushing the empty beer cans to the side.

"It's a house. No. More than a house. It looks like it used to be a mansion, but now it's all empty. Right here at the park, can you believe it?" She relaxed into his chest.

"What I can't believe is you," Russ whispered, his voice husky. "Are you really my wife? Can I be that lucky? You and this perfect little child, in my life forever?" His fingers threaded through the moist curls on Anna's neck, finding each other in the thick chestnut brown mass. He pulled her face toward him and kissed her. Very slowly. Very deeply. The tingling around her mouth could be felt all the way down Anna's body. If she had been standing, she would have fallen. With a glance at Claire, who slept on, she allowed her body to curl against Russ'. The copse of trees hid them from the squirrels that darted from tree to tree on some desperate mission. The waves lapped just loudly enough to create a rhythm for their lovemaking, there in the protection of the tiny, private alcove with the wind fluttering in the trees around them.

Chapter 39

Careful not to spend too much money now that they were saving for a house, they were constantly on the alert for pastimes requiring nothing more than a tank of gas. They discovered Pine Ridge County Park with shelters that could be had by the first people to arrive there in the morning. On a weekend morning they would bundle Claire up and set out before 8:00 to claim their favorite, Shelter #4. Sometimes Norma, Junie and Al, if he was currently part of the picture, would join them and by 8:45 the smell of bacon and eggs filled the air along with toast, slightly burned over a wood fire.

Their excursions broadened, taking them into the nearby rolling hills past dairy farms that spotted the landscape. A roadside sign proclaimed that they were in "The Heart of Rural America."

"Hey, look. An ice cream stand, Charlie's Ice Cream, made in our own dairy," Russ proclaimed. He cut over, making Claire's seat skid along the back of the seat where it was hooked. Anna pulled Claire over where she had been. Why was she so nervous? Claire was just fine. She felt she was being a ninny. They all got out of the car and approached the window. "They have fudge ripple, my favorite. I'll take a double, what would you like Anna?" Russ asked.

Anna looked at the flavors. She really hadn't had much ice cream in her life. Sometimes she and Russ bought a pint of vanilla or chocolate, but their tiny freezer compartment didn't keep it very well, and it took up most of the space. "What is Neapolitan, again?" she asked.

"It is delicious," said the girl behind the counter. "It has chocolate, strawberry and vanilla." The girl's eyes were bright and her dark hair was pulled back into a ponytail. She looked like Claire might look when she got older, Anna hoped.

"I'll take a single Neapolitan," Anna said.

"Would you like a spoon to give your little girl some?" The girl asked, smiling.

"That would be really nice, said Anna. Thank you…what is your name?"

"My name is Marcy Ellis. I started working here when school let out for the summer. Now, I just work weekends so I can keep my grades up. I go to high school in Silver Spring. It's right down the road about five miles."

"Thank you, Marcy," Russ said. "Maybe we'll take a ride down to Silver Spring. What is it like?"

"Oh, I guess you could say it was just a typical little town—a village actually. I like it, though. It has a good school. It's called Archibald Institute after the guy who donated the land for it. Everybody goes to all the football games and we have a movie theater that gets all the latest movies. I like the musicals best."

"Oh, I do too," Anna said. "We're looking for a house. I wonder if we could afford one in Silver Spring?" She gave Claire a spoon of ice cream to divert her from the cone she was reaching for.

"There is a house for sale right on our street. It's…let's see…it would be 112 Scott Street, right off Main. You could be my next-door neighbors. I could baby-sit for your little girl if you wanted." Anna smiled as she and Russ exchanged glances.

"We'll have to take a look. Thanks Marcy," Russ said, licking a drip from the second scoop of his cone. "The ice cream alone is worth the drive." He winked at Anna and offered Claire some of his chocolate ripple.

Claire was only too happy to help them finish their ice cream. She yawned as Anna put her back into her car seat. Silver Spring—such a pretty name. *If there were more people there like Marcy,* Anna thought, *it would be a wonderful place to live.*

"What do you think?" asked Russ. "Should we take a look?"

"Let's drive down. It's only five miles, and it sounds really nice," said Anna.

They entered Silver Spring under a canopy of trees that looked like they were bowing to each other over the road. On their right was the yellow brick Archibald Institute—the Silver Spring high school Marcy had mentioned. A boy and a girl were strolling down the path toward the sidewalk, holding hands. His other hand balanced books for both of them. His purple sweater had a large A on it. "Look at that cute couple," she said to Russ. "What sport do you think he plays?"

"He's probably on the ballet team," Russ snorted, reaching past Claire and squeezing her knee. Anna grinned and swatted him playfully.

A little farther down the street was a town park with a bandstand. A sign announced concerts in the park on Wednesday nights. Tidy, white houses surrounded the park. "Wouldn't that be great to hear the music right from your front porch?" said Anna.

"I doubt they get Tommy Dorsey playing out here."

"Oh look, there is a church on every corner here. Baptist, Presbyterian, Methodist, Lutheran. One on each corner, surrounding the park. Look! The Silver Springs Library! Passing the large, stone building with its stained-glass windows." Anna could just imagine the rows of delightful books inside as they approached the next light.

"Here's Main Street," said Russ. "Should we try to find the street that girl lives on? I think she said it's right off Main."

"Yes, let's look. It was an easy name, maybe Smith?" Anna speculated.

"Scott, I think. Should we turn left or right?"

Anna craned to look each way. "Let's go left. It looks pretty up there." Past the cluster of small shops and the Market Basket Grocery, the street swelled into an inviting hill. The houses on the hill were obviously those of the founding fathers of Silver Spring. Huge porches wrapped around Victorian beauties. One even had a turret.

"There it is, Scott Street." Russ made a sharp turn to the left, and Anna grabbed at the ice cream spoon and napkins as they went flying. The For Sale by Owner sign was about half way down the street. Russ slowed as they pulled up to a Wedgwood Blue frame house with a trellised porch on the front. Two tall pine trees flanked the porch steps, and Anna could see a garden of shade flowers around the stoop that led to the back door. Anna looked at the yellow two-story house on one side and the red brick on the other, wondering which one was Marcy's home. Having a girl like Marcy right next door would be swell. Surely Marcy had to have a nice family. They got out of the car, pulling Claire, now drowsing, from her seat. She fell right back to sleep on Anna's shoulder as they approached the porch. A red glider looked inviting in the afternoon shade. A full-length beveled glass door, with its starched lace curtain, provided a view of a front hallway with a dark wood railing, leading to the upstairs. Soon the smiling face of a small, gray-haired woman poked through the window. She looked up at Anna, beaming as she saw the sleeping baby. She opened the door and motioned toward the cozy glider, "Sit down, my dear. You must be tired carrying the little one. What can I do for you?"

"We saw your For Sale sign. Well, actually, we met your neighbor, Marcy at Charlie's Ice Cream, and she told us there was a house for sale. We're in an apartment now, but we hope to buy a house soon." Anna babbled as Russ walked around the side of the porch, pretending he knew what to look for in a foundation.

"Oh, Marcy is a love, that one. An extremely good baby-sitter, from what I hear. She motioned toward the yellow house. Lovely family too. What is the little one's name?"

Anna smiled, "We call her Claire. And I am Anna, and this is my husband, Russ."

"I'm pleased to meet you. My name is Lavinia Lux."

"Do you mind if I look around the back, Mrs. Lux?" Russ asked.

"Not at all, in fact I will show you the whole place. Would you like to start inside?"

The big, comfortable living room had not only a sun porch off of it, but a small room that could be used as a den or first floor bedroom. There was a full dining room and even a half bath off the kitchen. Upstairs there were two more bedrooms joined by a bathroom. The fixtures were old, but the Luxes had taken wonderful care of everything. All the wood shone with polish and the claw-foot tub gleamed. It was a house that had been loved. Anna and Russ smiled at each other, afraid to ask the price.

Russ finally jumped in. "What are you asking for your place?"

The price she stated was more than fair, but they had been warned about getting something that they couldn't put a 20% down payment on, and this one was a little too much for that. Mrs. Lux noticed their quietness as they followed her out the back door and past the garage into a little enclosure with a fishpond. Anna stood staring at the large, shimmering bodies gliding among the lily pads. Mrs. Lux smiled, "How do you like the place?"

Anna and Russ caught each other's eyes. "We really like it, but I'm not sure we've saved enough yet. We don't want to get in over our heads. We are looking for something where we can put 20% down," Russ said.

Anna nodded.

"It is just what we would like to have some day, but we just bought a car, so maybe it is a little too soon," Anna said, the disappointment obvious in her eyes.

“It’s been a wonderful house for us, but now that my husband has passed away, I am looking for a nice little apartment. I really don’t need the money right away, so maybe I could hold a mortgage at a good rate and between the savings on the closing costs and the lower interest rate, your payments might not be any more than if you had the whole 20% down. Frankly, I’d like a family like yours to live in this house. Both of my children grew up here and went to school at Archibald.”

With Claire dozing on the daybed, they sat down at Lavinia Lux’s table and when Mrs. Lux, who had done the books for her husband’s business as it happened, drew the figures, Russ concluded that they could swing it. “Do you want it, Anna?” he asked. Her shining eyes answered the question.

“Could I look around just once more?” she asked excitedly. As she climbed the stairs again, her mind imagined all the nights they would carry Claire up the stairs in their very own house. By the time their eyes met again in Mrs. Lux’s living room, the same word was on both of their lips. Yes.

Chapter 40

The house was wonderful. Anna couldn't believe that they had their own yard with pine trees framing both sides of the long, narrow lot, giving an air of privacy to the place. There was even a creek at the far end of the lot, far enough down so Anna didn't think she'd have to worry about Claire. Right now, she was climbing on everything, so it was almost lucky that they had so little furniture in the house. Their living room furniture looked lost in the large living room, and their little kitchen set was almost silly looking in the dining room. Mrs. Lux left her stove and refrigerator, which was lucky, since Anna and Russ' apartment came with those. There was enough hamburger stew for three meals cooking on the stove right now. It was true that the sink was stained with rusty streaks, but a lot of cleanser and elbow grease removed it to a shadow. The old heating system clanked at night, but it had the sound of an old friend to Anna already.

Mrs. Lux also left the cozy glider Anna had admired on the front porch. Although it was deep fall, Anna loved to sit with Claire in the late afternoon sun as she was doing now, waiting for Russ to turn into the driveway. In the few weeks they had been settled on Scott Street, Russ had found a new group of riders to share the expenses of the drive to the plant. The thing that had not changed was the stop on the way home—now at a bar halfway between Silver Spring and the plant called, ironically enough, the Halfway House. This stop usually delayed Russ' arrival for 45 minutes or so, but tonight he was especially late. The shadows were getting long across the porch and the sway of the glider was putting Claire to sleep. With her first birthday coming up, Anna had stopped nursing her, so she held a bottle in her hand, having finished her chicken and barley more than an hour before. She usually sat in her highchair and chewed on zwieback crackers while Russ and Anna ate, then they adjourned to bath time and Claire's bedtime story. Her favorite was Woofus, the Woolly Dog. It had rough, black fuzz where Woofus' coat was and Claire loved to rub her finger on the fuzzy part while saying Wooo, which

Anna and Russ knew meant Woofus, although Russ said it really sounded more like a train whistle.

Chilly now, Anna lifted Claire, who smiled a sleepy smile. In the kitchen, the stew was more than ready. Anna turned the heat down and glanced at the clock. Russ was really late. Maybe she should bathe Claire now, and let her greet her Daddy in her pajamas before going to bed. Frowning, Anna stirred the stew and turned the heat down even lower. Fresh baked biscuits waited on the warm stove top. Anna broke one in half with a free hand and took a bite. Claire, now awake, opened her mouth for a bite too. Anna popped a piece in her mouth. "Come on, little one. We'll take a bath and soon Daddy will be home." Anna's voice was cheerful, but she felt a kind of shivery tightness in her throat, which she knew would disappear as soon as Russ arrived. Claire had splashed in the tub with her rubber duck, had her hair washed, piled the round rings on the plastic cone at least ten times when Anna heard the car. The knot forming in her stomach, almost akin to nausea, loosened and she chided herself for being such a worrywart. She waited for Russ to bound up the stairs to the bathroom, but instead she heard a knocking at the front door. Tension got a new grasp on her as she plucked Claire from the tub and quickly wrapped her in a towel. Russ was at the door, but he was not alone. Supporting him from both sides were Ron, the guy he rode with to the plant, and another man, maybe a rider from the car pool she'd never met before. As she opened the front door, she saw that Russ hung between the two, his eyes barely open. She covered Claire's eyes.

Ron spoke first. "Ma'am, there has been an accident, and Russ is in bad shape. He said he wanted to come home, but I think he needs to go to the hospital."

"Yes, take him to the hospital, Ron," Anna agreed, seeing her husband's unfocused eyes. I'll get someone to watch Claire and meet you up there. Anna wondered what happened, but the first thing was to get some help for Russ, whose eyes had gone completely closed now. As Ron and the other man headed for the car, Anna saw that it wasn't theirs. She rushed upstairs and put Claire's pajamas on, then next door to the Ellises'. "Is Marcy here?" she asked breathlessly.

Mrs. Ellis patted the distraught mother's arm. "She should be home in just a little bit. What can I do to help you, Anna?"

"I need someone to watch Claire. My husband 's been in an accident. They're taking him to the hospital."

"I can help you out until Marcy gets home. Now, let's get Claire into her bed and you get yourself together. Jim will drive you to the hospital."

Back in her new house, Anna felt her fingers shaking as she passed Claire to Mrs. Ellis and tried to brush her hair. "Thank you so much," she called as she bounded down the stairs, struggling into her jacket. As they pulled into the hospital's parking lot, Jim offered to wait for her, but she sent him home, feeling that she would welcome the walk home after she made sure that Russ was all right. *Maybe she should have brought something heavier than this jacket,* she thought, as a cold shiver ran through her, even in the brightly lit hall.

"I'm Mrs. Wilson," she said to the girl behind the admittance desk. "My husband was just brought here. He was in an accident."

The sandy haired nurse scanned a sheet on the desk, marking Russ' name with her fingertip. "Here he is, Mrs. Wilson. He had multiple fractures that they could see, and they are checking for other damage right now. Would you have a seat over here and we'll call you as soon as they bring him down."

Ron, sitting in the waiting room, was now wearing some bandages. He stood and took Anna's arm. "Are you okay?" she asked him. "What happened, Ron?"

"We were coming out of the Halfway House, and Russ just pulled onto the road without looking. There was another car coming just then, and the guy tried to stop but he couldn't. Russ pulled back too much and pretty soon we'd hit that retaining wall that runs along the road there. No one was going very fast, but Russ took the hit. The guy was nice, got out of his car and helped me move Russ. I don't think he was hurt at all, and I had only some minor bruises. Russ was the one." He shook his head.

"I'm glad you weren't hurt too," Anna said. "Thanks for bringing Russ home. Who was the other guy?"

"If he mentioned his name, I didn't get it."

Anna glanced expectantly at the door, but it didn't open. "I'll stay here with you until they let you see him. My wife is coming to pick me up, and we'll give you a ride home."

"Thanks for the offer, Ron, but I want to walk home. I think the fresh air will do me good. I do appreciate the company, though, and the offer."

Anna couldn't have told anyone how much time went by before a gown-clad doctor came into the waiting room, calling her name. "Mrs. Wilson, I do have some good news for you. Mr. Wilson's head injuries don't seem to be critical, although we will certainly keep an eye on them. His legs were both broken, and we've set them, but there are injuries to discs in his spine that may not be reversible." He watched her face to make sure she had understood him.

"Are you saying Russ may not be able to walk again?"

"We have to consider that a possibility. Sometimes there is regeneration. We will try to remove any pieces of shattered bone fragment after we've had a chance to build him up a bit, but we can't count on surgery to repair his spine. I'm sorry."

"Can I see him?"

"He'll be down in a few minutes, but don't be disappointed if he's not very alert."

If Anna hadn't expected Russ, she wouldn't have recognized him on the gurney that was pushed down the hall. His dark hair was shaved off, with stitches on the right side of his head. Both legs were in casts elevated by what looked like pulleys. But more than anything was the awful stillness that hung over him. It made her realize what a large part of Russ was defined by his graceful movement. There was even a kind of animation in his body while he slept. Making sure it wasn't bruised, Anna took his hand and held it as they rolled him into the room. She arranged her face so her worry wouldn't show. He would need all of her support now. It would be hard for Russ to adjust to a life without walking. But the doctor didn't say it would be for sure. Maybe he would get better and walk again. Anna held that thought. At least he was alive.

"Don't stay too long," the nurse whispered to Anna. "You both need your sleep."

As if he knew that they were alone, Russ' eyes opened the moment the nurse left the room. Anna felt the pressure of his hand in hers and looked into his hazel eyes. "I'm sorry, Anna." Russ whispered.

"It's okay," she answered. "Just get well. I love you."

His lips formed words he wanted to add, but his eyes closed and reluctantly, Anna left the room. Pulling her sweater around her, she headed for the brisk night. The same trees she and Russ had seen arching Main Street when they came to Silver Spring formed a canopy over her, and soon she turned onto Scott Street, her lungs full of fresh air, heading for their new house and their little girl. When she entered the back door into the brightly lit kitchen, she saw Marcy on the phone.

"Mrs. Wilson," Marcy said. "It's the hospital for you."

Anna's hand took on the feel of melting butter as she took the receiver. She couldn't imagine what good news could be at the other end of the line as she took the phone. The voice was sympathetic. "Mrs. Wilson, we are sorry to tell you that a blood clot from your husband's leg traveled to his heart. We did all we could, but your husband…passed away. You have our deepest sympathy."

Chapter 41

A surprising number of people came to the funeral, considering how new they were in town. Although they'd only been to the Community Church a few times, the members came in support of the new widow and her beautiful little girl. Flowers banked the far wall of the reception room, filling it with a sickly-sweet aroma. Between the arrangements was the coffin, which Anna avoided looking at directly, although it played in her peripheral vision. Unaware of what was happening, Claire beamed and giggled for those who came to pay last respects. Marcy's family had rallied the Scott Street neighbors, although it was the first Anna had met several of them. Norma and Junie came out, dropped off by yet another of Norma's "friends" and stayed with her for the week. Norma ate plates of the food that kept coming to the door, although Anna was hardly aware of when it was mealtime. Junie hovered anxiously and played with Claire. Calls came from Pennsylvania, but only her brother Joseph could afford to make the trip for the funeral. He and several of the neighbors served as pallbearers.

The doctor offered her medicine to calm her and to make her sleep, but she was in a type of trance without any drugs at all. She made the choices she had to make, although not always rationally. In spite of Norma's advice to the contrary, she insisted on getting an innerspring mattress for Russ' coffin. She dressed and attended the wake at the funeral home's prescribed hours and took care of Claire when she got home without really experiencing any of it. She smiled when appropriate, thanked people for their concern, patted the hands of visitors who shed tears, but she shed no tears herself. Surprisingly she slept soundly, not waking until Claire's calls brought her back from a sleep she didn't want to leave. "She's amazing," said the churchwomen as she thanked them profusely for their offerings, while looking right through them. Mrs. Schott called as soon as she heard what had happened.

"Come and stay with me, Anna. I would be so glad to have you. Johnny is seldom here anymore. He travels so much for the bank, he does. In fact, he is sometimes up in Buffalo, working with bank folks. He could bring you back here with him when he comes home." Anna thanked her for the offer; it was tempting just to leave, but she couldn't make that type of decision. She was the one who now had to make a home for Claire.

When it was over and the last of the casserole dishes were returned to well-intentioned donors, she tried to assess their, no HER, financial situation. She called the insurance agent, who said he'd be over and explain the whole thing to her. The look on his face when he came to the door warned her that the news would not be good. He had looked into death benefits at the plant, but Russ was too recent an employee to qualify. Anna nodded. There would be dependent survivor benefits for Claire from social security, which would help but only in a supplementary way. "What about our life insurance?" Anna asked.

"You do have a small policy which Russ has had since he was a child, but unfortunately, your husband cashed the larger policy in when you bought the house. I assumed you had discussed that." They hadn't.

"The car insurance should help. The car was totaled and I don't drive so I won't be replacing the car."

"Russ certainly should have carried insurance on the car, but frankly, Anna, he didn't. From the account of the accident, it sounds fortunate he didn't collide with the other car– or get sued by his riders. It could be said to be fortunate that you don't have more assets. I am sorry to have to deliver this news, but you have to be aware of your situation."

Anna stonily absorbed all of it, sitting down to go over the monthly bills. It looked like there would be about twice as much going out as coming in. After a quick tabulation, Anna calculated that once Claire's benefits started coming, they could last about six months. That was without a lawsuit. Clearly, she would have to get a job-but it would have to be one that paid enough so she could afford a babysitter for Claire. What that would be, she couldn't imagine. She had never worked out of the home. Maybe she could clean people's homes. Would that pay enough? And what if Claire got sick? How could she afford insurance? What if SHE got sick? In panic, Anna's mind raced over the possibilities. For the first time since Russ' death the numbness subsided and fear crept over her.

Anna was determined to keep the house. She talked to Mrs. Lux, assuring her that she would keep her payments current, no matter what it took. Mrs.

Lux, eager to help, suggested extending the mortgage longer to lower her payments since it was already at 30 years and she probably wouldn't live to see it paid off anyway. Anna gratefully thanked her, keeping the lower payment as an option if she didn't get a job which paid enough to cover everything. She could probably close off the upstairs of the house and move herself and Claire into the tiny downstairs bedroom to save money on heat. Of course the full bath was upstairs and it would be very cold to bathe. She considered a small electric heater, warming the room only when they needed it. Anna was already good at inexpensive cooking. That was a big part of how they had saved the money for the down payment in the first place. She'd be willing to forego any treats if it meant they could stay in their house. She had to look for work, and care for Claire.

The want ads in the Buffalo News were no good since it was too far to take a bus, and the car was beyond repair. Even if she had a car, since the accident she could not imagine driving. It had to be something local, or a place where other people from town worked. The Pennysaver advertised local jobs, so Anna read it from cover to cover, checking each tiny ad for the answer to their problems, no, HER problems, she corrected herself. She was no longer part of a WE. Fearful, she found nothing but the usual part-time jobs for kids after school and some farming labor. Dismayed, Anna paid another round of bills and watched her bank balance go down.

Full of a kind of nervous energy, Anna moved Claire's crib into her bedroom. She wasn't sure if she felt lonely during the long, often sleepless nights or if she just wanted to make sure her child still breathed through the night.

One day, just about the time Russ would get home if things were still normal, a man stood at her front door, wearing a concerned look. "Mrs. Wilson," he said. "The guys at the plant took up a collection for you. Russ was a good guy. We're really sorry about what happened." Finishing what seemed to be a prepared speech, learned with difficulty, he held out an envelope.

"Why thank you," Anna replied, touched by the gesture. "This will make our situation better, and the fact that you did it makes it better already. Can you come in for a cup of tea?" Anna didn't really have anything else to offer. Russ had liked his beer, but never drank it in their house.

"Thanks a lot, but the Missus is expecting me." He removed his hat. "Respects to you, Ma'am." With that he was gone. Opening the envelope, Anna found that they had one more month of leeway.

She went back to her job search, wondering if anything would come up that someone would hire her for. She went on one interview for a receptionist job right in town, but when they learned that she had absolutely no experience and not even a high school education, the manager shook his head sadly, telling her perhaps she should learn typing at a night school class. Anna would certainly be willing to do that, but how could she, when she needed a job to pay the bills right now?

It was almost a month before she saw it. BURNETT PLASTICS INNOVATIONS. New Plastics Factory Fab Opening Soon. Willing to Train, Day and Night Shifts Available, Full Benefits, Competitive Wages, and Productivity Bonuses. Hard Workers apply to 23 Newman Street on Monday between four and six for personal interviews. WILLING TO TRAIN. Maybe they really meant that. FULL BENEFITS. That meant insurance for her and Claire. Night shift might mean that she could work while someone, like Marcy perhaps slept with Claire. Anna didn't even think of when she would sleep. She just focused on the interview.

As the day arrived, Anna wondered what to wear. They said hard working. Perhaps she should not dress up then, but would that make her look like she didn't know what to wear at an interview? Actually, she didn't know what to wear to an interview and this one was so important. By 3 p.m. she stood in her slip with everything she owned on the bed. Choosing a blouse and skirt, just before Marcy arrived, she brushed her hair and ran to open the door. Claire held out her chubby arms to Marcy, who had won her over completely, and Anna leaned to kiss her daughter, pulled her coat on and headed for the street.

The storefront on Newman Street had been newly rented for the interviews. Although Anna was early, three other women, about her age, already sat in folding chairs balancing application forms on clipboards. Anna recognized a dark-haired woman from church or maybe it was the funeral; she didn't know. She returned her smile and got a clipboard from a gum-chewing receptionist. She filled out the information, wincing when she came to the prior experience and educational record parts. The first woman was called in before 4, and by that time the room was filling. Only two chairs were empty, and the woman being interviewed vacated one of those. The friendly, dark-haired girl was called. Her name was Nancy Goodemote. Anna still couldn't recall where she had met her. Perhaps she should pretend she'd worked somewhere other than for relatives. No, she dismissed the thought. She wouldn't know anything about a workplace and it was foolish to lead them to think she would.

"Anna Wilson," the receptionist called between gum pops. She waved Anna to a small interview room. Anna clutched her clipboard with white fingers, jamming to her body. The man behind the desk was only slightly older than she was, she imagined.

"Hello. Mrs. Wilson, is it?" he inquired.

"Yes, my husband just died," Anna replied. *Why did she blurt that out?*

"And you have a child?"

"Yes, Claire is a little over a year old," Anna smiled.

"You are new to Silver Spring, from what I see here." He scanned her application.

"We just bought our house on Scott Street from Mrs. Lux," said Anna.

"Our company is going to bring a lot of employment to the Silver Spring area, Mrs. Wilson. We are one of the biggest marketers of luxury plasticware in the USA. Have you heard of our dishware?" Of course, Anna had. There was hardly a home without Burnett products – everything from storage dishes to children's pull toys. "We're starting a whole new product line, Mrs. Wilson, and Silver Spring is where we've chosen to put our new fab. That's exciting, isn't it?" Anna thought it was if it resulted in her ability to pay her bills and care for Claire. "It sounds like a job would make a big difference in your life, Mrs. Wilson. Do you have insurance at present?"

"No, I don't, not since Russ died."

"Well, you will be glad to know that we have a comprehensive hospital and doctor plan with a drug benefit for our workers' entire family. Your worries would be over, on that score. Would you describe yourself as a hard worker?"

Relieved that they were on a topic she could talk about, Anna leaned forward and shared her years with her father then her sister. "I am young and strong. I think I could learn to do almost anything," she concluded.

He nodded, obviously pleased with her answer. "This job would involve some warm temperatures. Do you think you're up to that? Of course, this is not a minimum wage job. We actually pay one and a half times the minimum wage, plus full benefits!"

Anna's mind calculated what that would mean per week. It would be enough, especially once she didn't have to worry about unexpected doctor bills. "What would I be doing?" she asked.

"Our new decorator line is made of brilliant shades of plastic, which is molded in the fab. Of course, our standards are very high, so when the molds don't form the toy perfectly, we need our people to change that. Sometimes it means removing the defective part, sometimes it just requires a trim. Our employees take turns off the line assembling the parts and packing them too. These are jobs that can be done by men and women alike. How does that sound to you?"

"I believe I could learn to do that," Anna affirmed. She was afraid to sound too hopeful.

"Do you have a car, Mrs. Wilson?" Anna's hopes sank.

"Well, I don't have one now." Her voice subsided to a mumble.

"How did you get to the interview?"

"I walked. I just live over on Scott Street."

"In that case, you will be glad to know that we'll be running a shuttle each way from this building to the fab at the start of every shift. There is a nominal charge." Anna couldn't believe her luck. Now if she only got the job, and at a time when she could get someone to watch Claire.

"Your ad said the night shift was available."

"Not only is 11 to 7 available, but there is a ten percent hourly bonus on that shift until we fill all the openings. Are you interested in nights?"

"Yes, I am—so I won't miss the time with Claire—that's my daughter."

"It sounds like you would be an excellent member of the Burnett team. We could have you working next week. How does that sound to you, Mrs. Wilson?"

It sounded wonderful to Anna.

Chapter 42

True to his word, Mr. Hintz—that was the interviewer's name—had Anna starting in one week. The excitement and nervousness over starting her first real job distracted Anna from the achy pit within her. There was a lot to do to get ready. With her mother's approval, Marcy was going to sleep over at the house, and by the time she had to get ready for school Anna would be home. Anna hadn't exactly figured out when she would sleep, but that seemed a small matter. Luckily, Claire took a good afternoon nap, at least most of the time. There were sheets of applications to be filled out. Anna was relieved to see both health and life insurance. There was a profit-sharing plan once she was employed for six months. Her fears about Claire's future were subsiding a bit. She needed coveralls too; she wasn't quite sure why, but she complied. (They were tax deductible, whatever that meant) She bought two pairs of olive-green ones, feeling that they wouldn't show any spots. They were big enough to wear something else underneath if she felt chilly in the winter.

Anna had tried to nap after Claire went to sleep, but she was too excited about this job to fall asleep at a time she never would have slept anyway. After Claire's bedtime, around eight o'clock was when the housekeeping got done and bills got considered, if not paid right away. Occasionally she even allowed herself the luxury of some time to read. Tonight, Anna packed her lunch into a brown paper bag to save further expense. Since heavy gloves were suggested, Anna brought some old ones of Russ'. They were too big, but her only pair was certainly not going to protect her hands, so they would have to do until after the first paycheck. She could pay for the first weeks of the shuttle after her first check too. That was going to be a big day. Wearing the olive-green coveralls, she took a last look at her daughter, playing blocks happily with Marcy, and headed off to become the breadwinner.

The shuttle showed up right on time, picking up about twenty people. As the bus chugged up the same tree-lined street Anna and Russ had found so charming, Anna looked around at her fellow workers, robot-like in their standard issue coveralls. As they entered the large, hastily constructed building at the outskirts of town, their eyes blinked in the light, garishly bright after the darkness outside. Anna fell into line with the other bus riders, mostly women she now noticed, as they trooped inside. Those who had coats were shown where to put them. The foreman, one of the few men she saw, strode up and waved them into a locker room. His voice barked over the noise from the machinery they could hear but not yet see. "There are lockers here for your things. We hope to have one for each of you soon, but right now you'll have to share. We'll have a fridge in here soon too." Stuffing her lunch into the locker, Anna thought she recognized a woman from the application office, although it was hard to tell since both of them had their hair pulled back with hairnets now. "We don't want any hair caught in the machinery," the foreman had said as he handed them out. Anna reminded herself to pull her hair back in a braid tomorrow. The girl returned Anna's quick smile as they were ushered into the roar of the machine room past another small group of workers who gulped water from bottles. One woman's hand reached for a small pill in her overalls, with a scarred hand. *Probably a headache,* Anna thought, *with all that noise out there.* She reminded herself to bring some aspirin tomorrow.

The foreman put on a small microphone as they approached the first machine, an apparatus almost as large as Anna's kitchen. It belched out small, plastic shapes which Anna recognized from toys she wished she could buy for Claire. Maybe there was an employee's discount. "You'll learn two machines tonight and switch off with ten-minute breaks. After a few days you'll learn a third and fourth until you can do the whole room. We're going to start you at a slow speed. Angela here will show you the ropes and you'll be into it before you know it." With that he took half of the group to the next machine. Angela stepped forward. She lifted a large, transparent shield over her face with gloves, which made Anna's look woefully inadequate.

"The first thing is, wear your shield. It's hot, you'll find, but this is what happens when you slip it off." She turned her face to show an angry red burn that jutted across her cheek. "The second thing is getting some good gloves. The shields are provided, but you'll have to provide the gloves. They should be flame retardant and have asbestos lining so hot plastic doesn't melt through to your hands. They need to be flexible too, since you have to reach up and break off any pieces that don't fall off before they clog the machine. You don't want that to happen since your bonuses rely on productivity, and if your machine is down for repair, it will cost you money. Now, let me show you how it's done." First, she brought out shields for everyone in the group. "You're going to get hot and want to take this off, but I'm telling you again, don't do it." She stepped up to a platform that enabled her to peer into the machine. She called the first person up. "The plastic starts flowing as I push this button. It should move from mold to mold, but sometimes the works get jammed and you have to give it a push so it moves on and doesn't spill onto the outside of the forms. If that happens it spatters, you're probably going to get burned and the machine will have to be stopped for cleaning. Lost money for everyone. It's your job to watch its cycle and make sure it gets to the next mold. Here is where you push it if it doesn't. Make sure you have your shield on, and don't linger any longer than you have to." One by one, she took each person up. Twice the machine needed the adjustment she described. Anna was glad, looking through her plastic shield into the guts of the huge machine that looked like it was ready to swallow her up, that it didn't happen while she was up there. The last person was asked to stay while Angela moved onto the next station. The molds came down into a large water vat soon after being filled, and the liquid plastic became solid with an enormous hiss. "Here's another place where you want to stay as clear as you can. The water won't hurt you, but sometimes the temperature change breaks off a piece of plastic. One of the girls lost her eye when one of those went flying because she had her shield open. They don't require it, but a hat is a good idea too. Two people had to make sure the plastic left the molds before they went up again to receive more hot plastic. Most of the cobalt blue spheres popped out of the mold and bobbed along in the water, but when they didn't a tool was used to dislodge them. Never touch the mold," Angela warned Anna, the next in line to try the job. "Even after its dip in the water, it will burn you like that." Her gloved fingers made a snapping motion. Just as she spoke, a blue ball stayed in its form as the mold arm lifted. Anna took the tool and popped it out, just in time. "That's just right," Angela called. "That's what you do!"

Inside her shield, Anna could see why people wanted to take them off. The heat from her breath added to the heat of the room was making her hotter than she'd ever been. Perspiration poured into her eyes, making them smart, running down her neck and into her clothing. Removing one glove, she could feel the collar of her overalls becoming soaked already, and although she didn't feel cold now, she wished she had brought some dry clothing for the ride home. Even without a hat, her hair was getting wet.

Posting two people at the water stations, Angela went on to the part of the machine where blue balls were sorted and either sent on for assembly, pulled out and repaired, or placed in a melting pot if they were beyond a quick fix. "Two of you will go on break at a time. Go to the bathroom if you need to, but get some water for sure. There is a fountain in the locker room, but it's not a bad idea to bring some extra water. Take one of these." She handed out the round pills Anna had seen the woman taking in the locker room. "They're salt pills and they'll help you retain the water in your body. It gets pretty hot in here." With that she assigned break time to two workers and put each of the others on a station. She stepped to the liquid dispersal station with a tall trainee. "I can see all of you from here and I'll assign the next breaks when those two get back," she shouted over the belching of the huge machine. The tall form took over, and in less than a minute the arm of the huge machine descended, and Anna had the momentary feeling that it would crush her. The molded blue balls all popped out, sizzling as they hit the water, so she guided them down the stream to the sorters. When a ball stuck, she or her partner wedged the tool under the ball, dislodging it. On one tray several balls stuck, keeping them both scrambling as the form threatened to return before they could get them all out. After each pair returned from break, they rotated with the machine still in full motion. During her break Anna wiped the inside of her shield as she waited for the water cooler. Just as she got her paper cup filled, the break was over. Tomorrow I will bring a full bottle, Anna promised herself.

The foreman returned as Angela moved on to the next machine with another group of trainees. "She'll be back to see how you're doing. We want you sharp on your job. If we have to stop the machine, it will mean lost money for everyone. All our bonuses are based on productivity." With that he moved on. Their training seemed to be over.

Chapter 43

At seven o'clock in the morning Marcy Ellis stood in her mother's kitchen drinking a glass of orange juice. A pile of school books was stacked on the counter next to her. Mrs. Ellis yawned as she reached for a cup of coffee and smiled. The arrival of Anna and Russ Wilson next door had changed her daughter's life. Here she was, all set for school on her own, after taking care of little Claire next door the first thing in the morning. Marcy was a seventeen-year-old to be proud of. Mrs. Ellis dropped an English muffin in the toaster, patting her daughter affectionately as she passed her. Marcy had been sleeping at Anna's for eight weeks now and she still couldn't get over the look of her empty bed when she passed her daughter's room in the night. "You look wide awake, Marcy," she said, smiling and running her hand through her bed-rumpled hair.

"I guess I'd better be." Marcy chuckled. "Claire is raring to go at six in the morning. She's sitting there in her crib with this big smile on her face. 'Hi dah' she says. It really wakes me up fast. She's so happy to see the day begin, it really doesn't give you much choice in the matter. By the time Anna gets home at 6:45, she's had her breakfast and is going full steam. Claire loves to climb. She has no fear. I don't dare to look away for a minute."

"I miss you when I go by your room," said Mrs. Ellis. "I almost panic for a minute then I remember you're working over at Anna's."

Marcy's eyes softened. "It doesn't even feel like work. I go over there and sleep there. Most of the time Claire sleeps through the night. When she doesn't, she's easy to soothe back to sleep. I can't say I don't appreciate the money; college will be coming up soon enough. I can't imagine how Anna does it, though. She is absolutely exhausted when she gets home. She takes a shower and has some coffee to get herself going, but I don't know when she ever gets a chance to sleep."

Next door, the shower and coffee had launched Anna's day once again. When she got home after a night of perspiring in the heat of the machines, she craved sleep more than anything other than water. The salt pills that were handed out on breaks were supposed to help, but Anna couldn't believe how her body demanded the water she lost during a shift at the factory. Out of curiosity, she had stepped on the scale after taking her shower and was shocked to see that she had lost six pounds since her last weighing. That made 14 pounds since she had started working there. That couldn't be all water, she decided. Her clothes did hang on her, but it didn't matter since she wore the coveralls while working. It was a good thing she did, because both sets now had mended holes where the hot plastic had burned through. She was making enough to pay the mortgage, feed them both, and even put a little away for emergencies now that the checks came in regularly.

Marcy always stayed while she showered. Anna didn't know what she would do without Marcy, and Claire loved her. Now that Claire was walking—well, running, actually, Anna felt she had to be in sight all the time. A playpen sat in the living room, but Claire balked at its confinement even when Ally the Alligator and her shiny blocks were in it. Anna had learned to block the stairs with chairs so Claire didn't slip away and climb her way to danger. Today she took her daughter, freshly dressed and fed by Marcy, on her lap and pulled Woofus, the Wooly Dog from the basket of books. Claire lived to feel the fuzzy texture on the page as Anna read about Woofus and his escape from his backyard. "I am a fuzzy dog and a brave dog, but I try to be a good dog too," proclaimed Woofus.

Anna felt the same way. Like the Wooly Woofus, she sometimes felt the deck was stacked against her best intentions. She was trying to be a good mother, but she always felt so tired. Lonely too, if she had the energy to think about it. Her attention span spent, Claire slipped from Anna's lap and pulled another book from the basket "*Aga re son ma*" she chanted as she turned the pages, telling the story in a language of her own.

Yes, lonely too. Russ had been the only love in Anna's life and his death left her cold and lonely in her bed. It pained her to remember the feel of the curve of his leg as she sat on her pillow next to his chair. His fingers would run through her curls and make soothing circles on her back. How wonderful it would be to slip into sleep in his arms, to share Claire's accomplishments with him…her first steps…her first words…the teeth that were popping in…the miracle of her smile. At times she almost turned to tell him something before the reality of the empty space hit her cruelly again. Her body longed for his, but all she could do was drift back to the days when they cuddled on the couch or kissed in the privacy of their room. She remembered the feeling of his body on top of hers. Anna smiled as the memories washed over her, leaving her warm in a way she had not felt for so long. Russ was smiling at her, carrying Claire, but in her reverie, Claire was not the age she had been when he had the accident. She was bigger, turning to him and talking. Anna still had to refer to it as "had the accident." She couldn't say DIED yet, even in her daydreams.

Anna's eyes fluttered open and searched around for Claire. She was alone in the room and at least twenty minutes had passed since she was aware of her daughter on her lap. Anna lurched to her feet, scanning the books scattered from their basket. "Claire, where are you? Here comes Mama," Anna called nervously. Her voice crescendoed as she found room after room empty. She tried the kitchen door, even though she knew Claire couldn't reach the handle. It was still locked. The entire first floor was empty. In a panic, Anna went to the hall where the chairs she used to block the stairs were still in place. In spite of that, a little voice came from the top of the stairs, "Petty, petty." Claire couldn't pronounce the letter r yet. Then Anna saw her. She was wound up in Anna's nightgown, waddling toward the top of the stairs. "Ma, Ma," she beamed as she saw Anna. She tried to move faster, but her legs were caught up in the folds of the nightgown. Anna pushed the chair aside, grasping the panic that welled up inside her.

"It is pretty, Claire," she said levelly. "Let's sing a song about how pretty it is. You stay right there, so I can see you while we sing."

"Pretty lady, pretty lady, all in blue, all in blue" Anna sang to the tune of Frere Jacques. Claire stopped for a moment and hummed some notes, but then her face burst into a smile and she took the final step toward the stairs, her foot catching in the fabric of the nightgown.

Chapter 44

"You better get yourself some rest or you won't be no good to yourself or anybody else." commented Josie Bertram as she and Anna stood by their shared locker in the break room washing salt pills down with Coca Cola.

Anna nodded faintly. She'd be the first to admit that the four hours of sleep she managed to get on a good day were not enough. She'd changed her showers to cold and waited for her days off to catch up on sleep. Luckily Claire slept well—usually from 8 at night until 6 the next morning. Anna moved her mattress into her daughter's room on her days off so she could hear her when she woke. She was on that mattress as soon as Claire dozed off, her body longing for sleep. She knew she'd sleep too deeply to ever hear her girl from her own room. Anna didn't see a way around it. She already felt she should be paying Marcy more for her overnight stays, but it took all of her babysitting budget to cover her weekly checks as it was. In an emergency Mrs. Ellis would watch Claire, but Anna shivered as she thought of the last emergency—the night of Russ' death. Her optimism was the greatest after a day off, but after a five day stretch with little sleep, she had no argument for Josie.

"These machines aren't for sleepyheads," Josie asserted. "Here. These will keep you sharp." She extended her hand with two small, red pills. Anna shook her head but Josie stuffed them into her pocket. "I don't want you getting hurt. That little one needs you." As her mind jarred back to the moment when Claire nearly fell down the stairs, Anna said nothing more. Wrapped in a nightgown she'd found in Anna's room; Claire would have stepped into the air at the top of the stairs if Anna had been a second slower reaching her.

Anna got frequent letters from Mrs. Schott inviting Anna to come with Claire and live with her. How wonderful it would be to have Mrs. Schott to talk to, and to be taken care of, but Anna couldn't imagine leaving Silver Spring. She had to make a home for Claire. This place was all she had left of Russ. "Do you hear from my Johnny when he's in Buffalo?" Mrs. Schott would ask in her letters. Mrs. Schott clearly held out hope of Anna and Johnny getting together, but Anna had not heard from Johnny apart from the flowers he and his mother had sent. She didn't know what she would say to him if he did show up. She was truly happy for the success he enjoyed—one of the youngest bank officers ever – but she wasn't about to use him for her own convenience any more than she would when he proposed nearly three years ago.

After Russ' funeral, Junie had come to stay for a few days, but now Norma was off with another of her flings and Junie was tagging along as usual. There was Josie too. Josie was a good friend at work now, but Anna had no time for the single life Josie enjoyed on her days off. The outpouring of meals and help from the people of Silver Spring had shifted to other, more recent tragedies, and much of the time, with the exception of the Ellises next door, Anna felt completely alone.

She had to make this work. Anna still hadn't taken any of the pills Josie kept offering, but she kept them on a high shelf in the bathroom. Just looking at them was usually enough to get her through an especially rough week.

The day it came was otherwise like any other. Anna was sitting at the old mahogany desk she and Russ had bought with the week's mail spread out in front of her. Its three drawers on each side made handy organization for her bills, check book, and the thing of which she was most proud—a brand new savings passbook for an account she'd started for Claire. Of course, it only had a pittance in it, but Anna was determined that something would go into it each month. She had sorted the mail into piles of advertisements, bills to be paid, and personal. The first two piles dominated, which was why the business sized envelope caught her eye. It had a Buffalo postmark and no return address. Her name and address were hand printed, however, so she knew it didn't belong on the bills pile. Although she usually saved any letters until she'd been through the bills and either paid them or put them in the top left drawer with the due date marked, she couldn't resist this time. Apart from an occasional card from family, most of her letters came from Mrs. Schott these days. She slit the top of the envelope. It had a security layer, so you couldn't see through it. It wasn't until it was completely open that she saw the check next to a single sheet of folded paper. A light blue check from M&P Bank for three hundred dollars. Puzzled, Anna opened the sheet of paper. In the same printing, she read, THIS IS TO HELP YOU OUT. LOOK FOR THE SAME EACH MONTH. There was no signature or explanation. Anna didn't recognize the writing either. On the signature line was a stamp by one of the bank officers. No clue who sent it. Anna had received donations from well-meaning friends and groups, but they were delivered in person or identified. And the part about each month? What did that mean? Anna could pay her mortgage with some left over toward groceries with this. Confounded, she put the check in the right-hand drawer and started arranging her bills by the due date. She kept sliding the drawer open as she worked, making sure it wasn't a figment of her imagination.

By the time she collected her next paycheck the unexplained check was still in the drawer, although it had seldom been out of her mind. The only person she could imagine having this kind of disposable cash and the will to help her was Johnny Schott. Johnny had even been willing to marry her and give her child a father. Johnny also worked in a Buffalo bank and could probably arrange for an anonymous gift like this. She decided to take it to the bank with her paycheck and see if they could tell her anything about it. At least she would know if it was real.

Anna and Claire got into the velvet-roped line at the Federal Savings, where Anna had her checking account. As Claire reached out for the shiny brass knob that supported the velvet rope, her Woofy dog fell to the floor. With Claire pointing and calling the dog's name. Anna dipped toward the floor. The next customer in line, a Sandy haired young man carrying a cash bag, retrieved Woofy just as Anna was called by a teller so tiny, she could hardly see over the counter with her enormous glasses—not someone Anna knew, to her relief. Anna had a deposit slip made out for her paycheck, but had kept the mystery check separate. As the teller counted the change into her hand, she placed the check on the counter.

"Could you tell me if this check is valid?" she asked hesitantly.

The teller lifted it to the light. "Well, I can tell you this. It is a certified check—just as good as cash if you are Anna Wilson, which I know you are unless you've been putting money in someone else's account. Would you like to cash this or deposit it?"

"Deposit it, I guess. Can you determine who sent the check?"

The teller looked over her reading glasses at Anna. "Officially, it comes from the bank itself. M&P is a Buffalo bank which doesn't have a Silver Spring branch. Of course, someone had to make the funds available, but there is no way of telling that from this check. In terms of sending money, the donor can only be identified if he or she wishes. Who gave it to you?"

"It's complicated," said Anna. "But thank you for your help." The teller credited the deposit and gave Anna a second deposit slip. Anna looked at the balance with amazement. She could actually pay all the bills in the top left drawer without waiting for her next paycheck…unless this was some kind of fluke.

Chapter 45

Winter was nearly over. It had been a hard one, starting with Anna's job at Burnett. The piles of snow needing to be shoveled while keeping an eye on Claire had melted away and tiny crocuses peeked through the newly revealed soil. Trees budded and one on the side yard showed signs of becoming a mass of pink flowers, even before it had any leaves. Anna had noticed these things although she really didn't have time to read the book on gardening she'd picked up at the library.

That day, last fall when Claire nearly fell down the stairs brought Anna close to quitting her job. Even with the windfall, she'd been afraid to trust the fairytale situation, so as each check came, she deposited it. As the checking account became substantial, she enriched the savings account where she put a small amount from each check for Claire. She opened a safety deposit box in which to store cash without calling attention to the growing funds.

Fearful of quitting, she allowed herself to consider the pills Josie had offered. Anna had not thrown them out, but she stored them on the highest shelf in the kitchen—the one only Russ had been able to reach. The next time she felt as sleepy as she had when that near disaster happened, she dragged a chair close to the cupboard and retrieved just one pill. It kept her awake all night. Not sleeping at all that night, the next day was even worse. Anna splashed her face with cold water on every break. As soon as she got home, without even eating she carried Claire to her room, locked the door, and sunk into her bed, cuddling her daughter. Fortunately, Claire was willing to cuddle with her mother although she didn't go to sleep right away at this unusual time. There were things in the room to play with—Anna's strewn overalls, a coat with a pocketful of Kleenex, and a pair of wooly slippers, much too big for little feet. Finally, she crawled back onto the bed and snuggled into her sleeping mother's arm with her Woofus book. The room was silent except for Anna's breathing and the occasional "good dog brave dog" as Claire turned the pages.

That was the worst night and Anna had gotten through it. She didn't know how many more times she could do that.

Shortly after, an opportunity presented itself. The Heritage Flower Shop had a Help Wanted sign in the window. Since she was already on Main Street picking up groceries, Anna decided it couldn't hurt to inquire. The bell rang as she opened the door and the smell of eucalyptus tantalized her nostrils. "Come on, Claire. We're going into this nice shop for a little bit."

"Lil bit," repeated Claire, smiling.

How wonderful it would be to work in a peaceful place like this, Anna thought, remembering the din of the factory. That din made it possible for her to pay her mortgage, feed her daughter, and get medical help when they needed it, she reminded herself.

A large woman with work gloves emerged from the back room. Her smile reached almost ear to ear. "Can I help you?" she asked.

"Help oo," repeated Claire. "Lil bit," she added. Her smile was almost as wide as the tall woman's.

"I was just wondering…I mean, I wanted to find out about…" Anna began.

"The job?" the woman guessed, putting Anna out of her misery.

"Yes, the job," Anna replied gratefully. "My name is Anna—Anna Wilson," Claire drifted closer to a shelf where silk flower arrangements were displayed in their pottery containers. "Claire, please bring Woofy and come here now." The little girl came right over, holding her book up for Anna to see.

"Well, it's a great job for the right person, but the hours are kind of goofy. We need someone to be here in the morning to receive deliveries before the shop opens and sort the flowers into the refrigerated cases. Our morning staff comes in at 9:30 so that would be from 6 to 9:30. Then we need an extra person in the evening to clean things up and take calls while the evening deliveries are made and organize orders for the next day. It isn't going to make anyone a millionaire, but we do pay $1 over minimum for the split shift. Oh, and there are some benefits—some sick days and a group health plan with half the premium paid."

Anna's mind whirled. She already had a babysitter she trusted, but Marcy wouldn't be able to watch Claire in the mornings and make it to school on time. Her face fell.

"Do you have a job now?" the tall woman asked, removing her gloves. She extended a calloused hand. "My name is Mary Donohue. I own the Heritage."

"Nice to meet you. My name is Anna, Anna Wilson. And yes, I do have a job working nights at Burnett. They have been fine, but I am finding it hard to do that and take care of Claire all day too. Claire is really good, but I am just so darned tired after working all night." As if to illustrate, Claire played happily with Woofy and a small note pad from Anna's purse.

"Does Lil Bit get up early?" Mary asked.

"Yes, she loves the morning," Anna replied, puzzled.

"Well, I can see she is well behaved, and in the morning, no one is here, so you could bring her with you. We have lots of storage, so you could leave some of her toys here and let her eat breakfast while you work. It would save on babysitting."

Anna couldn't believe what she was hearing. With her babysitting time down to three hours in the evening, she'd have money to pay her part of the health premiums. She wouldn't have to pay for the shuttle either. She could walk to the Heritage. Oh, the possibility of sleeping through the night like other people! And to have time with her daughter when she wasn't struggling to stay awake! Anna had lost 17 pounds since taking the job at Burnett. Her fallen face broke into a happy grin.

"Mary, this sounds wonderful to me. I just have to check with my babysitter. When do you need me to start? I will have to give notice to Burnett too." Anna became more excited the more she thought about it.

As Mary Donohue watched Anna and Claire leave the shop minutes later, she shook her head. "*I certainly didn't plan to hire someone who would bring a child along*," she chuckled to herself. Her words of accommodation to Anna surprised her as if someone else had said them. She was aware of Anna's widowhood. the way people are in a town the size of Silver Spring. "She doesn't seem like a very experienced worker. I wonder what I was thinking?" Health care was never intended to be part of the job either: in fact Mary had originally imagined hiring two very part-time people at minimum wage, but it was obvious Anna would need health care with that little girl. "I guess I must have fallen for that Lil Bit," she rationalized, realizing that something about her reminded her of Nancy, her own daughter now long grown. She actually looked forward to seeing both Anna and her daughter on a regular basis. The smile remained on her face.

Chapter 46

The first call of the night at the Heritage Flower and Gift Shop was an order for another Mother's Day bouquet, this one from Sylvia Huntington for her mother who was in Marshall House Assisted Living. In the months Anna had been working in the shop, she'd learned more than most people knew about the residents of Silver Spring. She knew that Martin Laurel always gave his wife Julie white roses on their anniversary—just like the ones she carried when they married thirty-eight years ago, he'd confided. Anna also knew that Patrice Zachary, a teacher at the high school ordered flowers for herself with a note that indicated they were from a secret admirer. There were parties, weddings, funerals, and, of course, the teen-age boys not sure if they should order wrist corsages or pin-ons for the junior prom. There had been hundreds of plants for Easter—tulips, pots of narcissus, elegant lilies, and the fragrant hyacinths, which Anna loved. Anna could imagine the rush for next Valentine's Day. With this thought, she realized that she imagined herself still working here when Valentine's Day came around again.

Anna had made her mark on the Heritage too. As Mary gained complete confidence in Anna, she'd given her more freedom and responsibility in the shop. Anna had instituted a "Flower of the Week" with advertisers at the Market Basket, bringing new customers in for flowers they'd previously thought too expensive. She'd also shown a talent for arranging, so if an order came in that couldn't be filled in time by the morning staff, Anna made it up. That was her favorite thing. She had loved sorting the delicate white Freesia, the romantic roses, the perky daisies and all the other flowers that came in the after-hours deliveries, but it was truly fun to combine those flowers, choosing just the right container to complement their colors, softening groupings with delicate baby's breath and slender ferns to make a beautiful arrangement.

A corner of the room was Claire's Corner, with a little table and a supply of her toys, which she used when Anna brought her in the mornings. That had worked out so well that often Anna stayed longer into the day, giving Mary a later start and giving Anna more income than she had counted on. Customers knew Claire by name, often receiving their bouquets from her little hands.

Regulars like Martha Caldwell often brought treats for Lil Bit, as everyone had taken to calling Claire.

When the phone rang for the second time it was Mary herself. "Anna, Bill Mason's wife Dorothy, has just died of a heart attack, and Bill wants to come in to order her flowers personally. Can you handle it? The funeral is on Wednesday at St. Al's."

"Sure, Mary. I 'll be glad to take care of him. When will he be in?"

"He wants to come tonight. He says he can't sleep anyway and he wants to do something. Thanks, Anna. Usually, I'd tell him to wait but he's a good friend and he and Dorothy were so devoted."

"I'll be here, Mary. That's St. Al's on Wednesday, right?" said Anna, jotting the date in the notebook by the register. The Masons' names were familiar to Anna. Bill, the son of the dentist, had married Dorothy, the sister of the Mayor. Dorothy had become an administrator at the hospital just across the street from the large Victorian house where they lived on Main Street, while Bill worked as a physical therapist in nearby Towanda.

They were always seen together, and it was common knowledge that they'd had at least five failed pregnancies before resigning themselves to the unencumbered life of a childless couple. When candid shots of the Cotillion Ball or a Charity Drive for the hospital were in the Silver Spring Gazette, the Masons were often featured in the group shots—bright-eyed. Dorothy was pictured perched upon high heels in a stylish dress, her curly dark hair pulled back with rhinestone clips. Red headed Bill was captured looking at her dotingly. Now, Dorothy has died. She was much too young. They were still in their forties, Anna speculated.

There was a gentle knock at the Heritage's door and Anna had the deadbolt disengaged in a moment. Even before she opened it, she saw his face through the etched panels in the door. Deep lines framed downcast blue eyes behind gold rimmed glasses and the reddish hair seemed to have more silver in it than she remembered.

"Come in Mr. Mason," said Anna. "I'm so sorry for your loss."

He came inside, and Anna had to look outside to assure herself that it wasn't raining. He had the look of someone who'd been in a rainstorm, everything about him pulling down as if with the weight of water. He looked around the shop as if he had forgotten just why he'd come here.

"Let me take your coat, Mr. Mason," Anna said, slipping it off him as he neither helped nor resisted.

"Mrs. Wilson," he began, his voice faltering. "I'm here…here to…" the voice trailed off.

"I know why you're here, Mr. Mason, and I am here to help you through this. You wanted to pick the flowers out yourself, I understand. Let me show you what we have and we can look at some pictures of other things we can order. Maybe there are some types of flowers that were special to her or both of you." He nodded, incapable of words. "When my husband died a while ago, I wanted flowers that reminded me of the time in our first apartment, when I went to the Botanical Gardens and got flowers for our kitchen table once a week. OH, we couldn't afford them," Anna said with a slight smile, "but they threw them out on Thursdays, and let anyone help themselves. That doesn't sound like a very romantic thought, but flowers that looked like that seemed right." A lump in her throat stopped her from saying more. Anna showed him the tall gladiolus, which he said were too tall for his Dorothy, who was short even in heels. The red roses, he said, were too bold and common for her. Finally, Anna helped him to pick an assortment of flowers that reminded him of everything from a corsage he'd given his Dorothy to the plant he'd given her at Easter. Anna pictured the foliage and the ribbons that would tie them all into a beautiful memorial. He didn't even ask about the price.

The poor man, Anna thought as he shuffled from the shop. Maybe he was older than she thought.

Chapter 47

Anna's screen door was always slightly ajar, but she could hear the squeal it made as someone started to open it. "Who's there?" she asked. "Come on in. We're in the kitchen." Anna and Claire were making cookies. Claire perched on the metal three-stepped stool, her special helping place, while she cracked the eggs, one at a time, into the bowl. If a piece of shell slipped into the bowl, she'd frown and point to it before Anna beat it into the dough. If none slipped in, she'd burst into a smile and place the cracked shell in the garbage bag while the mixture took shape.

"Are you in there? Anna? Claire? It's me, Junie."

"Junie? Oh my heavens. Come in! Come in!" Anna called, tapping the mixing spoon on the edge of the brown pottery bowl.

"We're making cookies," added Claire. "They are almost ready for the oven."

Junie stuck her head into the kitchen, heaving her heavy suitcase to the floor and rushing into Anna's arms. Anna couldn't believe the change in her cousin. She must have lost 40 pounds since Anna last saw her. "Oh, Anna, you don't know how good it is to see you. Junie's arms reached around Anna's small frame." She stood back and appraised Anna's new haircut. "Anna, you are downright beautiful. And Claire." The little girl licked the spoon she'd retrieved from the counter, smiling through the cookie dough.

"Talking about beautiful! Junie, you look terrific! Oh forgive me. Let me get you something to drink," Anna said, wiping her hands on her apron. "There will be cookies pretty soon, but how about a cup of tea right now?"

"That sounds just great. I feel like I've been on that bus for days—well actually it has been quite a while," Junie replied.

"Tell me everything. Where did you come from on the bus, and how did you get from the bus? And where is Norma?"

Junie smoothed her trim, navy blue travel suit and sat on the offered chair. Her hair was curled around her face in golden curls and she wore a becoming shade of pink lipstick. “The bus I started on was from Richmond, although that was two days and several buses ago. And THAT is where Norma is. With Harold.”

“Harold? I thought his name was…uh Charley?” said Anna.

“Oh, there have been two since him,” said Junie. She wanted me to stay, but it’s been hard being with the two of them. They’re always thinking of things to get me out of their hair for a while. So, I thought to myself, *I’m going to save all the money they give me for snacks, lose some weight, and get myself to somewhere where I can get a job.* “Do you think I could find a job in Silver Spring? And would you mind if I stayed here while I got started?”

“You bet, you could. Oh, Junie, I am so glad to see someone from my family again. I would always have room for you here.” Her voice quavered at the last part. “I have a wonderful job at the Heritage Flower Shop now. I’ll ask Mary if she knows of anything in the area.”

Chapter 48

My Darling Peggy,

It is your birthday today, and I wonder how you are? Are you good in school? Who are your friends? Most of all, are you happy? I so hope you have lots of love in your life. You have my love, although I will probably never be able to tell you.

Your little sister Claire is growing up. She is quite the little lady now, nearly eight years old. At the shop where I work, The Heritage Flower Shop, they still call her Little Bit, even though she isn't such a little bit any more. Sometimes, I think she knows more than I do. I wish she could know that she had a big sister out there.

Junie now lives near Silver Spring. She is managing the dress department at the Simon Fashion Stop now. She gets to take wonderful trips to buy their latest styles, which she gets at promotional prices, so she always looks stunning. If you could remember Junie, you would not believe her. She was always beautiful, but now she is slender and has such confidence in herself. She stayed with Claire and me for a while when she first arrived in Silver Spring.

Svelte. It means fashionably thin, and that's what Junie is now. That is a new word I learned in my class. I am finally getting the diploma I didn't get when I was a teenager. I should be finished in a few months, and who knows what I will do after that. You stay in school, honey, and learn everything you can.

My life is really very good now. I am paying the house off every month, and every room is wallpapered or freshly painted now. Claire has a savings account for her education which gets a little money every paycheck. There is another loan, given to me when I really needed it, that I will be paying off soon.

The missing parts of my life are Russ and you, my little girl. I miss you both every day, and carry you both in my heart.

With much love,
Your mother

Anna folded the paper and placed it into the red satin Valentine box with all the other letters she'd written to her first daughter.

Chapter 49

In the ten years since her father had died, Helene Lord never had a good word for him. It was unusual for Helene to have a good word for anyone, in fact. Edwin had learned to stay out of her way. Although she was still attractive by anyone's standards, it was hard for him to think why he had thought it would be good in any way to be married to her. They'd had separate bedrooms for years. When he wasn't at the office or seeing merchandisers for the mill, he filled his pipe, a comfort he had adopted since his marriage, and slipped into the back parlor with a good mystery or the financial pages of the paper. Often, the sound of Peggy practicing the piano would set a background mood. Sometimes a scotch, straight up, helped provide the peace he longed for too. After the required forty-five minutes of practice, Peggy would join him, sitting by his feet with a book of her own. Edwin thought Peggy was probably hiding out from Helene too, and they shared a companionable silence, which drove Helene mad.

"Edwin, do you have that smelly pipe out again?" Helene squalled. "I swear, this house smells like a men's club. It just reeks of that filthy stuff." Helene wasn't totally involved in her mission tonight. She paused for a moment and smoothed her blouse in front of the mirror.

"Um hum," replied Edwin, barely looking up from his book. Usually he and Peggy would share a conspiratorial glance at this point, both of them knowing that Helene would shortly close the pocket doors that separated the two parlors and leave them in peace. Probably one more tirade would come first. Tonight Peggy didn't look up from her book at all.

"Peggy Elaine, are you hunched over again with your head in a book? You'll end up with glasses this thick and a derriere that won't even fit in a chair. You should be practicing correct posture. You have to pay attention to your looks. young lady, or no man will look at you twice." With this the pocket door slid shut and Helene was on to whatever she did with herself instead of being a wife and mother. Peggy still didn't look up.

“Oh Peg, don’t take her seriously. She just likes to blow off steam,” Edwin said, watching his daughter more closely. “Come on, now, don’t let her bother you.”

Looking up from the page she hadn’t turned in over twenty minutes, Peggy’s brown eyes met his across a space that suddenly seemed much wider. “She told me today,” she said simply.

“Told you wha…” he began, but he had a miserable feeling he knew. “What did she tell you, Peg?”

“She was yelling at me for not drying the crystal goblets well enough this afternoon.” As Peggy began, she was suddenly back in the kitchen with Helene, hearing her voice as if it came from a loudspeaker.

“If you were my real daughter,” Helene had shrilled, “you wouldn’t be so coarse. I swear, you are just like your mother. No eye for elegance at all. At the rate you’re going you’ll be fat by fifteen. And look at those nails. Have you polished them at all this week? How will they look for your piano recital?”

“If I were your REAL mother???” Peggy repeated.

“Oh hell, I didn’t want you to find out like this, but I guess it is time we had a talk. I’m sure you must have suspected we couldn’t really be mother and daughter. I mean, look at your hair—just like Anna’s. And you have just about as much interest in your looks as a cleaning woman. God knows I have tried. You’ve always had the best clothes, lessons on the piano, and we’ve tried to tame that wild hair, but the apple never falls far from the tree. You are her all over!”

“Anna? You mean Aunt Anna? Are you saying that Aunt Anna is my mother?”

“Well, not in any way that counts, that’s for sure! It is Edwin and I who gave you a home and the best opportunities. All she did was get knocked up. And do I get any credit for taking you in? Giving you two parents? Not in this family, I don’t. They act like I was the one who did something wrong.”

“Aunt Anna is my mother?”

“Are you a little slow or what? I just told you she was your birth mother, but don’t let me hear you ever calling her mother. She’s just your aunt. I am your mother and don’t you forget it. Now, get those glasses good and shiny.”

As the afternoon replayed in her head, Edwin took the sobbing girl in his arms. He thought of all the questions she would have and hoped that he would not be the one to answer them.

Chapter 50

Silver Spring. celebrating its sesquicentennial, was decorated like a bride about to walk down the aisle. The lamp posts along Main Street supported huge baskets of flowers from which streamers in red white and blue waved. Each store had sponsored a window-painting contest, which brought entries from each class in the school and darn well would have even if they hadn't gotten time off from class to do the murals. The Silver Spring Journal had articles every week on the history of the town and even those who knew nothing before recognized that the original town was called Fiddlers Green. Miss Hensley, at the library had a whole wall of featured books on the history of Silver Spring—all hundred fifty years of it. Seamstresses were busy sewing period costumes and the men were busily growing beards for the occasion. They better well do so, since there was a fine if you were caught clean-shaven. The school band was practicing music written 150 years ago and spent many early mornings on the football field practicing for the big parade that would take place for the occasion. Mars' soda bar was featuring the big Green—a lime soda that was so big you got another one free if you could finish it. Norine Dorriall was teaching large groups of adults hundred-year-old dances like the reel in addition to her regular retinue of ballet and tap for the community's younger dancers. The town was caught up in sesquicentennial fever.

In the Heritage Shop the sales were unprecedented, partly due to another of Anna's ideas. Getting bowls from Mrs. Larcom's antique shop, an authentic antique arrangement could be had for the many parties and dinners being held in honor of the town's history. Often these were raffled off afterward making tidy profits for Mrs. Larcom, The Heritage Shop and the benefiting group. With 12-year-old Claire in school, Anna had become the manager of the Heritage and Mary was like a sister, or maybe an aunt to her, rather than her employer.

Anna's period dress was a blue floral print with puffed sleeves and a bonnet to match. She'd used the old treadle sewing machine to make matching dresses for Claire and herself. Junie had to have one too. Not officially a resident of

Silver Spring, she did work at Simon's Fashion Stop in Silver Spring and lived in Loren, a town only ten miles away. Anna was delighted to make a size 8 dress for Junie, who now had a ring on her finger and a date to get married to Fredrick Simon, the owner of the store where she worked.

Boys were starting to notice Claire too. On her Anna's curls were slightly relaxed into waves. When Anna looked into her eyes, they might be Russ' hazel eyes right down to the dark fleck in the right one. She was having a little trouble with science, but was a wonderful writer and had won the Forensic Society speaking competition. She'd never given Anna a moment's worry and she didn't seem to have the disdain for adults so many adolescents advertised.

Financially, Anna was in the best situation of her life. The house was nearly paid off. She'd made extra payments as her position at the Heritage had changed. The checks that still came from Johnny were cashed and stored in her safe deposit box at the bank. In two more months she would have all the money she'd used from those checks replaced. She'd asked Mrs. Schott for Johnny's address, which she stored with the saved cash for the day, soon to come, when she would proudly return it all to him.

Things were pretty good, Anna had to feel. The sharp pain she felt at Russ' death had subsided over the years, and yet she'd never felt inclined to respond to a number of nice fellows who had asked her out. Once or twice she'd actually gone, usually because Josie had given her no choice. Although the man was usually just what Josie had promised, Anna was always glad to see the evening end so she could get back to Claire.

This beautiful fall day found Anna tending the flowers on Russ' grave. Even at the beginning, when she barely had enough money for the bills, a small amount was reserved for a small plant for him. Then, as the season went on, she would water and feed it until it was the size she wished she could afford. Although she wasn't usually superstitious, Anna knew as the flower grew, she saw it as part of their life together, still alive and growing. This year the flower was a geranium-actually, three of them with blooms all over them. Anna had picked it because it was known to withstand heat, and it had been a very hot summer. The impatiens she'd planted last year had been hanging over the pot each time she came. Although they perked up when she watered them, she lived in fear that Russ' flowers would die; they seemed her last link with him. She caressed the top of the smooth granite marker, relatively new to the site. When Russ had first died, she'd only been able to afford a small, flat marker.

Now a handsome, engraved stone marked his resting place. Russell Abram Wilson, Beloved Husband and Father, she read to herself.

Anna emptied the last of the water in the watering can, then strolled over to the faucet where it was stored to wash her dirty hands. "May I use that? If you're finished, of course." Anna rose from the faucet to see Bill Mason, his hands as dirty as hers were. She smiled, recalling the time he had come into the Heritage when his wife had died. He'd been in for all the major events of their life together ever since.

"Here you are. You'd better get some water on those hands too. It'll take a while to clean those fingernails." He looked down at his fingers rimmed in black as if he'd just noticed them.

"I guess some gloves would have been a good idea," he said. Anna noticed a small smile, and felt glad that he could smile now. He surely couldn't that night. "I'm not really good at this, but it feels like something I have to do."

"I know what you mean. I nearly panicked when the flowers on Russ' grave almost died last year. It's as if keeping them alive keeps something of us alive."

Suddenly Anna had his full attention. His eyes were the clearest blue she'd ever seen behind his rimmed glasses. They were kind eyes, if still somewhat sad. "Yes," he said. "That's it exactly. Thank you." With that he took the watering can and headed toward the next aisle of graves. Anna watched him sprinkle way too much water on some petunias in a pot, then, forgetting the watering can, he got in his car and left. Anna walked to the gravesite he had left. Dorothy's grave. The inscription was long and as Anna read it, she felt somehow like she was intruding. "My worldly goods: a fair trade for just one more day with you," she read. The petunias floated in their watery pot. Anna retrieved the perlite she brought to absorb some of the moisture. She added it to the pot, happier with the plants' chance to survive. For good measure, she added a bit of fertilizer to the pot, quite sure he would not have thought of that. Then she spotted a brown wallet, nearly hidden behind the pot. Bill Mason's for sure.

Chapter 51

The Mason home was on Anna's way home from the cemetery. If Bill wasn't home, she would have to call, but it didn't hurt to give it a try. The house was one of the prettier structures in town; white with black shutters. An enclosed porch was surrounded by deep pink rhododendrons that looked like they could use a bit of trimming. The lawn was neatly mown, but the roses on the trellises by the side of the drive were calling to be deadheaded for another bloom. She guessed these had been Dorothy's responsibilities.

Anna turned into the drive slowly. She rarely drove and the truck was a loaner from the Heritage. She saw that Bill's white Buick was parked outside the two-car garage.

She collected the wallet and walked past a blooming magnolia tree to the back door. She heard a muffled "Just a minute," as she pressed the doorbell. When he came to the door, Bill wore an oven mitt, a frown playing on his freckled face. "Oh, Mrs. Wilson, come in please," he said awkwardly, pulling his hand from the mitt to open the door.

Standing in the back hall, Anna couldn't help but notice cabinets filled with antique dishes. The closest one was full of cobalt blue depression ware. She moved closer. "These are beautiful. They are Mount Pleasant, aren't they? I have just three pieces that were Russ' mother's."

"It is Mount Pleasant. It took me a long time to collect those-a lot of trips to Pennsylvania and Ohio. I'm missing one candle holder, a sugar dish and some divided dinner plates."

"One of my pieces is a sugar dish. It doesn't have a lid, though."

"They are rare, even without lids. Your mother-in-law gave you quite a gift," said Bill.

"It always surprised me that she got them in soap powder boxes. Now they are being collected. They should have bought more soap powder," Anna smiled. "I won't keep you Mr. Mason, but when I collected the watering can, I found your wallet by your wife's grave."

Bill dug into his pocket, clearly unaware of the missing wallet. “I am so grateful, Mrs. Wilson. Apart from the money, I can’t imagine replacing all the cards and such. Thank you so much. I would offer you a cup of coffee, but the stuff I make is more of a punishment than a treat.” He looked at the oven mitt. “I am having a war with the kitchen as we speak. I should know better than to use that oven.”

“Maybe I can help you. What is the problem?”

Bill led her into the kitchen toward what looked like a brand-new range. “The direction book is around here somewhere, but I can’t get the thing working for the life of me. My nephew gives me these boxes of meat for my birthday and I end up putting them back in the freezer and heading for McDonald’s.”

“Let’s see. You’ve got the temperature at 375. Do you bake it or broil it?” They consulted the directions and Anna showed Bill the oven/broiler switch that would activate the oven.

“I feel a little foolish. I’m doubly indebted to you now, Mrs. Wilson. You’ve saved a man from starvation and financial disaster. Can you stay and share a steak with me?”

“No, I have to be at the Heritage in an hour and I need to stop at home. Thanks for the offer, though.” Anna smiled at his obvious new empowerment as she headed out the back door.

Chapter 52

The sesquicentennial celebrations officially went on for a week, but the citizens of Silver Spring held the event in their hearts for much longer. There were the beards, reluctantly shaved by men who found that not shaving appealed to them. The scrapbooks and newspaper clippings of long ago were unwilling to be relegated to dusty shelves again. At the Heritage, Anna added up the receipts of the quarter with delight. Profits had tripled over the same period the year before. Maybe, Anna hoped, people would feel that they could not do without fresh flowers in their lives. It was certainly a milestone. Anna's own finances had reached a milestone as well. The last time she'd counted the money to repay Johnny, she needed just $50 more, and with this paycheck she had it.

Even for Silver Spring, famous for its wintery weather, it was early for the storm that was brewing. Nevertheless, she went to the bank with her biggest purse to cash her check and visit her safety deposit box. "You'll be wanting the privacy room, Mrs. Wilson?" asked the head teller, but it was more of a statement than a question. Anna nodded and produced the duplicate key to the box. She felt the weight of the money as she lifted the box to a table. It was nearly full, representing a lot of savings over these past years. Anna counted it out. Exactly right when she added the final fifty-dollar bill. Anna smiled. She couldn't wait to see the look on Johnny's face when she returned his money. She was taking the bus to the city this afternoon. She'd made an appointment with Johnny's secretary. There was uncertainty about carrying so much cash, but she decided against a check. In a town like Silver Spring a check that large would be common knowledge in a day or so.

She wrapped her handkerchief around the bulky bundle and stuffed it deep within her purse, piling her other belongings on top of it. Checking her watch, she saw it was almost time for the bus, so she signed out of the privacy room, secured her ticket and, hugging the purse close to her side, left the warmth of the bank for the wintry blast outside. The snow was coming steadily, and Anna appreciated that the sturdy vehicle she was boarding was running on time. By the time they arrived in Buffalo, the snow had thickened to the point where it made her feel dizzy to watch it as the wind whipped it into swirls. Anna had only been driving occasionally, and she was very glad she'd decided against driving to the city today.

Feeling the reassuring bulk deep within her purse, Anna took the elevator to an impressive mahogany suite on the 7th floor. JOHN SCHOTT, REGIONAL VICE PRESIDENT announced a gold plaque on the door. There had never been a doubt in Anna's mind that Johnny would be successful, and she was proud to see the evidence of it today.

"Mrs. Wilson, Mr. Schott will see you now," announced an efficient-looking woman in a brown worsted suit. Johnny bolted from a massive chair behind a ponderous desk as she came into his office.

"Anna, Anna, Is it really you?" He swept her up into the biggest hug she'd had in years. When they'd caught up with the parts of their lives Mrs. Schott hadn't shared, in her letters, Anna approached her reason for being there. Face glowing, she reached deep into her purse and withdrew the handkerchief wrapped cash.

"Here it is, Johnny. Every cent you ever sent me. You've been my guardian angel for all these years and now I can pay you back!"

John looked quizzically at the pile of cash, "What is it you are paying me back for, Anna?"

"The money. The money you've sent me every month. The money that allowed me to leave that horrible job at the factory. The money I lived on and fed Claire with before I was able to earn enough myself. The money…" Anna's voice trailed off as she realized Johnny had no idea what she was talking about. "I-I was so sure it was you," she stammered. "Who else could it be?"

"I wish it had been me. There is obviously someone out there who cares a lot for you and thought of a way to show it. I wish it had been me." His face was downcast. "Let me at least treat you to dinner, although I can see you can certainly afford it," he said, smiling.

"Oh, Johnny, I wish I could, but I have a bus to catch. Claire will be home in a couple of hours and I want to be there when she gets home." Bewildered, Anna carefully re-wrapped the money, and put it back in her purse.

Outside the wind had picked up, forcing Anna to lean into it on her way to the bus terminal. Even her winter coat couldn't stop icy fingers that jabbed her ribs and her new brown boots totally disappeared in the accumulated snow. The schedule inside the terminal showed the bus to be on time, she noted gratefully, clutching her purse with stiffened fingers. Only an hour and a half to home, or so she thought as she boarded the bus, relishing its blasting heater. She passed by a scrawny man who leered at her hopefully, choosing instead a seat behind a frail white-haired woman and in front of a fedora clad middle-aged man with his nose buried in a magazine. All told, there were twelve people on the bus, none of whom would get home that night.

Chapter 53

Claire found the house empty when she returned from school. She knew her mother was going to the city for an important appointment. It had something to do with a loan she was able to repay. Had Claire come home at the usual time, she would have expected Anna to be there, but Claire was home early. Seeing the torturous wind increasing, the superintendent had decided to end the school day early, giving the extensive bus routes extra time to deliver their precious cargo. Living close to school, Claire walked home with her best friend, Claudette. Walked or more accurately, was blown. By the time they came to Maple Avenue where their paths parted, they both had red cheeks and cold hands. They decided to head home rather than hanging out at one of their houses as they often did.

Claire finished her homework easily and brought the mail inside. What was that expression about "neither snow nor sleet stopping the mail?" It seemed right today. She waved at Marcie Ellis, who had been her babysitter as far back as she could remember. Marcie was grown up now, but was home for a visit. Claire flicked the radio on as she opened the fridge, noticing that it was close to dinner time. She often got things started when Anna worked late, but today she hadn't expected to do so.

Claire's attention was now fully riveted as the voice changed from female to male.

"This is Michael Bradford on route 219 between North Dayton and Silver Spring where a Greyhound bus missed an icy curve two hours ago and ricocheted off a stone wall to roll down a steep cliff. We are waiting for details about the passengers, most of whom were on their way to Silver Spring or Punton, PA. We have word that the driver has been killed, but his name is being withheld pending notification of next of kin. Route 219 is closed to all but emergency vehicles until the survivors have been located and transported to the nearest emergency facility in Silver Spring."

With this the music resumed. Deaf to it, Claire darted out the back door to the Ellis home, not even bothering to grab her coat.

Chapter 54

Claire blew into the Ellis house with a blast of cold wind. "Claire, what in heaven are you doing out in this storm without a coat," chided Mrs. Ellis.

"It's my mom. She was on that bus that crashed on the 219. People died on that bus, Mrs. Ellis. They know the driver did."

Mrs. Ellis cradled Claire just as she gave way to a meltdown of tears. "Now, I'm not going to tell you not to worry. This is definitely serious, but let's find out all we can about it and do what we can. Marcie—turn on the TV. Let's see if there is anything on the news about the bus crash."

In spite of the snow, there were TV cameras at the site, photographing nameless forms on stretchers being pulled from the demolished bus. No names were given, and some of the stretchers were completely covered. All were being taken to the Butler Hospital in Silver Spring.

"That's where we will find something out," said Marcie. "We'll go to the hospital and wait for them to be brought in. We will be there before they are." Claire nodded docilely, but it was clear she was not really functioning. "We'll get your coat, Claire, and I'll drive." Scrambling into her own coat, she led the shocked girl next door.

The Butler ER was a mob of people—reporters, cameramen, worried relatives, and a fair share of curious onlookers. Mrs. Ellis made her way to the desk. "This young lady's mother was on the bus. Her name is Anna Wilson. Do you know if she is being brought here?"

"The emergency vehicles are due any time now. We won't have definite information until they arrive. I am so sorry." With this the nurse reached for the constantly ringing phone.

Outside, the crowd volume increased as the first truck pulled up. Three stretchers were lifted from the back, each with an IV attached—a person still living. There were two men and a white-haired woman. No sign of Anna's curls. A fourth stretcher was completely covered. Claire stared ahead in a blessed stupor, but Marcy gulped. The families of the first three were informed of the status of their loved ones. The fourth stretcher held the body of the driver, whose family had been contacted already.

In half an hour all the rescue vehicles had arrived. Two more bodies were identified and everyone else was in surgery or triage. The crowd had thinned, filtering much of the crying and anxiety. Only one passenger was unaccounted for…Anna Wilson.

Chapter 55

As the bus skidded out of control, Anna winced at the screams of her fellow passengers. She clutched the armrests tightly as the bus tipped, trying to clench her purse between her knees. Her mind was full of Claire. If she didn't make it through this, who would Claire have? Would Junie take care of her? She hoped so. The driver managed to coax the bus back to the road, but the wheels hit the ice once more, and the bus shifted, grazing the huge rock surface at the right side of the road. Screams intensified and fragments of prayer could be heard as everyone was catapulted to the other side of the bus. The purse was still between Anna's knees as the bus slid back to the left, but its center of gravity had been lost and it leaned precariously over the side of the road, hesitating only slightly before it succumbed to one roll, then another. Bodies, luggage, and belongings formed a hurricane of movement to a cacophony of cries, murmurs, and screams.

When Anna opened her eyes, she was curled on her back on the roof of the overturned bus. Seats hung upside down above her. Other seats had dislodged, falling on passengers less lucky. No one else seemed to be moving. "Hello, anyone," Anna called weakly, but there was no response. In the silence, she straightened her legs as much as the space allowed. They still seemed to respond. There was a hard pressure on her ribs, but it turned out to be her purse, wedged between her knees and her diaphragm. She fastened it over her shoulder. Testing her movement, Anna started crawling across the ceiling toward the back of the bus. She squeezed under a seat, still partially attached to the floor above her. She crawled over a brown fedora, now under her on the roof of the overturned bus. Her last thought before darkness set in was that you could kick those emergency windows out if you could get your feet in the right position.

Sometime later she was out of the bus without any memory of how that had happened. Time must have gone by. A lot? A little? She didn't know. With a singleness of purpose—to get home—she scrambled over the snow banks, through the blowing snow. Time and place merged in a whirling of snow. Sirens in the distance, coming to help were swallowed by the howling wind. Dizziness. Confusion. And Cold. Always the Cold. Anna trudged on, determined to survive.

When the outline of a house emerged from the storm, it looked like a mirage. With the last vestige of her energy, she lunged for the door, sensing help and warmth within it. With no bell in sight, she hammered with her fist, her voice rasping, "Help, help." She had to make them hear her over the howling wind. She saw a heavy coal shovel propped up against the house. They would make a louder noise. She swung it at the door, hearing a satisfying THUNK. With her eyes on the door, she never saw the heavy icicle formation that loosened itself from the second story roof to plunge down on top of her.

Chapter 56

"I sure am glad to be home," gasped Betty Witt, releasing her white-knuckle grip on the car's door handle.

"It was one hell of a ride back from town," agreed her husband Harold as he turned off the ignition. For the last half hour they'd barely been able to see the road, blinded as they were by the whirling snow. They'd crept along, hoping that no one was behind them or stopped up ahead.

Betty lifted her long skirt and waded through the drifted snow, wishing her fur-topped boots were even higher. "What's that?" she asked, pointing to a spot in the snow right near their back door.

"It's red, looks something like blood," he answered. "I think something is wounded. There's a regular track here, and blood, lots of blood. The snow is all packed down as if something crawled and it goes behind the house."

"Don't go back there, Harold. It could be anything. At least take your gun."

"I'm just having a look. Go in the house, Bets. I'll be in in a minute." He started to follow the trail behind the house and she heard his voice. "For crying out loud. It's a woman. Betty, go call an ambulance. She's lost a lot of blood." Reaching the end of the scarlet trail, he dropped to his knees beside the crumpled form in his backyard. Anna's face was a pale contrast to the streams of blood oozing from under her knitted hat. She wore a warm tweed coat and gloves, but her legs were spotted with frostbite. Pushing her sleeve up a bit, he felt a steady pulse although she seemed unresponsive when he tried to make her hear him. "Bring a blanket," he yelled to his wife.

Anna's first thought when she woke to the smell of antiseptic was of Claire. She was in bed in a bright room. Where was she and where was Claire? That question was quickly answered as she saw her daughter's anxious face peering over the side of the bed. When she tried to move her neck to get a better look, she couldn't.

"Don't try to move. Your neck is in a brace, and you have so many bandages on your head you look like a sultan," Claire said excitedly. "Mom, I'm so glad you're awake. You took the longest time. Everyone in the bus crash was accounted for except you. Then this nice couple found you unconscious behind their house. We've been so worried."

Anna squeezed Claire's hand, trying to reconstruct the events that put her in the deep snow…the bus…the snowstorm…turning over in the bus…she couldn't remember more. Then another thought—the money. She was carrying a lot of money—money intended for Johnny Schott, at least until he told her he had never given her the money at all. Now she owed that money to someone else—someone she didn't even know. She tried to say Claire's name, but only an undetermined syllable came from her mouth.

"Don't try to talk, Mom. They have your jaw wired shut. They think the icicles from the second floor of the Witts' house came down and hit you. You're lucky to be alive."

Anna pushed the cobwebs of her mind far enough to see that her right wrist was in a cast. The door opened and a tall, smiling young woman with Sharon Schwartz RN on her name tag bustled into the room carrying a tray with a large fruit smoothie and a straw. "It looks like you won't be eating much for the next couple of weeks, so we've put everything you need into this drink," proclaimed the nurse.

Anna sucked on the straw on command, but her mind raced to what was in her purse and what it had contained. "Puurrr," she attempted. Claire glanced at Nurse Schwartz as if to say, "Should I tell her?"

"Mom," Claire began, "The bus crashed four days ago. You've been in a coma since then. Two people died in the crash—the bus driver and an elderly lady from New Castle. The hospital is full of others who were hurt, but until Mr. and Mrs. Witt called and said they found you in the snow behind their house, no one knew where you were. We were so worried about you." Unable to continue, Claire lay her head on the pillow next to Anna's and gently touched the fingers extending from the cast.

"Other than the jaw and the broken wrist, you have a lot of frostbite on your legs and a serious concussion," added Nurse Schwartz. "Now, don't you worry. We're taking good care of you. Now drink up. You will need your strength."

Who was taking care of Claire? Anna wondered. As if on cue, Claire popped up and said, "Now. If I know anything at all about you, YOU are worried about ME. I have been staying next door with the Ellises, and now that you are out of the coma, everything is great with me."

With her biggest worry out of the way, Anna went on to think again about her purse and all the money in it. She tried again to form a question, but the sound she made brought no response but "Shhh!!! no talking. You need your rest now." Apparently, that was so, since that was the last thing she remembered that day.

Chapter 57

"Yes, the last of the bandages was taken off last Thursday. Thanks for asking." Anna replied to Sam Gatlin, smiling as she wrapped the pink ceramic bootie filled with daisies that he bought for his new granddaughter. It had taken a while. She did have a concussion from the ice that fell on her at the Witt's house the night of the bus crash. She now had a crazy hairdo, shorter than it had ever been before. Some of the hair was barely grown out from the stitching on her scalp. She'd found some cute caps to cover this awkward stage and pinned a flower to the right of the brim. Jaunty was what most customers called it.

There was a lot to be thankful for. Other than the occasional headache, her recovery was complete. Claire seemed to have grown from a child to a young adult so quickly and she had a regular babysitting job watching three rambunctious boys. Things at the Heritage couldn't be better. Mary worked less and less now. Her confidence in Anna made the possibility of days off and trips taken a reality. As a result, Anna had the freedom to try out some of her own ideas. It worked for both.

Only two things clouded Anna's life. One was the money she'd had when the bus crashed. It had never been found, even when the crash scene was thoroughly searched. Winter had turned into spring and the loss of it still brought a gagging lump to Anna's throat. She had to accept that there was nothing she could do about it.

The second thing she could do something about. Since the accident, she had been unwilling to drive. The doctor had sounded so excited when he told her she could drive again. She hadn't told him that the whole idea made her feel ill. It made no sense at all; she hadn't been driving when the accident happened. Mary's old Ford truck was still in the garage and Anna had the use of it at any time. In good weather, she preferred her bike and Silver Spring was small enough that both she and Claire could walk most places. Nevertheless, she decided it was time to confront the situation.

It was still a cool early spring, but you wouldn't have known it from the perspiration on Anna's forehead.

The roads were clear at this hour, so she got the keys from their hook by the door, got into the Ford and pulled out of the driveway. So far so good. The village presented no challenges. There were stop signs every two blocks in Silver Spring allowing no chance of breaking the 30-mph speed limit. Anna felt amazingly in control. A bit farther and she was headed for 319, the route out of town. Maybe she'd take a ride up to Miller's stand. Some early fresh vegetables should be available. Anna coaxed the Ford up to 45 then 55 as she cruised down the highway. Just before Miller's Anna recognized a white Buick pulled over to the side of the road. Standing near the open trunk was Bill Mason, a flare in his hand. Anna slowed the Ford and pulled up behind him.

"Are you all right, Mr. Mason?" she called.

"Feeling a little foolish," he replied, "it looks like I forgot to fill my gas tank."

"Well, that is easily taken care of. I just passed a Shell a mile back. Do you have a gas can?"

"That I do. It was supposed to be for an emergency. I guess this is it." He smiled.

"Hop in. I am glad to have someone help me celebrate," Anna declared.

"Celebrate? Is it your birthday?" Bob inquired from the passenger seat.

"No. It's my first time driving since I was in the accident. I have to say, it is not as bad as I thought it would be," she shared as they made their way up the road. "Oh…here we are…I guess we won't be shopping for the best price today."

In a matter of ten minutes they were back at his car, which started after a few sputters. "It seems to be a full-time job for you to rescue me," said Bill. "I think the least I could do is provide a real celebration. Would you consider having dinner with me on Saturday?"

For the first time since Anna lost Russ, the prospect of a dinner date didn't sound like something to be avoided. "I would love to," she replied. "About six?"

"I will pick you up at six. And I will make it a point to have gas in the car," he said, causing Anna to smile.

Chapter 58

Anna changed her dress again, donning the blue pleated one with a white collar. Why had she ever consented to this? A date? Why was she going on a date? This dress made her look like a hopeful schoolgirl. If the doorbell had not rung at that moment, she would have changed again.

Get yourself together, Anna. It is not a big deal. Dinner is—well—dinner. He's just grateful that you saved him from having to cook one night this week.

"Mom, there's someone at the door," called Claire, amusement obvious in her voice.

"I'll be right there," Anna called and she put one foot in front of the other until she was at the top of the stairs. She could see Bill seated in the living room looking nervous. Well, he was not the only one. Anna grabbed a sweater from the front hall and put the facsimile of a smile on her face.

"Hello, Bill. How are you?" What a great opening line.

"Mrs.…I mean Anna. Good to see you. I hope you're hungry. I have reservations at the Spring House."

"No one has ever found fault with my appetite…Bill." Anna was having trouble remembering to call him by his first name. "Have you met my daughter, Claire?"

Claire sprung up, a silly smile playing around her mouth. "Hello, Mr. Mason. I think we met at the Heritage Shop. It was practically my pre-school."

Bill smiled the way everyone did when they met Claire. He took his glasses off, wiped them with a handkerchief, and gave her his biggest smile. "Little bit," he began, "You've grown up. I hope you don't mind that I've invited your mother for dinner. She saved me from starvation a while ago and found me stranded without gas just this week. Maybe you will join us next time."

Claire gave her mother an encouraging grin.

The Spring House Restaurant was undeniably the best one in Silver Spring. It had a reputation for aged prime beef and seafood flown in fresh each day. As Anna and Bill were led to a table next to a fountain, designed to look like an underground spring, several couples looked up to say "Hi Bill" and others just nodded. Anna knew who these people were, but they weren't social friends as they had been to Bill and his late wife, Dorothy. In truth, she had no social friends other than Ellises and Josie. Everyone else knew her as the flower lady or as Claire's mother.

Everything on the menu looked expensive and Anna reflexively went to the lower part of the entree offerings. "The spaghetti and meatballs look good," she said.

"When was the last time you had spaghetti and meatballs?" Bill asked.

"Oh, a few days ago. It's a favorite of ours."

"When was the last time you had lobster?" he asked.

"Lobster? I don't think I've ever had lobster. Besides, they don't even have a price for it on the menu. They might not have it at all."

"I'm guessing they have it. They just don't want to commit to a price. I think it is time you tried lobster. And what shall we have to drink while we wait? I happen to know that they have a delicious strawberry daiquiri. How does that sound?"

It sounded to Anna like something she'd never had, but it looked very pretty when it came—quite a lot like a freezie cone, only in a beautiful stemmed glass. The top had a dollop of whipped cream with a strawberry on top. She sipped on the straw inserted into it and liked what she tasted. This was more like dessert than a drink. It was delicious and she was thirsty. Bill smiled as she drained the glass.

"Mr. Mason, here are your rolls," said the waitress sometime later. "I must apologize. Your lobster will be delayed a bit. We had a little mishap in the kitchen." She rolled her eyes. "We'll be offering you a complimentary drink while you wait and your salad will be right out."

The second daiquiri tasted even better than the first, and Anna found herself chatting with Bill about owning property in Silver Spring, about the school vote coming up in a few weeks, about the future of the Heritage Shop, and about life without the spouse you loved. Those were the topics Anna remembered. Actually, the more they talked the less she remembered the details. They laughed a lot and seemed to feel similarly about so many things.

For the first time since his death, Anna got into the details of Russ' death. "I never had a real sense of closure about Russ' death," Anna admitted, "how it happened and whether it was his fault."

All of a sudden, the happy repartee of the evening seemed to stop. Maybe it was that the lobster had arrived. When the waitress removed the cover to expose the steaming lobster, Anna didn't know where to start. There were a couple of tools she was puzzled by as well. One looked like a nutcracker. She tentatively suspended her fork over the breadcrumbs at the center of the lobster. Bill gently guided her fork to the tail. "Right there is the best part," he said, loosening meat from its red shell after cracking it open. He took a piece and dipped it into a dish of melted butter. Anna did the same. How delicious. Different from anything she'd had before – a texture all its own – at the same time firm and yielding. Next, Bill directed her to the claws. "These have a different texture, but still very good." Anna agreed.

The lobster was served with a twice baked potato that seemed to have everything under the sun on top of it. Anna tasted sour cream and saw green onions and cheese. They were sprinkled with something that matched the color of the lobster's shell—paprika, Anna guessed.

As Bill dropped her off, she thought she'd never had such a meal in her life. She was missing some of the details of their conversation, but she had a sense that she had shared more about what was important to her than she had in a very long time. He made no attempt to kiss her, but smiled and thanked her for a wonderful evening as she glided into the house.

Claire popped out of her room. "Did you have a good time, Mom?" she asked.

"I did, Claire, I really did," said Anna.

Chapter 59

Standing bewildered in his kitchen the next day, Bill Mason was a lost man in a foreign land. It had been years since his wife, Dorothy died; still he gravitated toward the Pizza Hut and free coffee night at the Sweet Spot. In the fridge was a macaroni and cheese casserole dropped off by Marcell Hoffman when she was "in the neighborhood" a few days ago. Marcell was relentless. Bill wondered how long it would be before some other unlucky fellow would lose his wife and become Marcell's newest prey.

As he took the casserole from the refrigerator, his mind shifted to Anna Wilson. Being with her had been the best evening he had since Dorothy died. It had felt, in all the time he had been alone, like he would never again have what people called "a good time". There were better days and worse days, for sure, but always the feeling that there was a hole in his days and nights which kept his world from being complete. Bill felt pretty sure Anna felt that way too. And yet the two of them had spent hours together and it felt like no time at all. She was everything the other women who stalked him were not—genuine, resourceful, independent, and perhaps unavailable.

Bill wondered what Dorothy would think about his preoccupation with Anna. He and Dorothy had lived every year of their marriage to the fullest. They each gave 100% to their jobs, and yet had always had another 100% to devote to their relationship. Snowmobiling made the winters fun. Their wide circle of friends kept them busy all the time. They loved summers at the lake. Only Dorothy's miscarriages marred the perfection of their lives. On that topic, Bill had never met a young lady he liked better than Anna's daughter, Claire. She was outgoing without being brash. She was intelligent without being condescending. And so pretty. Like a little Anna. Bill realized his thoughts had digressed from Dorothy.

So why was he hesitating? Shouldn't he be over on Scott Street right now? Anna was surely home from work. There was no doubt that she had loved Russ unconditionally in spite of some of the rumors that circulated about his too-frequent time at the bar. It is always hard to compete with someone who died, and that was especially so in this case.

Realizing exactly why he was not heading to Scott Street, Bill scraped the macaroni and cheese into the disposal and headed out the door to Pizza Hut.

Chapter 60

Valentine's Day and Easter had been a boon to the Heritage Shop. Anna's three day back to work schedule had turned into a sort of marathon. She didn't even have time to eat the sandwich she had brought for her lunch. Now, it was nearly 5 and she had committed to working at the German Dinner at the church from 5–6:30—the last shift. The Ellises were coming with Claire; maybe she could arrange a take-out. As she slipped into the church basement, she saw brightly colored tables, well attended. The roast pork smelled delicious and Anna heard her stomach growl as she passed the table laden with apple strudel. Her head ached, dully, but she put a smile on her face and approached Annalise Werner, the chair of the event. "What can I do?" she asked.

"I could use someone to put the sauerkraut on the plates, Anna. Carl, your shift is over. Anna will replace you. Thanks, Anna." Annalise turned to another arriving volunteer, and Anna took Carl's place on the line. Next to her, Trudy Morgan was putting spazle on each plate.

"We're asking people if they want sauerkraut," Trudy said. "Not everyone wants it."

"Two with sauerkraut," said Ken, the waiter for the right side of the hall. Two plates came down and Anna put a scoop of sauerkraut on each one.

"One without sauerkraut," said Ken. The moment without work made Anna think of how really hungry she was. She looked with longing at the German potato salad. She inhaled its vinegary smell as she leaned toward it.

"Will there be enough for take-outs at the end?" Anna inquired.

"I wish there was," said Annalise. "We are completely sold out and may even have to make a run to the Market Basket to buy some more desert. The strudel is running low."

Anna started mentally inventorying the contents of her refrigerator. There was a little left-over spaghetti and some soup. She'd been too busy to shop in the last week, and Claire had taken the last of the bologna in her lunch today. Oh well, there was always peanut butter.

"Were you hoping for take-out? I was too." Suddenly Bill Mason was standing in front of her. Anna broke into a smile then felt almost immediately self-conscious. It had been almost two weeks since her dinner with Bob and he hadn't called her. Anna had reviewed the evening she had thought was such a success over and over. Admittedly, there were gaps in her memory after her two daiquiris, but she still felt they had a wonderful time. Maybe she'd talked too much. She did remember how the flow of conversation had halted so abruptly when she shared her unresolved feelings about the accident that ended Russ' life. She probably shouldn't have done that. Anyone could tell you; you don't talk about your former husband when you start dating again. The thing that bothered her so much was the fact that it mattered so much what Bill thought. This was just the type of thing she didn't need in her life.

"Two with sauerkraut," Ken said, and Anna scooped some on both plates. Bill was still standing there.

"What do you say we catch something to eat after you're finished?" he asked.

"Two with sauerkraut," Ken was back and Anna couldn't sort her feelings out.

"I'm finished at 6:30," she told Bill. He nodded and turned toward the door.

Chapter 61

It had been three days since Anna and Bill had shared submarine sandwiches after the German dinner. Julie's Pizzeria was hardly a romantic hideaway, and yet she was experiencing wonderful feelings for the first time since Russ died. She and Bob had devoured submarine sandwiches and laughed about…well, everything. His incompetence in the kitchen—her failure to schedule a time to eat…everything. And then three days passed again with no word from him. By the time the phone rang three days later, Anna was jumping at every call.

Anna caught the phone on the second ring, and immediately wondered if she appeared too available. To her surprise and disappointment, it was a woman's voice on the other end of the phone.

"Mrs. Wilson, this is Betty Witt. How are you?"

Anna immediately recognized the name of the couple who had saved her life after the bus crash. "Mrs. Witt, how nice of you to call. I am doing well; the doctor tells me. Sometimes I still have a bit of a headache when I have stayed up too long, but overall, I couldn't be better—thanks to you and your husband."

"I am so glad to hear that. One of my daughters said she hadn't seen you in the Heritage last week."

"I am back to work, but only a few days a week right now. I expect to be back to my regular schedule after my appointment with the doctor on Thursday. I just started driving again last week."

"That is good news, for sure. There is another thing I wanted to ask you about. The snow seems unwilling to give up this springtime, but with the thaw last week, we saw something in the backyard, just a ways from where we found you. It is a purse, brown with a gold buckle. I haven't opened it yet until I talked to you. Is it yours?"

Anna's heart leapt. Her lost purse was found! Was it possible the money was still in the purse? She had a fleeting impulse to ask Betty Witt to look in the purse, but quickly changed her mind. "You've rescued me again, Mrs. Witt.

There are several things very important to me in that purse and I thought it was gone for good. I am due at work pretty soon; would it be okay with you if I picked it up, after maybe 6:30?"

"That would be fine. I'll put it aside by the fireplace for you. It is pretty wet after being under that snow for such a time."

Anna sorely wanted to skip going to work and race right up to the Witt house, but Mary had been so wonderful about Anna's accident, Anna couldn't let her down at the last minute. She finished dressing and made it to the shop on time.

By three o'clock Anna felt as if she had been at the Heritage for a week. Although she was usually totally absorbed in her work, today she checked her watch every fifteen minutes. She was finished with the orders for the next week when the bell over the door rang. Looking up, Anna saw Bill. "Well, hello," she said, feeling uncertain about their next step.

"Just the person I hoped to see," Bill said. "I know you know a lot about flowers so you can steer me to just the right ones for someone I had an enjoyable time with this week." Anna flushed and seemed to lose her usual ease with words for a second.

"I'm sure the person in question would enjoy any flowers that came from you. In fact, I'm sure they feel no flowers are needed. The dinner was a gift in itself. As I recall you saved me from starvation."

"I am counting on the flowers to let this person know how much I enjoyed her company and how anxious I am to see her again. Do you think these daisies would convey that message?" He pointed to the new shipment in the refrigerated case.

"I am somewhat biased since I dearly love daisies, but, Yes, I think they might relay what you intend them to." All of a sudden, the day that had dragged so slowly was accelerating.

"I'll take two dozen in that case. Perhaps you would be so kind as to deliver them for me?" Anna laughed. The day was suddenly so different.

"This is the second gift I've received today. Betty Witt called this morning and said they found my purse under the melted snow in their yard. I am going to her house after work today to pick it up."

"I saw you were worried about it when you woke up in the hospital. It looks like that worked out all right." Anna nodded, hoping he was right.

By 6:30 Anna found herself back at the Witt house. She hardly remembered the pretty clapboard structure, but she looked up at the roof and pictured icicles hanging two stories up—icicles she'd never noticed on that snowy night. The door she had pounded on opened as soon as she opened the truck's door. Mrs. Witt had a beaming smile on her face.

"Anna, you are looking wonderful and that hat couldn't be cuter," said Mrs. Witt. "Come in, now. I have tried to dry your purse out as much as possible. Can you stay and have dinner with us?"

There it was. The imitation leather was puckered as it dried out after months under the snow. Anna could hardly hold herself back from snatching it and opening it right that moment. "I have to get home to my daughter, Mrs. Witt, but thank you for the offer."

"I have some tea made for us. Let me just go get it." With that Betty Witt left the room. Anna's eyes were locked on the purse. Maybe she could just peek inside. As she thought of it, Mrs. Witt returned with a tray. "Now, I have hot water here. Do you prefer Darjeeling or Earl Gray?"

"I like them both, Mrs. Witt," Anna said, squirming in her chair.

"Let's do the Earl Gray, then. I just got a new order of that. Now…How about lemon? Do you like lemon in your tea?"

"Lemon is fine, thank you," Anna reached for the cup.

"Honey, perhaps?" said Betty, moving the cup beyond Anna's reach.

"No honey, it looks fine just as it is," Anna replied, trying to keep the anxiety out of her voice.

"I believe the water is very hot. You had better let it cool, my dear," said Betty.

"Oh, I like my tea very hot," said Anna, burning her tongue with the first sip.

It seemed like hours before she finished the tea and was heading for her car with the purse in hand. The moment she reached the car, she fished into the damp purse to see what was within it. She felt the handkerchief near the bottom. The day fulfilled its promise. By nightfall Anna had two dozen daisies, a date with Bill for the following night, and a purse containing a soggy, but intact roll of bills.

Chapter 62

Anna had hundred-dollar bills spread over the floor in her bedroom. Now and then she just had to look at them to make sure they really existed. She thought of all the years they had arrived and how hard she had worked to keep from using them. They were her safety net for sure. She felt free to count them as Claire was at band practice after school. Anna didn't know how she could possibly explain all this money to her, so she'd always been careful not to get it out while Claire was around. She didn't even know how to explain it to herself. US currency, it turned out, survived being buried in the snow quite well. Her driver's license looked good too, but she had already replaced that.

She didn't know if the Witts knew they were returning more money than Anna had ever had in her life. It seemed to be rolled in the same handkerchief she had used to contain it, and the ribbon she'd used to tie it looked intact. But what should she do now? She really didn't know how to go about finding the person it belonged to. She'd been so sure it was Johnny.

Tonight Anna and Bill were going to the Fireside. Claire was babysitting after her band practice, so it would be just the two of them. Since the night of the German dinner, Anna and Bill had spent at least four nights together every week, and each time was better than the last. At times he just came to her house as she healed—carrying some of the take-out from places he knew so well. Other times it was just a walk. Nights like tonight, it was dinner out. But tonight he sounded so very serious when he called her to confirm the time. When he said he had something important to tell her, Anna's curiosity soared. But he didn't sound very happy about it, sending Anna's speculations plummeting. Was he losing interest just as her interest was accelerating? Lately, she had allowed herself to consider a new, different direction for her life, although she'd never before imagined another man in it. A woman with a child was not what every man was looking for, she reminded herself. *Just keep it casual*, she counseled herself.

Shaking these thoughts aside, she dressed for dinner at the Fireside. She had a new white blouse, trimmed with lace, which she had bought at Simon's with Junie's discount. That made the gabardine skirt she often wore with serviceable blouses to the Heritage look a little different. New clothes had rarely been in the budget to this point. Her glance fell on the now-dry bills piled in her bedroom, and thought of the possibilities they offered before censoring those thoughts. She gathered the bills and tucked them into two pull-out, hidden columns in her secretary, her prized piece of furniture.

In the bathroom, she addressed the issue of her hair. Its natural curl served her well now that she kept it shorter, but she combed and smoothed it, seeking a more sophisticated style, securing it with a pearl comb. She looked at herself closely for the first time in months…no, years. Her mouth was a little wide, but she had a nice smile, which crept up into her eyes. The freckles she had hated so much seemed to have faded. She had never regained the weight she lost at Burnett Plastics, so the few clothes she had fit her well and complemented her trim body. People were always telling her she was pretty, but, until Bill, she'd dismissed the comments, feeling that they applied to a time in her life which had ended.

Seated in Bill's Buick, Anna felt the tension emanating from its driver. Bill's eyes were riveted to the road, rather than lingering on hers as they usually did. His body seemed stiff too, awkward…making her feel the same kind of restraint. She couldn't brush away the feeling that this would be their last date, although she couldn't for the life of her think what had happened.

The Fireside had gotten to be their place. It wasn't quite as fancy as the Spring House, but they liked the chopped salad and its special warm yeast rolls. During the winter a large stone fireplace had provided a crackling fire. Now the windows were open, inviting the scent of early spring lilacs into the room. Bill's eyes seemed glued to the familiar menu. They'd often joked about how they looked at the menu needlessly since they both always ordered the chicken parmesan. Tonight, there was no joking. The waitress was approaching the table, but Bill waved her away. He took his glasses off and rubbed his eyes, seemingly willing to do anything to delay what he had to say.

Anna couldn't stand it any longer. "Bill, is there something you want to tell me?" She prepared herself for the worst.

"There is…there is…and I've been trying to figure out how to do it for a long time," he said regretfully.

A long time, Anna thought. *Has he been planning to end it for a long time? And I never had any inkling?*

"I've been telling myself that people don't need to know everything about each other, but I can't make that stick any more. There is something you need to know no matter what the consequences are."

"Something about you? What could there be about you that could result in the look on your face. You are the kindest and nicest person I've ever known."

"I don't know if you'll still think so when you hear what I have to tell you."

"It can't be worse than what I've been imagining." Anna smiled. "Are you a secret homicidal maniac? Are there bodies strewn in the closet behind your bone china collection?"

Bill hesitated. "In a way, that might be better…" he paused awkwardly. "…you know…the night Russ had his accident on the 319?"

"I'll never forget that night…but what does it have to do with you?"

"Well, I was on the 319 that night…and the other car involved with Russ' accident…that was me."

"What do you mean?" A frown crossed Anna's brow.

"I was coming back from the city when Russ pulled out right near the Halfway House. When I saw him, I swerved into the other lane. There was no one coming, thank God. Russ pulled over to the right and went right into a tree at the side of the road. By the time I parked the car and went back. the guy who was riding with him got out. He just had a few scratches, but Russ was hardly conscious. Another guy had stopped—someone they worked with—and the two of us got Russ into his car. They drove off—to the hospital, I imagined. When I got home, I called the hospital and they said his name was Russ Wilson and he was being treated for multiple fractures. It wasn't until the next day when I learned he had died. I'm not very proud of what I did then. I did nothing. I went to Russ' wake, looked you and my friends in the eye, and never told anyone that I was in the other car."

"What could you have done?" Anna choked.

"I don't know, but I should have tried. I couldn't get it out of my mind. I told myself I hadn't caused his accident, but I had nightmares in which I drove right at him, watching his body break, and then there was you, his widow, and that little girl."

"Claire…"

"Yes, Claire. I saw her at the wake. So bright. So beautiful. What would her future be? That's when I started sending the checks."

"The checks? You mean it was you sending me money every month?"

"It was all I could do. It made me feel better to know that I was helping the two of you. I watched Claire grow up in a nice, clean house with enough of everything and I felt better…less of a coward."

"What about your wife? What about Dorothy?"

"Dorothy never knew. We shared most everything, but I could never tell her that. I was so ashamed. The money came from a trust fund from my grandmother we never had to use, so I never told her. When you and I started seeing each other, I should have told you right away. But I didn't. I felt sure that would be the end of it if I did, so I kept putting it off. I'm so sorry…I'm so, so sorry." Bill was unable to continue.

"Bill, I never spent all of the money, but having it gave me the confidence that if things really got bad, I could fall back on it. I can never thank you enough for that. After I got on my feet financially, I saved until I had it all back again. I felt sure I knew who sent it. When the bus crashed, I was on my way back from trying to return it, but it turned out it wasn't him. Then I lost it while wandering around after the crash. It was only with the spring thaw that my purse was found and the money was right there where it had been the winter before. I have your money and I can only thank you for the peace it gave me."

"You don't hate me? Can you forgive me?"

"It wasn't your fault. I…I know Russ was in the habit of drinking too much. He pulled into the road, probably without looking. I had to accept that a long time ago."

"So you'll forgive this old coward for deceiving you so long?" Bill's eyes were wide with wonder.

"This coward, as you call him, is certainly not old and has become an important part of my life. That money accomplished just what you wanted it to. And now I'll return every dollar back as soon as we go home tonight."

"I'll accept it on one condition."

"What might that be?"

"That you'll let me use it for a honeymoon trip."

"A honeymoon trip? We aren't even engaged," Anna teased.

"The only thing missing there is a ring. That can be fixed at Kalee's Jewelry tomorrow."

Anna paused for a moment. "I think I could squeeze you in tomorrow." She smiled as Bill reached over and took her hand.

"That calls for a strawberry daiquiri," Bill beamed as he waved the waitress to their table.

Chapter 63

The Heritage had never placed so many flowers at a wedding site as those in the United Chapel on June 26th. Ropes of gardenias wound their way along the altar, culminating in a huge floral heart. Bouquets of heliotrope with shimmering bows graced each pew. Bouquets of orchids and roses had been ordered for Anna and her two attendants, Junie and Claire. And there was a basket of single stem flowers—one for every guest to take at the conclusion of the ceremony. Anna proclaimed it too extravagant, but Bill maintained that the Heritage had supplied him with so much happiness that he could never repay it.

For the first time in her life Anna had a formal dress designed just for her. Tiny pearls nestled in the simple, ecru lace shift with fitted sleeves designed to a point on her hand, calling attention to her glittering diamond ring. A square neck framed her face and revealed a graceful neck, now visible with Anna's new, shorter hairstyle. She wore a tiny cross, sent to her by Mrs. Schott. "Something borrowed, it is," she had said. Anna didn't have something blue, but Bill's eyes were blue enough to fulfill that.

Junie, now married, tucked a miniature arrangement of roses with tiny explosions of net into Anna's hair. "There you go," said Junie, securing the flowers with enough pins to keep a dirigible in place. The lilting tones of the organ came through the door as Claire entered the room. "Love Divine, All Loves Excelling" drifted in, the words sung by Josie, who volunteered her wonderful alto voice for the occasion.

"Mom, you look beautiful," said Claire, handing Anna the largest of the three beautiful bouquets.

"Thank you," was all Anna could say as she hugged her daughter. She couldn't believe how grown-up Claire looked today. Like Anna's, her hair had been professionally styled for the first time. The slightly gathered skirt of her dress rustled and shimmered, reflecting pink and tan tones. She twirled on her new high heels. How did she know instinctively how to navigate them? No longer a baby and not even a little girl any more – a young woman.

Following Junie, Anna put one foot before the other and made her way to the white carpet. It looked like at least a mile to the front of the church, but peeking over Junie's right shoulder she saw Bill waiting. Faces of neighbors and friends blurred as Anna saw only Bill and suddenly the distance seemed like nothing. With a smile on her face, she strode confidently the rest of the way to the altar and took her place, her rightful place, by his side.

Ninety pictures later, the band started the dance that would be the first of their lives as man and wife. They had tried a few steps in his living room in preparation for this moment. Mentally counting, Bill twirled her under his arm and dipped her low for the finale of the song. Immediately, a cheer rose up from their guests. First a few then nearly everyone came up to the dance floor, not to dance but to surround them, enveloping them in happiness. Looking up at her new husband and surrounded by so many people who cared about them, Anna thought herself lucky beyond belief.

Anna had ten days off from the Heritage. Mary was coming back to fill in while she and Bill went on their honeymoon. The location of that honeymoon was still a mystery to Anna. Bill had told her she would need a passport and clothing for warm weather and she'd complied. Dressed in her new traveling suit, Anna waited by the door, flanked by Junie, Claire, and two suitcases with almost all the clothing she owned, much of it new thanks to Bill. The Buick pulled around the corner, Anna heard the tin cans friends had attached to his back bumper. The window had Just Married inscriptions. No one would fail to recognize them as newlyweds. She clung to Claire as Junie shooed her into the car and off they went into the mystery of their new life.

The first stop was the Sheridan where Bill had a reservation for the night. The porter took their bags and led them to the bridal suite where Bill dismissed him with a tip. The first room was like a living room with overstuffed chairs mounded with soft pillows. Indirect lighting made the room glow and yet seem intimate. Sheer curtains framed beautiful windows. Once again, flowers were everywhere—bouquets on every table. The thick rug hugged Anna's feet as she slipped out of her shoes and put her purse on an elaborately carved table.

"That is for you," Bill said, pointing to an envelope on the table with a silver letter opener next to it. As Anna picked it up, there was a knock on the door. Bill answered and in came a rolling cart laden with food and drink. Holding the envelope, Anna asked Bill what was on the cart.

"Just some snacks in case we work up an appetite," Bill replied, "and of course some strawberry daiquiris. I credit them for getting this all started," he grinned. "Now open your envelope Mrs. Mason."

Anna slit the envelope with a silver letter opener, and her eyes widened. "Greece? We're going to Greece? Mt. Olympus? The Temple at Delphi?"

"First thing tomorrow. Those Gods and Goddesses got you through some rough times in your life. It's time you see where they hung out."

As Bill's arms went around her, Anna thought her life couldn't possibly get any better. It wasn't very long, however, before she found that it actually could.

Epilogue

House for Sale

The red Chevy slowed in front of 93 Prospect Street in Silver Spring. A large yellow Lazzard Realty-For Sale Sign sported a diagonal PENDING banner. The house's white clapboards looked freshly painted and the crisp black shutters framed large windows. Flowering bushes nestled around the stairs. They were well trimmed. A smaller sign near the front door read: Bill and Anna Mason.

Three women got out. At the windows Anna's lace curtains framed the view into the house. "I remember when Anna got those curtains," said Junie. "She felt they were a terrible extravagance, but Bill talked her into getting them."

"They cost as much as our budget for the whole month when I was growing up," said Claire.

"Anything that made her happy was okay with Bill," Junie replied. "And what about that trip to Greece for their honeymoon? Anna had never been farther than New York before that. She made up for it after they were married, that's for sure."

"I wish I could have been part of her life then," said Peggy.

"Not having you in it was the only thing missing at that point. Anna was so happy when you got married," said Junie.

"I guess I hoped that the little lace handkerchief that came in the mail was from her," Peggy mused. "All it said was 'Something Old' with no signature."

"Mom carried that handkerchief when she got married to my father," said Claire.

"And now each of you carried it at yours."

Claire smiled and glanced at her wedding ring, sparkling with diamonds. "She danced in her high heels at my wedding," she said, recalling the day. She loved Steve and was so excited when I got pregnant the first time. Claire opened the front door. “I can still smell the lemon oil. That was my job when we moved in here.”

“You liked living here, didn’t you Claire?”

“Oh, yes. Bill was wonderful and Mom was so happy.”

Light streamed through the lace framed windows onto the large oriental rug. Swirls of teal blue and red formed intricate patterns in the thick wool. “She found this rug at an estate sale in Evans,” Junie recalled. “She had the cleaners pick it up and they didn’t send enough men to carry it. They didn’t make the same mistake when they dropped it off.”

“Probably the worst job they ever had,” stated Claire, wiggling her feet in the thick wool.

Peggy picked up a framed picture of a smiling couple with plumeria leis around their necks. “This was their first trip to Hawaii. She must have been in her element with all those flowers.”

“No doubt about it,” said Junie, smiling. “They even rode bikes down Mt. Haleakala. And here’s one on their trip to Alaska.”

“I remember Mom talking about the train ride and the glaciers they saw on that trip. When they were there, it was light all the time.”

“Land of the midnight sun,” mused Junie.

“Here they are tubing down the river in Jamaica,” Claire said, pointing to another framed picture. “I want you both to take all the pictures you want as well as any things that remind you of her.”

“Oh my gosh, here they are! The frogs!” Claire pulled Peggy to the room divider which housed frogs of every imaginable description – ceramic frogs, metal frogs, artistic frogs, wooden frogs. Claire picked up a metal frog with a goofy grin. “This one comes home with me. He’ll sit on my window sill over the sink. Come! Have a frog or two or twenty-seven!”

“What is a home without a frog or two or twenty-seven?” Junie laughed.

“I’m packing them,” Claire stated. “I’ll put one in everyone’s stocking each Christmas.” Claire’s family had continued to convene at her daughter, Elaine’s home each Christmas. The stockings Anna had made so many years ago made an appearance at each one.

With this Peggy looked around the room overwhelmed by all the figurines, vases, miniatures, cut glass and china that crowded the many shelves.

“There is certainly enough for all of us and a few hundred more people.”

“We have Bill to thank for a lot of that too. He was quite the collector. Wait until you see his gun room and the cupboard full of his mother’s hand painted dishes,” said Junie.

“Didn’t Aunt Anna get rid of any of that when she married Bill?” asked Peggy. She hesitated, realizing she’d fallen into the name she’d known for her mother as she grew up.

“Their common philosophy was if one is good, ten is better, and twenty is terrific, and THAT,” Junie concluded, “is why we are here.”

Many hours and numerous boxes later, a throaty laugh came from the family room where Junie was packing.

“What is it?” asked Claire.

“I never noticed this plaque before,” replied Junie, still laughing. “Listen to this…AGE AND TREACHERY WILL ALWAYS OVERCOME YOUTH AND SKILL.”

“I can see them buying that,” said Claire.

“Along with a few hundred other things,” replied Junie.

“I think that’s why Mom liked miniatures so much,” said Claire.

“Why is that?” asked Peggy.

“Well, with the same space, you can purchase four times as many miniatures.”

“We’ve been at it for hours and hardly made a dent,” smiled Peggy.

“There is no possibility we can keep all of this, but hopefully everyone will have things that are significant to them,” Claire replied. I’ll meet the auctioneer tomorrow and they will start cataloging and transporting things to their auction gallery. They have a website where they advertise things before the sale. Be sure to put aside anything you want before then.

“I’m taking the Christmas village houses if you don’t mind,” said Junie. “I can’t think of Aunt Anna without picturing the village beneath the Christmas tree.”

“I’ll look forward to visiting it at your house,” Claire said.

“I’m adding her *Greek Myths* book to my library,” said Claire. “What do you want, Peggy?”

“I already have what I want. The letters. All the letters she wrote to me during the years we were apart. She gave them to me when Helene—my mother—died. She was so afraid to contact me, but Dad let her know that Helene had told me about her years before. She’d written letters every year.

They were all in a red satin box in her closet. They are like a diary, in a way, telling me how important I was to her, even when she couldn't acknowledge me."

Claire reached out and took Peggy's hand. They stepped out and closed the front door for the last time. As they backed out of the driveway, Claire's gaze fell on a sign, nearly obscured by the rhododendrons. "Two old crows flew here," it announced, with two elderly birds grinning at each other. *They really did*, thought Claire. "*They really did*," and she smiled.

CPSIA information can be obtained
at www.ICGtesting.com
Printed in the USA
BVHW052058010623
665232BV00009B/282